Borne in the Blood

Edited by Carol Hightshoe

WolfSinger Publications Brackettville, TX

Acknowledgements

Revision in Red © 2024 Charles M Saplak
The Vampire's Ice Cream Shop © 2024 Tim O'Neal
A Charmed Life © 2009 Rob Nisbet
Originally published in: My Weekly magazine Wellbeing Special April/May 2009
Betwixt and Between © 2024 Karen Keeley
Beauty Treatment © 2017 Liam Hogan
Originally published in: WeirdBook Issue #34, Feb 2017
A Gift for our Friends © 2024 Jean Martin
Unsanctioned Transfiguration © 2024 Sam Crain
Blood & Beauty © 2024 Brian MacDonald
The Cyclist of the Full Moon © 2024 Lindsay Oliver
Blood of Heaven © 2024 DJ Tyrer
The Witch Bottle © 2024 Tim Newton Anderson
I Am Awake © 2024 Mariah Southworth
Blood Token © 2024 Deby Fredericks
Ben was Struck by Lightning © 2023 Michael Paige
Originally published in: The Horror Zine Magazine Summer 2023
Sanguinary Kin © 2024 Chris Horrell
Family Tree © 2018 Mike Murphy
Originally published in: Fantasia Divinity Magazine Issue 21, Apr 2018
Sins of the Forefather © 2024 Kay Hanifen
Unfinished Business © 2024 Joe Stout
The Price © 2024 Dana Bell
Virgins R Us © 2024 A.P. Sessler
Praxis Tattoos © 2024 Jamie Zaccaria
Mortal Karlat © 2024 James Tallett
The Iron Née of Life © 2024 Anka B. Troitsky

For permission requests, please contact WolfSinger Publications at:
editor@wolfsingerpubs.com

Cover Art created by Carol Hightshoe
using Midjourney Generative AI and stock photos

ISBN 978-1-944637-49-1
Printed and bound in the United States of America

Table of Contents

Revision in Red

Charles M. Saplak

Colin the Wanderer, Minstrel of his Time, Temporary Bard to the Court of King Hasurpass, took yet another swig of tart, dry wine as he settled back into the overstuffed chair in the upper chamber of the northeast tower of Castle Craddauren, a blank book and quill pen on his lap. He was enjoying the warmth of the fire, basking smugly in the glow of his own triumph and genius, when the ghost appeared and took shape.

It started as a figure in the fire, a trick of flame and shadows; then it coalesced into a man, wearing a leather field uniform and chain mail. The ghost stepped into the room to stand before Colin. He was tall, nearly five feet, eight inches, bearded, with straight brown hair and light blue eyes. His skin was covered in deep, bloody cuts. He carried a sword, steel but not highly polished, not a broadsword, but more of a foot soldier's, a sword which looked to Colin to be nearly thirty inches long and covered from tip to hilt with caked blood.

The ghost pointed this sword toward Colin as it groaned, "Storyteller…"

Colin raised his glass toward the ghost and nodded. "My compliments," he said. "You're more real-looking than most such phantoms. A residue of King Hasurpass's good wine, no doubt. But since I prefer to write alone, please, back into the bottle."

The ghost furrowed his brow and flared his nostrils. His eyes burned as if the shade had embers from the fire stuck in his visage.

"Scribbler," the ghost said, sneering. "Liar. Falsifier. Perjurer."

Colin made a disdainful face. "You damage me," he said with effortless sarcasm. "Back into the bottle, shade, before the light of cock-crow burns your skin."

The ghost lifted his sword and took two wavering, faltering steps (although his feet didn't seem to touch the floor) toward Colin. "Would cock-crow burn me, wastrel? Truth would burn your tongue."

The shade lunged forward with the sword and passed it through

Colin's neck; Colin felt as if the bluest, most ancient, most crystalline of ice had just passed through his flesh.

That got Colin's attention. He looked at the pages before him; he must have spilled his wine, for there were crimson stains on the leaves.

"I was there for your story tonight, Mouther of Rhymes," the Ghost said. "How great the story of Hasurpass! How fascinating the tale of his bravery! How noble his self-sacrifice to come to this castle to liberate people from the tyranny of the evil King Ishka!"

Colin gulped as he stared up at the swordsman's face; there was threat there, yes, but something else also: sadness.

"The people need an epic of Good King Hasurpass, and how he banished the Cowardly Ishka…" Colin mumbled, apologetically.

The specter flickered in the moonlight and fingered his sword as if he meant to take another swipe at Colin, but instead he raised his hands in frustration.

"Mouther of Lies. Bearer of Slander. Peddler of Mind-Murk. Author of Acidic Falsehood. The 'Good' Hasurpass; the 'Cowardly' Ishka. If you fix these lies in song…"

"My song contained no lies. I've woven it around facts, I've framed it with truth. How would you know what happened so many years ago?"

"I know for certain," the Specter said. "For I am King Ihska."

"Of course," Colin stammered, eyeing the sword with a worried eye. "The ghost they whisper about… Now, King Ishka, Your Highness, you must remember a story is just a story…"

"Yes, about the story you presented tonight," Ishka's Ghost said. "'O sing a song, oh Muse, of how the land was liberated by noble Hasurpass, how the tyrant Ishka was banished. Sing of the Siege of Castle Craddauren…'"

The ghost sneered and spat toward the fire, then turned back toward Colin to continue his harangue.

"How you story-mongrels love sex and violence: ribald tales of snatch for the back rooms when warriors swill wine and suck the marrow from chicken bones; poetic epics of war for formal dinners when virgins and clergy are present."

Ishka's ghost pointed its sword toward Colin's heart. "Knew you any battle? Is the blood of a warrior just a little red spice for your stories? Do you know how blood smells in the dark? How it froths out of a man's chest when that chest has been laid open with steel, and that man lies crying on the battlefield? Do you know how blood dries and crusts on a corpse in the course of a day?"

As Ishka's Ghost spoke the tower room dissolved around Colin's sight. Colin was able to look around and see the siege of Castle Craddauren, as it had taken place so many years ago. Here was the detail he had so sorely lacked! Here was the blood which could color his epic rhymes! The creaking of the leather saddles and shields… the clanking of sword and spear…the snapping of gaily-hued battle flags in the chill breezes of morning… Oh, to be a writer and have these life experiences! What fabrics could be woven from such fiber?

"Yes, yes," Ishka's ghost cooed. "Come in, there's more, and all for you, Great Bard. Come in and take what you need. Dip your pen in the red, quickly now, and place these realties on the page."

Colin's quill began scratching across the paper on his lap, as if possessed. This was the story for which every writer pined—the great romance, the excitement, the drama—The Siege of Castle Craddeurann!

"Wonderful, isn't it, Scribbler?" Ishka's Ghost said. "Now look closer…"

Colin continued to write down in verse exactly what he saw. Now what was this? Hasurpass and his army? They were not the noble liberators written about in all versions of the tale so far.

Freebooters, criminals, rapists, looters, lower than mercenaries—and their leader? Hasurpass had no legitimate interest in Castle Craddeurann, nor in the lands surrounding it. Like many such, he'd been closed out of inheritance of his father's lands, shut out by the eldest son. Like many such, he'd taken to wandering, to make his fortune by whatever way…

"Now closer still," Ishka's Ghost murmured. "Look. What is a siege? What was this episode that you should write of it? Is it the great engines of war, towers and catapults? Is it a mark in a history text? Is it banners and campfires and battles at the castle walls?"

Ishka's Ghost gestured with the hand which didn't hold the sword.

"See now, Scribbler," the ghost said. "See the siege from my perspective."

The fields of soldiers disappeared, and Colin's viewpoint was inside the walls of Castle Craddauren. No dogs barked; no cats sat preening in doorways or windows. A boy sat naked from the waist down, plucking up hanks of brown grass and chewing them. A sleepy-eyed Granny held a yellowish baby which neither twitched nor stirred in her arms.

Colin's pen continued to scratch out its red tale.

"What is it that *you* want, Scribbler? What makes existence good for one such as you?" Ishka's Ghost asked.

Colin took on a faraway look; the disillusions of one man's life can sometimes be more distant than history.

"What would make existence good?" Colin repeated. "A great story. Something that would last hundreds of years. To have all eyes on me. To have people say, 'That is the story from Colin the Minstrel, have you heard it?'"

Ishka's Ghost nodded. "So you know what is good, Scribbler; do you know what makes life bad? Do you know the worst part of losing a battle? Do you know the pain of being a King?"

Ishka's ghost stood still, yet wavered in Colin's sight, as if these events of the past still sent waves through him, as if his substance were inextricably tied to that long-ago siege.

"When your people suffer, Scribbler," the Ghost answered his own question. "When your land is hurt. Each subject's life is like a drop of blood from The King. War on the land is like fire on the King's skin."

"So you took action," Colin said. "The story is famous."

Ishka grimaced. "Oh, the story you tell, the story Hasurpass wants told, that's well known. That Hasurpass had a policy to let all women and children out of Castle Craddeuran, that he was merciful, but the tyrant Ishka would let none leave."

Behind the ghost's shoulder, Colin could see a scene by firelight, such a scene as no decent writer could describe in detail without squeamishness. It involved a woman and her children who had tried to sneak past the siege troops. It put the lie to tales of Hasurpass's mercy.

"Yes, you wrote so convincingly that Hasurpass caught the cowardly King Ishka sneaking out of the castle disguised as a woman, and that he tried to steal some food from a campfire and was discovered. And then Hasurpass challenged Ishka to a duel, which caused Ishka to flee in fear and shame, never to be heard from again."

Colin felt a tinge of shame at the lie he'd told.

"So what really happened?" Colin asked.

Ishka gestured behind him, again to a scene of the past. A cloudy dawn, with drizzle falling.

There the castle gates opened, and a lone figure walked out. Hasurpass's camp was near idle, with only a few sentries stirring. Soon tent flaps were opened and some of the freebooters came spilling out, watching the figure approach.

Colin could see it was Ishka, in a leather field uniform, with his chain mail, his steel sword (the size and shape of a foot soldier's sword, such as he had trained with in his youth).

He also carried a white flag of truce.

Hasurpass was summoned, and the two men stood face-to-face.

"'Good King Ishka proposed a duel, the survivor to take Craddeuran,'" Colin whispered. He dipped his pen and wrote as he watched.

For a moment it was as if Hasurpass was considering Ishka's challenge. At the Castle parapets, Ishka's subjects silently watched.

And then Hasurpass raised his sword, turned to the looters at his back, and screamed, "One hundred pieces of gold to the man who gives me Ishka's head!"

Colin could see the ghost standing before him; could see the thousand or so cuts on his body. Beyond the ghost, in the distant past, Colin could see the scene of that gray and rainy morning.

With his right hand Colin wrote the red tale of how King Ishka got seven of his attackers before he met his end.

Colin's hand continued on, pinning the crimson tale to the page before him. As he did this, Colin felt sick. Whatever Ishka had or had not been, he had been human. And to see a human being hacked to death in the rain and mud…

Ishka's Ghost stood back and let the minstrel continue with his text.

"Know you the epilogue, Scribbler? 'Without their leader the Castle fell.'"

"But how could history be so different from what happened?" Colin asked.

"Winners write the history," Ishka's Ghost said. "But such an outlandish lie? I couldn't allow that story you told at the supper tonight to become fixed in time."

"But that's the story everyone knows," Colin said.

Ishka's Ghost pointed toward the pages on Colin's lap with his sword. "And now you've written another. This new tale could last hundreds of years. It will be the story every one associates with Colin the Minstrel."

Colin knew the Ghost of King Ishka was correct. He rose, and didn't even need the book. It was all fixed in his mind. And he would make sure all he encountered would hear it.

After rising Colin took one last glance back at the chair before the fire, which was now glowing embers.

A figure sat there, a quill pen in one hand, pages covered with a revised epic, the true story of Ishka and Hasurpass, written out in blood from the place where an icy sword had opened a vein in his neck. But that lifeless writer was not important.

Colin entered a new existence, one which would last hundreds of years, as he would wander the corridors and towers and catacombs of Castle Craddauren, telling all he found the compelling epic, the story of a lifetime, the true story of Ishka and Hasurpass.

So too did Ishka enter a new existence. He was quieted, and his ghost never seen nor heard again.

And for Hasurpass, the Usurper "King," who had been so treacherous?

His problems were just beginning.

~ * ~ * ~

Charles M. Saplak has been publishing fiction and poetry for the past 30 years. He has two collections of reprinted fiction available on Amazon: QUIET, YET SOMEHOW WRONG, which is all horror stories; and DISPATCHES FROM INFINITY'S BORDER, a collection of science fiction stories. In addition to his ongoing efforts at writing, he occasionally contributes illustrations to current magazines.

His social media is @cmsaplak on X (formerly Twitter), as well as book reviews and essays on www.cmsaplak.com.

The Vampire's Ice Cream Shop

Tim O'Neal

On opening day, towering bunches of red balloons framed the shop's ornate glass doors. At 10 a.m. the shades shot up. Bright lights clicked on, illuminating a spotless dining area with Formica tables and scarlet vinyl booths. The checkerboard tile floor shone. A long lunch counter with red vinyl stools, gleamed before a refrigerator case and an antique soda fountain. Dark red lettering on the window announced it as The Iced-Heme Shop.

But, like anything new in Berkeley, California, the little eatery on Shattuck Avenue caused an instant uproar. Before it'd even opened, citizens organized protests, condemning the new store and its sale of blood products. They marched in mobs, carrying pickets and signs. Dressed in their tie-dye, flannel, tattoos, and piercings, they chanted angry slogans, accusing the proprietor of everything from bestiality to cannibalism.

The mysterious owner, who'd previously avoided all public scrutiny, unlocked the glass door and emerged with a flourish. The large crowd went silent at their first sight of him. A paper hat tilted at a rakish angle atop his frizzy white hair. A dapper elderly gentleman, he carried a gold-tipped cane topped with an egg-sized garnet. He wore a neat buttercream suit with tailcoat. He spun a sun parasol that matched his clothes perfectly. Merry wrinkles seamed his boyish face and his eyes twinkled as he grinned, revealing two sharpened incisors in his mouth.

"Good morning, everyone," he greeted the protesters. "I am Maximus B. Lazarus, the—"

Insults and jeers cut short his opening speech.

"Monster!" a woman in black yoga pants yelled.

"Meat is murder!" someone with matted dreadlocks howled. The crowd picked up this refrain and chanted it.

"Please, please," Max said, waving his long-fingered hands. "I do not sell any meat—"

"You're using animal *blood*! Same thing!"

"Please, all the heme in my products is responsibly sourced—"

A paper lunch bag filled with human excrement sailed through the air and struck Max, leaving an ugly brown stain on his spotless buttercream jacket. More hurled refuse followed—banana peels, overripe fruit, and even a crumpled beige brassiere.

Crushed by this rejection, Max withdrew from the onslaught. He pulled the doors closed and retreated to the solitude of his wooden casket propped up in the storeroom. He climbed in, lowered the lid, and sobbed.

~ * ~

At 2:45pm, the etched-glass door of the shop opened again. A pink-and-green haired teenager, wearing a bright yellow hoodie, bearing the legend: 'Preferred Pronouns = they/them,' entered. The teen's name was Denver, an intersex senior at Berkeley High School.

Denver approached the lunch counter and swung onto a red vinyl stool.

"Hello," they called into the empty parlor. "Anybody home? I'd like to buy an ice cream, please. Hello?"

A rattling clanging thump sounded from the back. A broom slapped the floor. Someone yelped in pain. Moments later, Max appeared, rubbing his head. He blotted his eyes with a bloodred handkerchief. "Good afternoon and welcome," he said. "I'm Maximus B. Lazarus."

"Hey there," Denver replied.

"Please forgive me. Opening Day has not gone quite as I'd planned."

"Oh no. What happened?"

Max sighed. "Well, I thought in Berkeley, people would be more accepting. They're legendary foodies, I figured they'd enjoy a bold new culinary experience. But they won't even *try* my product."

Denver nodded. "Yeah, there're closed-minded people everywhere. But as Oscar Wilde said, 'Diversity of opinion about something means it's new, complex, and vital.'"

"I met Wilde once way back," Max replied. "Extraordinarily nice fellow. Always dressed to the nines."

"You *met* Oscar Wilde," Denver said in disbelief. "As in *the* Oscar Wilde? *No*!"

"Yes, he threw the most fashionable parties. Quite outré."

Denver met Max's twinkling eyes. Something passed between them and they cracked up. Perhaps it was the tension of the failed opening day, but their mirth continued for some time.

Once the chuckles subsided, Max dabbed his streaming eyes. "Thank you. I needed that."

"Sure. Oh, wow. It's warm in here," Denver said, fanning themself and swiping away tears. "If you say you met Wilde, then just how old are you?"

Max considered this. "Roughly three-hundred years, I suppose."

"No, really?" Denver asked, eyes narrowing. "Are you kidding me?"

"Well, in truth, I'm a bit older," Max said. "But what's a decade, here or there?"

When Max didn't elaborate, Denver spoke. "Can I ask something else?"

"Of course."

"*Sooo*, with your age, and the blood ice cream, are you, like, supposed to be a vampire or something?"

"Something like that," Max echoed softly. His pale fingers toyed with the knot of his silk bowtie.

"And what about those things people say? Like drinking human blood, avoiding garlic, dissolving in sunlight? Is any of that true? Aren't vampires dangerous?"

"Certainly not." Max chuckled again. "Vampires are nothing like all that nonsense. No, the real threat is the Happiness Leeches. The Miserable Masses. Like vampires, they've gathered many names over the centuries. But they pose a far greater threat than I."

"Happiness Leeches? What's that?"

"Oh, they're dreadful shades. Every pleasure is anathema to them. They draw their energy by depleting others' joy."

"Yikes! What do they look like?"

"Like anyone you'd pass on the street. That's what makes them so frightening."

Denver nodded. "I bet my Aunt Wendy's one. She's always upset about something."

"Resist them, my friend," Max said. "Otherwise, they'll steal your happiness and fracture your soul. Too many times and it will destroy you entirely. I know from centuries of experience."

"That's terrible, Max. I'm sorry."

Max shrugged. "Tell me about your aunt."

Denver pushed a lock of green hair out of their eyes. "She's the most miserable person ever. We don't often see eye-to-eye on things. And she never allows my nonbinary friends to hang out at our house."

"I am grieved to hear that," Max said. "Please know you and your friends are always welcome here. My shop is a safe place for all."

"'Preciate it," Denver said. "So what brought you out here to California?"

Max opened his mouth, then closed it. He chose his words carefully, "I was no longer welcome back home amongst my fellows."

"I get that," Denver said. "My family doesn't approve of my lifestyle either."

"Indeed. I've been looking for somewhere I could run this humble iced-heme shop. Somewhere the Leeches won't stop me." Max abruptly clapped his hands. "But enough about me. You came here for a sweet treat, not to hear my whole sad tale."

"Yes! Let's talk ice cream," Denver said.

Max frowned. "I'm afraid I don't sell that. Only my own sweet treats. There's the rub."

"As long as it has sugar, sounds good to me," Denver said with a grin. "I love trying new sweets."

"Well, we're in business, then." Max drew himself up as tall as his five-five frame allowed and recited. "My recipe is a centuries-old family secret from Transylvania. It comes in twelve flavors including plain hemoglobin or anemia, for those who prefer a lighter taste. The mint-chip iced-heme tastes like the mint jelly and lamb at Easter. I even have rainbow sherbet." He winked. "Now *that's* a taste you won't forget!"

Denver nodded. "Go on."

Max inhaled, eager to finally deliver his well-rehearsed sales pitch. "All my blood products are ethically sourced. It's more eco-sustainable than regular ice cream! I figured the foodies here would appreciate that. And not a single drop is from humans," he insisted. "So those jackals outside have no right to call me a cannibal. I even offer a *vegan* option, made with plant heme and coconut cream. To be most inclusive."

"Yeah, I don't think those people outside knew any of this," Denver said.

"Still interested in trying a bite? I promise it tastes like the regular stuff, except better."

Denver shrugged. "I came here looking for something sweet and cold that wasn't boba tea. I'm sick of those rubbery tapioca balls."

"Then you're in for a treat—a banana-split iced-heme special, coming up."

Max busied himself, filling a paper boat with three scoops of different iced-heme, topping it with nuts, cherries, and carnival-colored sprinkles.

Once he'd finished this towering confection, he presented it grandly to Denver. "One banana-split special for my first customer. On the house."

"Oh gosh, thanks," Denver said, scooping up a bite. "Looks amazing."

Max leaned in, eagerly awaiting the teenager's reaction.

"Mm. Wow! That's delicious. Super thick and rich," Denver gushed. "You're right, Max. It is better than regular ice cream. You said the blood gives it that lovely flavor?"

Max beamed. "The secret ingredient. Think about it. There're more nutrients in blood than milk. It's so dense with iron, fats, and proteins, they all contribute to the richness of my product."

Denver took another thoughtful bite, rolling it around their mouth like a fine wine. "Hmm. You've got a real winner here, Max."

"I am delighted to hear it," Max said. "Please do tell your friends."

"Oh, I will," Denver said, standing. "Don't give up yet, Max. People will change their minds. Those fools outside don't know what they're missing."

~ * ~

But around lunchtime the next day, more trouble found Max. Two dour nuns entered, prayer beads clicking at their hips. One sister was large and round as an igloo. She reeked of garlic. The second was small and shriveled like a mummy. A tall grim-faced priest completed their entourage. With his prominent cheekbones and dark scowl, the vicar could've starred in his own horror movie.

Max knew them to be Happiness Leeches the moment they entered; he sensed them draining all cheer from his shop. But still, he greeted them warmly.

"Welcome, friends," Max beamed. "How may I serve you? Care to try some fresh iced-heme? Cold and sweet, it comes in twelve flavors—"

"I don't think so," the larger nun snapped. "Not after the complaint we received."

The small, wrinkled nun smacked her weathered lips like a turtle.

"My, a complaint? What about?" Max asked, wringing his hands.

"Our parishioner alleged a *vampire* was selling perverse sweets in this already hedonistic city. We came to investigate."

"A v-vampire?" Max coughed into his elbow. "Well, I wouldn't know anything ab—"

"So with the power vested in me," the priest boomed, "I'll perform an exorcism here."

"An *exorcism*?" Max squeaked, wringing his long-fingered hands. "Surely, that won't be necessary."

The larger nun frowned thunderously.

"I'm afraid it is," the priest intoned. "We must bless this establishment and cleanse it of all evil spirits."

Max waited for them to ask his consent. When none came, he shrugged. "Do whatever will put your mind to rest. But you won't find any evil spirits here. Just tasty frozen treats."

For the next hour, Max looked-on bemused, as the three visitors went about their esoteric business, sprinkling holy water across the tables and checkerboard floor. The priest waved an oversized cross and chanted mumbo-jumbo.

Max turned back to polishing his brass cash register. He wasn't overly concerned. As he'd told Denver, all those superstitious tales of ridding vampires were simply born of fear of the foreign. Xenophobia. The only superstition that might do anything was pounding a wooden stake through a vampire's heart, but that'd finish off *anyone*.

However, twice, Max caught the smaller turtle-faced nun, throwing covetous glances at his freezer case. So as the trio finished up, he scooped up three servings of chocolate iced-heme and placed them on the counter as a peace-offering.

"You had me worried about those evil spirits zooming about. Please, try some iced-heme with my thanks," Max said.

"I think not, my son," the priest droned, frowning. "We don't indulge in heathens or hedonism. Come, my sisters."

With a swirl of black cloth, he departed, followed by the larger nun and the cloying scent of righteous disapproval. However, the older woman glanced back hungrily at the paper trays of chocolate iced-heme and smacked her wrinkled lips. She winked and raised one mummified hand in a covert friendly wave.

Max waved back, enheartened by her gesture. Did it mean his shop might finally catch on? Might it endure the Leeches' assault on good cheer? Maybe. But it'd succumbed to their efforts all the previous times he'd tried…

~ * ~

Aside from the ragtag protesters out front, The Iced-Heme Shop had no further visitors until 2:45p.m. When the bell above the door tinkled, Max glanced up from his gathering despondency and endless polishing.

Wearing red suspenders and hot pink denim pants, Denver bustled in with two other teenagers. Max beamed and straightened his crisp bowtie. He swirled a white apron around his neat suit and doffed his paper hat.

"Welcome back to The Iced-Heme Shop, dear guests."

"Hey, Max," Denver said, sliding onto a ruby-colored stool. "I told my friends about you. Meet Lennon and Briar."

Denver indicated the young woman on the right. Briar had a half-shaved head. She wore a cut-off jean jacket, revealing a tattoo of interlocking female gender symbols on her bicep. On Denver's left, the short boy, Lennon, wore an oversized tie-dye shirt and large round glasses that magnified his soft brown eyes.

Max beamed. "Wonderful. And what would everyone like today?"

"Denver mentioned you have a rainbow sherbet," Lennon said, pushing up his specs. "That sounds good."

The other two gave their orders.

"Coming right up," Max bustled over to the freezer case.

"How're things going today?" Denver asked.

"It's been a long day. Haven't sold a single cone. Unhappy people came in to rant about the evils of my shop."

"More Leeches?" Denver asked.

"Precisely."

"That's too bad."

"Don't take them too seriously," Briar advised, her voice sharp.

"These are the same precious Berkeleyans who tried to make it illegal for homeless people to sit on the sidewalk. I mean, *really*?"

"At least you're still open," Lennon added. "That's something."

"I'm quite surprised," Max said. "With all the protesters, I thought the police would've shut me down and dragged me off."

"What, BPD?" Briar scoffed. "Naw, don't worry about them. They've arrested me in enough demonstrations, I know they don't have any real teeth." She drummed her chipped, polished nails against the lunch-counter.

"I never imagined the public would react as they did to my shop," Max said as he served up three paper boats of iced-heme.

"Naw, Berkeley people will protest *anything*," Lennon said. "That's just how they are."

"Yeah," Briar interjected. "The proletariats always get their panties in a twist whenever something different comes along. Look at any controversy across history—women's rights, for example. That fight's *still* going on."

"She's right, Max," Denver said, digging into their iced-heme. "Your new take on ice cream upsets the expected status quo. People react to any new idea with fear and anger. Remember, they almost burned Galileo for suggesting Earth *wasn't* the center of the universe. I still predict the rest will come around soon."

"Thank you, folks" Max said. "I appreciate your encouragement. But unfortunately, I am lacking in the custom necessary to keep my fledgling business afloat."

"Hmm, if they are trying to shut you down," Briar said between bites, "those protestors are going about it all the wrong way. When you try to silence something, it only grows louder. But I'm sure coming back for more of this stuff. It's delish!"

All three teenagers made hearty sounds of enjoyment as they finished their desserts. They scraped their spoons along the soaked paper trays, paid, and stood to leave.

"Keep the faith, Max," Denver said. "We'll find some more people to come with us next time."

Max watched the three depart, passing the chanting protestors outside. Briar flipped the finger at them as she passed. The crowd had dwindled somewhat. Were the enraged demonstrators losing interest? Would the curious soon start coming in? Because the shop needed more customers to remain in business.

Max's spirits drooped at the idea of having to pack up and move *again*…

He sighed and straightened his bowtie. He went into the backroom to prepare a larger batch of iced-heme for tomorrow. He would remain optimistic whatever mischief the Leeches conjured up this time.

~ * ~

Three days later, Max had another unexpected visitor. A paunchy middle-aged man in a black suit appeared in the doorway. The man wore dark sunglasses and a stoic expression. He glided forward on expensive loafers. A nametag on his breast read: Alameda County Food Inspector Walter C. Price—obviously another Leech coming in to dampen the shop's cheer.

"Good afternoon, sir," Max greeted him. "Care for some iced-heme?"

"No, thank you," Price said stiffly. "I'm here on official business. Our department received a complaint about your establishment—"

"Another one," Max sighed.

"So I'm here with the Public Health Department to inspect your facilities," Price finished. His aviator shades bored into Max. "May I?"

"Please, have a look around," Max said, lifting the folding countertop.

Price produced a clipboard and snapped on blue gloves. For the next two hours, he combed through every cranny, following his checklist. He noted the temperatures in the freezer case and walk-in refrigerators. At one point, he even laid down flat in the back room, reaching into the netherworld beneath the fridge, but found nothing—no evidence of dust bunnies or any other pests.

He stopped once upon seeing Max's humble pine coffin, leaning in its backroom corner.

"What's this?" Price demanded.

"Oh, that," Max said. "Er, nothing. Just extra storage space. A joke, mostly. Please investigate if you wish."

The inspector frowned and opened the lid, finding the interior empty. The aviator shades peered at Max for an explanation.

"When you run an iced-heme shop, people expect a certain amount of the, *ahem*, macabre," Max said.

"If you'll follow me to the front, we'll discuss my findings," Price ordered, snapping off his gloves and clicking his ballpoint pen.

Max shadowed him like a prisoner shuffling to the gallows.

"First of all," Price said, "Compared to the health nightmares I've seen in other kitchens, your shop is one of the cleanest I've seen in the county. Very well done."

"That's kind of you, Inspector."

"Indeed it's rare when I can't find any food safety violations." Price paused. "I commend you. Despite the oddness of your product, it seems you prepare it in good order and obey best practices."

Price signed a blue and white inspection certificate on his clipboard and handed it to Max, who accepted with trembling fingers.

"Display that in your front window to show your compliance," Price said. His leather shoes slapped against the immaculate tile. "Good day."

For the first time in two hours, Max exhaled. His shop had survived this latest assault. Even the health inspector hadn't found a reason to remove him. All his endless polishing had paid off and thwarted the Leeches.

Incisors glinting, Max beamed.

~ * ~

After school, Denver stopped by The Iced-Heme Shop. Inside, other teenagers hunched around the tables, socializing and studying. Several had even picked up their middle-school siblings and brought them along. The younger children, of course, were thrilled to hang out with their "grown up" friends.

Denver slid onto the last available red stool. "You got a good-sized crowd in here, Max."

Max slid a deluxe sundae over to Denver. "I believe my shop is catching on as people grow accustomed to the idea. Every day the crowd outside shrinks a little more."

He gestured to where a couple protestors still loitered with their drooping picket signs.

"That's terrific, Max!" Denver dug in a spoon and scooped up a large mouthful of whipped cream, bananas, and a cherry. "Yumm!"

"All thanks to you and your friends," Max said. "Say, with the increase in business, I could use some help around the shop. Would you, Briar, and Lennon like to work here?"

Denver stared in disbelief.

Max continued hurriedly, "But I would understand completely if you didn't want to upset your aunt—"

"Are you kidding? We'd love that!" Denver exclaimed. "Jobs at this place? That'd be *super* cool, Max. Yes, thank you!"

Max winked. "Since you three brought in so many new customers, you're almost founding members of my little shop."

"I'm all for it," Denver replied. "Plus it'll give me a chance to annoy Aunt Wendy. Brilliant! I'll ask Briar and Lennon about it right now. Max, you're the best!"

Denver gobbled down the rest of the sundae and bounced off the red stool, eager to tell their friends the good news. Max smiled, sharing in Denver's happiness, unaware of the trouble that would soon assail his iced-heme parlor.

~ * ~

A month after Opening Day, Max drifted among the tables, spraying the spotless surfaces with disinfectant. *Eerk-eerk-eerk*, squeaked the yellow plastic handle. The bell above the door chimed and a sixtyish woman in a somber ankle-length dress entered. An immaculate sheaf of silver hair hung stiffly to her bony shoulders. Her blue eyes glowed with wrath. A multifaceted amethyst brooch flashed like a dragon's eye at her throat.

The intensity of her rage made her regal and Max recognized her instantly. Standing before him, was the Queen of Misery, herself—the Supreme Regent of Leeches. Mother Superior of Despondency. The air temperature in the shop plummeted.

"You," she began, her voice scraping like an icepick. She jabbed a finger at Max.

"Er, yes, madam?" he asked, clutching the yellow squirt bottle to his chest. "I bid you a pleasant aftern—"

"Be quiet!" she ordered. "How dare you offer my godchild a job in this *place* without my permission?"

Max blinked. "Pardon me? Who?" Then realization filled his face. "Ah, you must be Denver's Aunty Wendy. They mentioned you. It's a pleasure—"

"No," she interrupted. "This ice cream shop is an absolute *disgrace*. You're feeding children animal *blood*. It's a blasphemous violation of family values!"

"Please, madam, you are mis—"

"Furthermore," Aunt Wendy castigated, "Denver visits this despicable place far too often and fills up on your poisonous desserts, never leaving room for dinner, and ruining their teeth. Our latest dental bills are atrocious!"

The shop had gone silent as customers watched the heated exchange.

Like a plummeting barometer, Max sensed the happiness fading from his shop. This woman, this incensed Leech, was sucking the customers' delight as easily as a vampire might guzzle down a quart of blood. As the queen fed, her voice deepened and became colder, metallic.

"You don't belong here. You never did. No one wants you here, old fool," she spat.

Max staggered and, for an instant, almost believed her. He could feel the bedrock of his whole endeavor—peddling edible joy—crumbling. If this conversation continued much longer, then the spirit of his shop, all he'd struggled to assemble, would crack and he would lose to the Leeches again, for no one would return to a café drained of its merriment, leaving behind an empty shell, which no longer provided the insulating shelter of escapism.

But he refused to lose this shop that'd brought such delight to him and other misfits. He'd found a *community* here that accepted him after his three-hundred years of peripatetic wandering. No.

Max summoned all the cheer he could muster from his polished shoes to his frizzy white hair. He conjured every particle of his positivity. He stared straight into the Queen's frosty eyes.

And smiled.

"You're wrong," he said.

The Queen blinked. Then she laughed—a sound as harsh as a bear trap snapping closed. "Wrong? No, Vampire. I am never wrong."

"If I may, madam," Max insisted, planting his polished loafers and straightening his back. "Your quarrel is not with me. Not here." His winning smile never flickered.

The Queen emitted an angry squawk, but Max held up a long-fingered hand, silencing her.

"You dislike that Denver spends time in my establishment," Max continued, "but your miserable asceticism is no way to live. My shop is a safe harbor for these young people. If they feel comfortable, then I refuse to banish them from passing happy afternoons here with their friends. All are welcome."

"Of all the nonsense," the Queen of Misery spat. Then, fast as a serpent, she changed tactics, "How irresponsible. You won't even accept the gluttony and immorality you've created? Can't you see the *harm* you're causing—?"

"We don't serve harm here. Only sweet treats. Try one. Please."

Her blue eyes narrowed. "I'd rather swallow a spoonful of misery."

Max spread his palms. "Then how may I ease your discomfiture regarding my presence?"

The Queen's voice shook with rage. "*Leave*," she cried. "Pack up your murderous iced-heme before you cause any more damage."

Every eye in the shop stared as Max beamed his boyish grin at the Mistress of Misery.

"I'm afraid that's quite impossible, madam," he said softly. "I've travelled too far and for too many years to surrender. I've found my permanent home and I plan to remain here indefinitely. Now, if you have finished your diatribe, I will ask you, with utmost politeness, to vacate my shop. And have a lovely day."

The woman's blue eyes flashed along with her amethyst brooch. "I'll do anything I can to rid this city of your *filthy* shop," she hissed.

"No you won't," a customer piped up. "We love this place too much."

"Yeah, Max is the best," another teen agreed, grinning.

More voices added their acclaim for Max and his iced-heme shop.

At the upswell of cheerful adoration, the Queen flinched in pain and screeched. Faced with smiles, she retreated as if splashed with acid.

"I will *ruin* you, Vampire," the Queen hissed. "Ruin! Count on it."

"We'll see. Until then, we'll be here," Max said. "In the meantime, please do tell your friends to stop by. We'll be waiting." His grin exposed his glinting incisors.

The Queen of Misery stormed from the Iced-Heme Shop in ill-concealed defeat.

When the door slammed closed behind her, the patrons cheered, applauding.

Pride flooded Max. With his customers' help, he'd faced down the greatest Happiness Leech and triumphed. No one—not the clergy, the dwindling protestors, nor even the Queen of Misery herself—could bully him from his beloved shop.

No, this time, he was home to stay.

"Right then. Who's next?" Max beamed, straightened his cap, and resumed serving customers.

~ * ~

Six months after the shop opened, the last angry demonstrators vanished, drifting away to protest other causes. Inside, the iced-heme parlor sported a festive air. Young people packed the interior. A hodge-podge of teenagers chatted at the tables, the lunch counter, or in small groups by the walls. Everyone was laughing and eating pink tinged iced-heme. A line of customers extended onto the sidewalk.

Sprays of red balloons bobbed from their tethers. Above the counter, a large hand-written sign announced 'Congrats, Max!!' Rainbow flags draped from the ceiling. Sunlight spilled in through the cut-glass doors—colorful spectrums danced across the floor. Plumes of joy floated on the air.

In his thick glasses, Lennon bustled around the shop, cleaning tables as quickly as they became available. With a hairnet over her half-shaved head, Briar hunched behind the counter, scooping out customers' orders. She'd rolled up the white sleeves of her button-down shirt, exposing her inter-locking tattoos. Denver stood proudly at the cash register, ringing up orders as fast as Briar slung them out.

Max materialized from the backroom. He wore a gaudy rainbow-striped bowtie with his crisp buttercream suit. The inescapable paper hat perched jauntily atop his frizzy white hair.

Denver noticed Max and started clapping, calling out, "Here he is, folks! Maximus B. Lazarus, proud owner of the world-famous Iced-Heme Shop. Let's give him a hand!"

The crowded eatery burst into applause. Whistles punctuated the cacophony.

Max blushed scarlet. He waved his long-fingered hands, warding off unwanted adulation, but still the noise expanded.

The crowd chanted, "Speech! Speech! Speech!"

Max tried to retreat to his coffin, but Denver shoved him forward. The applause swelled. As the clamor faded, Max gulped.

"Thank you, my friends," he began, voice shaking.

Someone wolf-whistled. Another person screamed, "We love you, Max!"

Max smiled into the sea of faces and bright wash of colors. "My friends, I don't have much to say except my sincerest thanks for your support these past six months. It's been a struggle, but together, we persevered and overcame adversity. And after far too many years of wandering, I've found my home, my *community*. I can't articulate how much I…"

Tears overcame him, choking his voice, forcing him to take out his scarlet handkerchief. This time, the applause roared as the guests cheered Max's short speech.

Denver patted Max on the back as people returned to their desserts. "Well said, Max," Denver said. "Hey, thanks again for giving us jobs. And for sticking up for us—with the protestors and Leeches like Aunt Wendy. All of it. I know it wasn't easy."

Max dismissed this with a flip of his red hanky. "I would never have done otherwise. I've been drifting too long. I'm grateful to have finally found my permanent dwelling. For the first time in my long life, I can finally be happy."

"Me too, Denver said. "And I hope your shop is here for the next three-hundred years. This city needs it *and* all it stands for."

Max nodded, too overcome to reply.

"Yo, Denver," Briar's voice interrupted. "What are you doing? Get your butt over here, I need some help. We got hella customers!"

"Gotta go," Denver said. "Thanks again, Max."

Denver returned to the cash register.

Max surveyed his shop. A year ago, he'd never have imagined this kind of success; he was much too accustomed to the constant drudge of packing up his belongings. But now, after long centuries of travelling, he'd finally triumphed against the Leeches. His eatery teemed with contented patrons.

Max beamed. With the help of Denver, Briar and Lennon, they'd created this community where all flavors of people were welcome to scoops of happiness at The Iced-Heme Shop.

~ * ~ * ~

Tim O'Neal is an Associate Member of SFWA. His stories have appeared in the British Science Fiction Association's *Fission #2 vol.1* and *Ember Literary Journal,* among others. He is an amateur juggler. Currently, Tim lives in Washington, DC and is working on a PhD in nutrition and chronic disease prevention.

A Charmed Life

Rob Nisbet

"I'm sorry about this Mrs Rodgers, but the doctor would like one more blood test."

"Now?" Silvia struggled to lift her head awkwardly from the pillow. "Ruddy vampire. Doesn't he know I'm about to have a baby."

The midwife smiled her sympathy but stood her ground, she would not be put off. Obediently Silvia lay back with a sigh, her left palm upwards while the midwife tapped at her elbow joint coaxing a vein to the surface.

"Just another little scratch Mrs Rodgers. I guess by now your arm must feel like a pin cushion." She mustered a professional smile as she inserted the needle. "Odd sort of scabbing…" She studied the other needle marks as she drew out a syringe of deep red liquid. "Doesn't look like dried blood, more like they've rusted over."

Silvia gave a sharp whimper and clutched at her bulging stomach with her free hand.

"Another contraction?" The midwife pressed a ball of cotton wool over Silvia's latest puncture. She placed the syringe in a dish and passed it to a young nurse who scuttled out with the sample for analysis. "Your husband had better hurry up or he'll miss the birth."

Silvia lay back on the hospital bed and tried to breathe normally. That's when the midwife noticed her wrist.

"Your bangle," she said. "A charm bracelet is it? Do you want to take it off? It looks very tight pressing into your wrist like that."

Silvia held the bracelet out for inspection. "It doesn't come off," she said, "there's no clasp."

"Must be." The midwife took a closer look. "Well, I never. How on earth did you get it on in the first place? Did you slip it on when you were younger and your wrist a bit thinner?"

"Something like that." Silvia said, but the truth was even stranger.

The midwife was feeling around the chain. "It's definitely too tight," she said. "Look here it's caused some sort of inflammation under the skin—a hard bump. We'll sort out baby first, but later we'll get a doctor to look at that wrist—probably have to cut off the bracelet I'm afraid. What metal is it? It's not silver—too dull, is it pewter, something like that?"

Silvia shrugged—she had no idea what metal it was—if indeed it was a real metal at all.

"Matches your earrings I see," the midwife said. She examined the shiny-grey hoops. "That's unusual," she said, "your hoops have no clasp or catch either—they look like a solid circle passing through your ear lobes. How's that done then, eh? Is it like two half circles that slot together?"

Silvia grinned, glad of the distraction. "No. I had my ears pierced when I was ten or eleven, they got quite messy and infected at the time—I couldn't wear my studs 'cos of this discharge. Anyway, this metallic pewter-like stuff was coming out of the hole where my ear was pierced, like a thin strand oozing out of the front and back of each ear. I didn't like to touch them, and in a few days the strands had joined together and thickened into these hoops. They look like earrings, but whatever they are, they're part of me."

The midwife gave Silvia a reproachful look; she clearly didn't believe a word. She tilted the watch that hung over her left breast and, as if on cue, Silvia convulsed with another contraction. "Won't be long now," she said. She pulled absently at her own ear lobes. "I could never stand the thought of having my ears pierced. It's funny isn't it; I can happily poke needles into other people all day but can't abide them near myself." She laughed, "You won't find me getting my belly button skewered."

Silvia felt the contraction ease—that had been the strongest one yet. She sighed. "You won't approve of Stan then, when he gets here. He's got piercings everywhere!"

The midwife glanced at the doorway to the corridor. The nurse should be back with the results from the blood test any moment—she knew how urgent they were. And the doctors wanted to be called if the iron level of Silvia's blood was still high. She turned back to her patient, turning on her reassuring chat. "These piercings of—Stan's, was that his name? —are they normal or did some metal extrude itself out of holes he made in himself?" She laughed, not expecting an answer. "Let's have another look at your chain—I read in a magazine that you can tell a lot about a person by their choice of charms on a bracelet."

Silvia held out her wrist for inspection.

"Why, they're just blobs," the midwife said. "Shapeless blobs—not charms at all."

But Silvia knew otherwise: At the time, she'd thought it just another stage of puberty when she felt the ring of bumps beneath her skin. She hadn't mentioned it, even to her mum or her friends—it was sort of embarrassing—another symptom of how her body was growing up. In time the bumps had grown through the skin of her wrist, segments of a perfect chain linked together to form a bracelet. Silvia knew it was a part of her, attached tightly round her wrist. Like her earrings, it had a metallic sheen but she'd no idea what they were really composed of, bone perhaps.

The bracelet looked tight, but it didn't hurt, so Silvia just accepted it as part of her arm. Just as she accepted the appearance of the charms over the years. There had been that car accident. Silvia wasn't expected to survive, but she pulled through—and had gained a charm in the process. They seemed to form at periods of her life of emotional overload. Her first experience of teenage love, the day her father died, her wedding—they may look like shapeless blobs to the midwife, but Silvia knew they were charms. Each one forged by her own body and added to the chain like a physical memory.

Several things then happened at once.

Stan appeared, flushed but grinning, shown through the door by the young nurse with the blood-test results.

The midwife nodded to Silvia. "I see what you mean," she said gesturing to Stan's pierced eyebrow, nose and the dull metal spike just below his lower lip. Silvia had said he was pierced *everywhere* but speculation of these locations would have to wait. The midwife took one glance at the test results—as before, iron levels and metallic traces in the blood were off the scale. She dispatched the nurse immediately to fetch the doctors—but she doubted they'd arrive before the birth. Silvia, with Stan at her bedside, was wracked by another contraction.

~ * ~

It was a girl. She had bewildered looking blue eyes, a downy film of dark hair and a healthy glow to her still-wrinkled skin. Silvia and Stan brimmed with joy at their new arrival.

The midwife washed her hands. The doctors hadn't turned up yet—luckily it had been a straightforward birth, no complications, and a beautiful new baby.

In the sudden bustle of activity not even Silvia had noticed the hard swelling at her wrist had erupted into new charm on her bracelet—another emotional experience made physical. Her metallic blood traces would now drop to normal for a while—as if to confuse the medical staff even further.

All attention, naturally, was switched to the new baby, who began to cry in Silvia's arms.

"She's got a good pair of lungs, that one," the midwife said. "That's a healthy sign."

Silvia cuddled her precious daughter close as her new blue eyes creased with her crying. And a glistening tear slid like quicksilver down her tiny cheek.

Originally published in: My Weekly magazine Wellbeing Special April/May 2009

~ * ~ * ~

Rob Nisbet has had around 100 stories printed in anthologies and magazines ranging from romance (using his wife's name) to horror. His wife has recently turned to crime. He also writes audio drama. He has adapted work by Philip K. Dick for radio and has had several audio scripts produced by Big Finish/BBC for their Doctor Who range.

Betwixt and Between

Karen Keeley

"Cassie, child—you be stayin' clear of that picket fence," Mama-Lu hollered. "You hear me, girl? You go over that fence and these eyes never see you again."

Cassie Fairchild nodded assent. Sixteen years steering clear of that picket fence, nothing more than a kept dog, a hound to do the fetching, cooking, and cleaning. Except better than a dog having been given the run of the yard, not chained to a doghouse, panting in the heat, begging for a piece of carrot, a dried-up old turnip.

Mama-Lu entered the house, every room begging for a breath of fresh air. The screen door slammed shut. The wind rustled the withered corn stalks in the adjacent field, and beyond that, the cool dark forest filled with savory pine, cedar, thistles and thorns.

Cassie grabbed one rope of the swing hung from the largest branch of the tall maple rooted near their artesian well. She sat down, both hands clasping the rope as she twisted her body in a circle, judging the height of the fence, realizing for the first time, it wasn't really that high, how easy for her to jump it, like a deer, and then what would Mama-Lu say? Oh, she'd have a fit! Cassie knew that. But what would really happen? It wasn't like she'd disappear—she was here, solid flesh and blood. It was Mama-Lu's way of keeping her chained to the property. Without Cassie, Mama-Lu had no one.

Cassie's imaginary friend Ryerson, brown as a nut and looking every inch the garden gnome popped up from beneath the withered cabbages, his boyish grin smiling at her. "Look what I found," he said.

Cassie pulled her mane of dark hair into a serviceable ponytail. She left the shade of the maple, shooed aside the chickens scratching for food and stepped over the cabbages. Ryerson held an eagle feather the length of Cassie's arm. "Found it over by the fence," he sighed. "Wished I could've seen it fly."

"Me, too," Cassie said. "I bet they're beautiful, all the world to see."

She and Ryerson sat cross-legged in the shade of the tall maple, imagining what it would be like to be a bird, soaring above the mosaic landscape, an invitation to explore. Later, when Mama-Lu called Cassie into the house, she said her good-byes to Ryerson as he slipped beneath the cabbages. It was siesta time, much needed during the hottest part of the day, a routine as rigid as Mama-Lu's unbending spine.

Sometime later Cassie woke to the sound of angry hooves pounding the dirt tract which led to her home. She peered through the open window high in the rafters, keeping to the shadows, and there, a band of outriders approaching, thick dust churning the air. The tallest of the bunch spurred his pony forward, the animal pressing against the picket fence. "We come for the girl, Miz Haven," he hollered. "Old Hector be sayin' he seen her when workin' in the corn field."

Cassie heard the squeak of the screen door; then Mama-Lu came into view, her trusted shotgun nestled in one arm like a newborn babe. Her calico dress flapped around her thin frame; her soft white hair feathered above her wrinkled brow. "Ain't no girl here," she hollered. "And I knowed you, Davie Spiegel—you get now and leave an old woman in peace."

Davie, assuming the role of leadership, spat into the dust.

"Hector's been known to smoke the wacky tobacci," Mama-Lu shouted. "We all heard his stories about Bigfoot and flying saucers. I been there when he's doing the tellin'. Now get, you'll find no girl on my property."

Davie straightened in the saddle, arched his back, sat taller on his dapple-grey pony. He spat a second time, a long brown gob of greasy tobacco landing in the dirt. "The General believes him. He's got Hector up at the compound, been feedin' him peyote. You know that for a truth serum, I'm sure."

Mama-Lu stepped forward, lifted her chin in defiance. "You try bridging that fence and I'll turn you and that prize pony of yours into chicken feed," she shouted. "Don't be thinkin' I couldn't. Come to think on it, I could do with a supply of feed, the chickens have been looking a might peaked."

Davie backed up his pony and glared stony eyed at the old woman.

Mama-Lu clenched her jaw. "The General can believe whatever

he wants," she hollered. "Sixteen years since my Jake passed, and him tellin' others, the two of them friends." Mama-Lu spat into the dirt. "Some friend doubtin' my word. I pay my yearly tithe, vegetables and fruit. Eggs too, when I got 'em. The General's got no right hasslin' me on my own property. Like I said, you get, and forget about a girl. There ain't no girl."

Davie dug his boot heels into the side of his pony. The animal reared up, spinning sideways, and then leapt away. The others followed, leaving a choking dust cloud in their wake. Mama-Lu shouldered the shotgun, turning back toward the house. She knew Cassie, hidden in the rafters, would've heard every last word.

~ * ~

At dinnertime, Cassie heard a knocking sound. "I'm hearing something strange," she said. "Like a faraway heartbeat."

"Can't hear nothin'," Mama-Lu snapped. "Eat your vittles and quit trying to distract me."

Cassie pushed her spoon around in the thin broth, knowing in her heart of hearts she could hear a heartbeat, or what sounded like a heartbeat. It was uncanny the way it called to her, a kind of musical riff disrupting her thoughts. Maybe Mama-Lu's hearing was about as busted as an old snuff jar after all. She was no spring chicken, was Mama-Lu. Cassie smiled to herself at that thought. If she spoke it aloud, Mama-Lu was liable to give her a quick smack across the cheek. Hurt like hell when Mama-Lu slapped her, always for something trivial, like breaking an egg when there were dozens more. Or traipsing mud across the kitchen floor after it rained—how in blazes was a body supposed to enter a home and not traipse mud when thunder and lightning stormed right outside the door, the whole world shaking.

Cassie twirled her spoon, her appetite gone. Not that she had much of one with this annoying heat. Six weeks since they'd last seen rain, and it was getting harder to coax plentiful buckets of water from the artesian well to water the garden. Maybe the well too, was drying up, much like the land, most of it parched. The corn field, ugly and withered, the yellow stocks burnt to a crisp, and no one willing to tend the crop except for Hector, just too dang hot.

"I gotta go to town tomorrow," Mama-Lu said. "You know what that means."

"Yes, ma'am," Cassie whispered. It meant a morning in the root cellar with her books to keep her company. She hated the root cellar though it was much cooler than being stuck in the rafters. Problem was, there were creepy crawlies down there in the dark, and her measly flashlight didn't always keep them away. She stood and cleared the soup bowls from the table, set them in the kitchen sink. She boiled water. Presently she set a pot of tea on the table and Mama-Lu poured.

"Those men what come, I expect you heard what was said." Mama-Lu's voice had taken on a caustic tone, her words slithering with venom. "The reason I got to keep you a secret. Those men would hurt you—hurt you bad," she sneered. "I may be one smart cookie with a few spells up my sleeve, but might is right, and that means, I'd lose you. You understand me?"

Cassie nodded, thinking—no, not really, but she knew better than to question Mama-Lu's musings. And there, that heartbeat, that knocking sound with its rhythmic *da dum, da dum,* it seemed to be growing louder. How could Mama-Lu not hear it?

Mama-Lu stood, picked up her teacup and headed to the sitting room, to her favourite chair piled high with soft cushions, the chair nestled next to the footstool. Cassie remained in the kitchen and washed the dishes, shadows lengthening, dusk falling across the yard. Sixteen summers gazing at that corn field, and the cool green forest beyond. Sixteen summers learning about the outside world from the many books Mama-Lu had stored on bookshelves, learnin' materials the old woman called them. Cassie supplemented the books with monthly magazines, propaganda as far as the old woman was concerned, delivered to the Kettle Creek post-office, one of the many stops Mama-Lu made when purchasing supplies.

Cassie dried her hands and went to the sitting room—Mama-Lu fast asleep in her chair.

Ryerson appeared from behind one of the bookshelves. "I hear it, too," he said. He sat cross-legged on the braided rug, wisps of his unruly locks curling over his shirt collar.

"I wonder what it means," Cassie whispered. She'd taken up her drawing pad, set it on her lap, busy making swirls and paisley patterns with her coloured pencils, a soothing activity which always calmed her, knowing the root cellar awaited her come morning.

"Don't worry," Ryerson said. "I'll keep you company."

"I know you will," Cassie whispered. She smiled, thankful for her imaginary friend.

Ryerson disappeared back into the bookshelf. Cassie stood, setting aside her pad and pencils. A sharp pain ripped its way through her mid-section and up the small of her back. She doubled over, the pain taking her totally by surprise. She raced for the upstairs toilet, threw herself onto the porcelain throne and there, blood leaking out of her, she let out a godawful scream. Footsteps pounded the staircase, Mama-Lu standing there wide-eyed with fright.

"Something is happening," Cassie groaned. "Something terrible!"

Mama-Lu took up a washcloth and gently washed between Cassie's quivering legs. "No child, it's part of the whirlin' way. Some call it a blessing, others a curse. I always knowed this day be a'comin'. Now it's time for the truth no matter how difficult the telling."

Mama-Lu made a fresh pot of tea. She and Cassie sat in their favourite chairs. Cassie concentrated on Mama-Lu's story: "You were born under a blood moon, a hunter's moon, the likes the forest had never seen. Your ma'm ran away from her forest clan, love taking her into the arms of your da, a tidewater drifter far from home, him collecting mushrooms and other wild herbs and roots. She knew it were wrong. But the ways of the heart rule stronger than common sense. Your ma'm came to me, knowin' I'd done the same, joining myself to Jake, me labeled an outcast, never allowed to return."

Cassie sat wide-eyed, watching Mama-Lu, wondering if the old woman had finally taken leave of her senses, the dreaded wasting disease eating her thoughts, making her spit out this drivel and nonsense.

"If any man knew of your existence, they'd done trap you. Force you to do their bidding," Mama-Lu said. "The worst of the men is the General—he's the one what's after rulin' this land with tyranny, clutching at the throats of others with an iron fist."

Cassie held her tongue, not wanting to break the spell now that Mama-Lu was talking. She still wondered about the blood, how that could possibly be a good thing? But Mama-Lu said it was natural—the next phase moving toward maturity.

"That Davie Spiegel, he's the meanest of all," Mama-Lu spat. "Oh, how he'd love to get his hands on you, make you a present to the good ol' General. Mark my words, Davie boy is bad blood. He comes from the rock walled cliff clan, a cantankerous bunch what moved here after the war, most of his relatives dead, only him and one brother left, if memory serves."

Mama-Lu sighed, took another sip of her tea. "I should'a been teaching you the whirlin' ways, me no better than the General, keeping you a prisoner, thinking I was protecting you. And I knowed better. The road to perdition is always paved with good intentions."

"We're not blood?" Cassie asked.

The old woman shook her head. "We come from the same forest clan, but we're not blood. I been using a camouflage spell to keep you hidden from the outside world. That day Hector saw you when working in the field, what Davie Spiegel got on about, made me realize my power is slippin', my ability to protect you is waning."

"A camouflage spell?" Cassie echoed.

"Think of the forest creatures, a baby fawn, the colour of the thicket, lying quiet. The fawn carries no scent, keeps it safe from predators."

Cassie nodded.

"Now listen," Mama-Lu said. "You'll be needin' to concentrate if you're to find your true path. Can you do that?"

Cassie nodded a second time. "What about tomorrow and the root cellar?"

"That'll have to wait," the old woman said. "We got much to do, and time is short."

~ * ~

Cassie came to learn Mama-Lu was born into the eagle clan. After meeting Jake, and falling for his broad shoulders, inviting smile, and unruly locks of raven hair, she kept her human form, settling down with the man she loved in the house he'd built. Cassie's ma'm too, transformed from her spirit as a wide-eyed prancing doe. But unable to control the nuances of her new body, she died only moments after Cassie's delivery. Her pa, heartbroken, disappeared into the night, never to be seen again. "But no matter," Mama-Lu said. "You were delivered into my arms; my Jake having been taken from me that very night. I took it as a sign, the cycle of life. I was grateful for your tiny presence even as I wallowed in my own grief."

"Tell me about the war," Cassie said. "What happened?"

Mama-Lu rubbed her tired eyes, turning her focus inward. "Sometime at the start of the last millennia, mankind destroyed not only his own, but most of the natural world, too. Some say it was retribution, Mother Nature sprinkling the magic what allowed all flora and fauna to take back what was rightly theirs. But even during the war, millions dyin' through pestilence and disease, there was some who escaped. They came together in towns and settlements, tryin' to resurrect some semblance of what was."

Mama-Lu explained, despite a second chance to mend their ways, humankind simply saw it as a shift in power. Some, like the General, embraced the darkness, using brute force and sheer terror to gain a foothold, dictating life and death over those weaker than themselves.

"Is that why you hate him so?" Cassie asked.

"He's the one what took my Jake," Mama-Lu said. "He knew me for what I was, Jake sharing that truth with the General, something he should'a never done. I said they was friends. But if truth be told, they was more than friends. They was blood brothers, both tidewater drifters like your da, from that clan far beyond the mountains."

The General ended Jake's life in a fit of anger, accusing Jake of treason against his own kind, referring to those like Mama-Lu as twixters, a play on words, no better than the raven, the trickster. "Your ma'm and me, we tried to bridge the natural world with that of man, a feeble attempt to try and teach others the magic, to show them we could live in harmony."

The night Jake was killed, he'd demanded the release of the young'uns kidnapped by the General, using Davie Spiegel as his instrument of torture. The young'uns were abducted from outlying farms and homesteads, Davie acting on rumour, innuendo, and gossip.

"Some of the children were born from the union of man and twixter, but not all," Mama-Lu said. "Through torture, they were made to revert to their spirit form. Those who were not twixter simply died."

Mama-Lu explained, once broken, the twixters were imprisoned in the General's compound, some kept as domestic livestock, others like the ponies and the mules used for transportation, others put to work in the fields. Many of the dogs were trained to guard the compound perimeter, all of it a desecration against Mother Nature's creed that all life should live in harmony. "There was hope in the beginning," Mama-Lu said. "But the General and others like 'im, soon put an end to that. And now, there are fewer twixters, what means the General has fewer children to find and torture for his own sick demented means."

"And all these years later, you still pay the yearly tithe—give that monster his due!" Cassie felt anger bristle the hairs at the nape of her neck.

"I pay my tithe on account I couldn't return to my natural state." Mama-Lu closed her eyes, rubbed her forehead, so much weariness about the old woman. "What you got to understand, child. It be like dialing into a different frequency, becomin' one with the animals, the plants and the trees. Exceptin' once blood has been shed, we be trapped in the betwixt and between, locking us in the form we be takin'. I needed to protect you until you come of age." She then spoke of the whirlin' ways. "Not all creatures partake of the magic," she said. "Some are content to remain as they are. If you reckon those chickens in the yard scratching in the dirt, they be happy bein' who they is. But some, like your ma'm and me, we wanted more."

"And you belonged to the eagle clan," Cassie whispered. "Oh, how I would've loved to be you—to soar high above the earth, gliding on the updrafts, feeling the wind in my feathers."

"You get your thoughts out of the clouds and down here, with me," Mama-Lu snapped. "All twixters has got a spirit, me the eagle, your ma'm the deer. Now we got to figure out your spirit, and then we got to get you gone."

"Gone!" Fear grabbed Cassie's heart. "I belong here, with you."

"If I didn't knowed better, I'd be taking you for an Arctic hare or a ptarmigan," Mama-Lu barked. "Ain't you been listenin'? All that fear inside of you."

"And who's fault is that?" Cassie snapped. "Keeping me yarded like a bleedin' dog."

"I'll take no cuss words from you, young lady. Now you listen up, what I got to say is important. My power is waning. I can't protect you. Not no more." Mama-Lu grabbed Cassie's hands and held them tight. "I expect Davie Spiegel will return. When he does, he'll find you. I can be tryin' to fight him but I knowed in the end, he and his kind will win. They always do."

Tears trickled down Cassie's cheeks. "I'm not leaving. This is my home!"

"All chicks gotta leave the nest," Mama-Lu whispered. "You just be doin' it a tad later than most."

~ * ~

The following morning, Mama-Lu brought her treasure box down from her bedroom and placed it on the kitchen table. She opened the lid with a gentle touch, laying out the contents, numerous feathers from owls, hawks, and eagles—all the birds of the forest. There then came the incisors and molars from the mammals: cougar, badger, beaver and wolf along with numerous vials of fish scales: salmon, trout, and pickerel followed by marlin and a shark.

"Where did you find all this?" Cassie asked as she lifted one of largest molars, rolling it in the palm of her hand, wondering if it was bear or cougar.

"Found some myself over the years," Mama-Lu said. "The more exotic items I traded for when drifters be passin' by, most stoppin' for water for themselves and their livestock. There's a heap sight missing. But what I got; it'll have to do. You pick 'em up, each item, hold it in your hand, close your eyes, and concentrate."

Cassie did as she was told. All that day she sat in the kitchen, waiting for a vibration, a tingle in the palm of her hand, but nothing. Each time she opened her eyes she felt foolish and silly, Mama-Lu nothing more than a foolish old woman, making up stories, the wasting disease happening after all. Cassie wanted to swipe the box from the table. Instead, she moaned, "My head hurts. I'm tired. I'm hot—I want to rest."

"Rest is for the dead," Mama-Lu barked. "We ain't got no time for rest or the dead. Again, whaddya smell? Whaddya see and hear?"

"I only hear that heartbeat," Cassie lamented. She covered her ears. "The sound you say you can't hear!" She kept her hands pressed to her head. That horrid heartbeat throttling her brain. She then heard the sound of clattering hooves, the squeak of leather harnesses, bridles and saddle stirrups. Horses' hooves tramping the dirt tract leading to Mama-Lu's property.

Outriders and a wagon approaching. "Damn," Mama-Lu said. "I was hopin' for more time."

"Time for what?" Cassie asked, releasing her hands, that heartbeat sound amplified.

"Time to deal with the likes of the General. Get to the rafters, and stay put."

Cassie left the table and climbed once again into the rafters, squatting in the shadows, peering out of the window, half hidden behind the gossamer curtains, and there, Davie Spiegel and his gang of outriders. In the mist of the ponies and the men, a buckboard pulled by two mules, both animals weary and broken, sat the General, his hands holding the reins. He hollered, "Mary Lou Haven, you come now. I got a bone to pick with you."

Mama-Lu lifted the shotgun from its perch on the kitchen wall and stepped onto the porch. "You be talkin' to me like I be a dog," she hollered. "A dog got more manners than you, old man."

"And you been misbehavin'," the General shouted. "Come out from under that overhang. I wanna know about the girl."

"I told your mouthpiece, there ain't no girl," Mama-Lu shouted. "You might be thinking you got a bone to pick. If so, come closer, tell it to my face." She knew Davie would have told the General about her threat to turn him and his pony into chicken feed—would the General take the bait?

Cassie sensed the confrontation, heard the quiver of fear in Mama-Lu's voice, a tremor she'd not heard before. She could see Mama-Lu's shadow, elongated on the ground, realizing for the first time, how thin and frail the old woman had become. *She's doubting her abilities*, she thought. The scent of aggression wafted over her. But more than that, a reeking stench of sadistic cruelty flooded from Davie Spiegel. "I'll do it," he said. "I'll get 'er and bring her here, plunk the ol' biddy under your nose."

The General scrubbed one fist under his bristly beard, pulled at the loose flap of skin under his chin. He then nodded, giving his assent.

Cassie raced the staircase down from the rafters, that giant heartbeat she'd been listening to, drumming loud in her ears. Any fear she'd felt for her own safety was gone. Protect Mama-Lu! She bolted through the screen door. In those few seconds, her strong young body transformed. She bounded across the yard, her paws hitting the dirt, her trajectory taking her through the garden, past the rope swing, up and over the picket fence. Then another leap and she landed on the General as he stepped down from the buckboard.

She ripped his throat, sharp teeth tearing at the General's scrawny frame, flesh and sinew slashed. Blood gushed forth, soaking Cassie's silver pelt. She shook the General, the scrawny chicken he'd become, tossing him aside where he landed in the back of the buckboard.

Davie Spiegel was reaching for his shotgun. Unable to revert to her original form, that power taken from her when she'd joined with Jake, Mama-Lu still had the ability to tap into some of the magic. She willed the dust and the dirt to take the form of an eagle, striking out at Davie with its deadly talons, blinding him.

Cassie turned and leapt again, rocking Davie in his saddle, his dapple-grey pony wide-eyed with fright, the scent of blood sending the pony into a frenzy. The animal reared. Both Cassie and Davie tumbled to the ground, Davie's foot caught in one stirrup. Cassie tore at Davie's throat, blood gurgling, the man flailing, the last vestiges of life draining away.

The outriders, not wanting any part of the conflict, turned their ponies and raced across the corn field, disappearing into the cool green forest. Mama-Lu smiled as she watched the General's mules pulling the buckboard, giving chase. Davie's dapple-grey brought up the rear, Davie's corpse pummeling the ground as his pony charged forward.

"They'll soon get their due," Mama-Lu said, knowing the scent of blood would find its way to the predators prevalent within the forest.

Cassie, blood dripping from her silver snout turned toward the old woman—Cassie's canine eyes the colour of obsidian—deep, dark, and sorrowful. "Go now," Mama-Lu whispered. "Go and find your kin."

Cassie leapt away, paws pounding the earth, the wind whistling in her ears, her heartbeat strong, her eyes comprehending the world before her with a newfound vision. Never more would she think of her ma'm nor of her pa. She raced through the withered corn stalks, the forest beyond offering a new kind of sanctuary—deep, dark, and mysterious, knowing her wolf instincts would keep her safe. There was no more need for Mama-Lu.

Ryerson materialized at the side of the old woman. She shielded her eyes from the last rays of the setting sun as she watched Cassie's majestic timber wolf form disappear into the forest, knowing she would never again set eyes on the girl.

"Thank you," she whispered, not knowing who or what she was thanking—only knowing it was necessary. She leaned the shotgun against the tall maple, gazing down at Ryerson, his job now done.

She bade him take his true form, a rotor-propelled maple seed which glided upward, him too, gone from her sight.

She then grabbed the rope swing and sat on the wooden seat. Anyone passing, would've thought the old woman had taken leave of her senses—all that snivelling, laughing like a banshee, but whether from grief or joy, who could tell? As the shadows lengthened, the picket fence collapsed, board after board falling like dominoes until all signs of its existence were gone.

~ * ~ * ~

Karen Keeley has published short fiction in more than a dozen anthologies: literary, speculative and crime. Recent stories appear in *An Ancient Curse Vol. II* (PulpCult publisher, an imprint of CultureCult Press) and *Tales from the Monoverse* (Last Waltz Publishing).

Karen makes her home in Alberta, Canada where she has a splendid view of the Rockies, that most formidable bulkhead running the length of western Canada and into the US. Find out more about her writing at www.karenmkeeley.blogspot.com.

Beauty Treatment

Liam Hogan

I tap my painted fingernails on the bar next to the empty glass, attracting the attention of the barman. He gives me the eye as well as a refill and I offer a small smile in return, acknowledging the interest but not rising to his bait. I'm here to hunt, not to be hunted.

There is a beast within, a beast driven by an insatiable hunger that forces me out into the night looking for fresh meat. Fresh human meat. The need makes me tingle, giving me a delicious buzz far beyond that of the cocktail placed before me, condensation running down its steep sides. I heed the call. Gazing into the mirror behind the bar, I tilt my head from side to side and flick my hair.

On the plus side, I've never looked so *damned* good.

~ * ~

It's been four months since my trip to the clinic off Harley Street. The one where the Doctor held out a box of Kleenex; an act of kindness that only made the tears flow even faster, while he sat back and patiently waited.

As I blubbed and blew a small part of my mind calculated how much this consultation was costing me. No wonder the good Doctor could afford to wait. But then, I wasn't exactly hard-up either, not with a hefty pay rise to go with my six-figure bonus, earned by outgunning the oh-so-macho-men at the exclusive wealth management company I worked for. It was this, and the feeling of somehow being a fraud, that brought me back to myself. I looked up at the square-jawed Doctor, at his immaculate hair, his smooth complexion, and knew, just knew, that he wouldn't—*couldn't*—understand, that any semblance of empathy was purely professional and paid for. I straightened my back, daring him to make a throw away platitude, an empty promise, an insincere disavowal.

He held my defiant gaze for a moment before crossing to a cupboard beneath the impressive array of diplomas and certificates. Fiddling with a set of keys he swung the mahogany door open, his broad muscular back masking the contents. My imagination did cartwheels. What could he possibly have locked away in there? But then, wasn't that what I was there for? A hope against hope, a cry in the dark for a miracle?

He placed an old cigar box on the desk and lifted the lid, the scent of cedar wood and tobacco long since smoked brought sudden memories of my grandfather. I found myself looking down at a square black and white picture: a woman, young but homely, holding a barely visible babe in her arms. The Doctor lifted the stack of photos and placed them gently in my hands, and slowly made his way back to his chair.

I leafed through the images, a flip book of an early childhood, black and white giving way to colour as the years advanced. At first, I noticed nothing unusual; the baby was merely a baby, small and unremarkable, as alien looking as they always are. But as the infant grew it was obvious this child was unlikely to win any beauty contests. His features developed as if they didn't all belong on the same face. The nose was too big, the eyes too small; a combination that conspired to make the child look piggish and stupid. A brief ballooning of weight as a teenager did him no favours and, though the weight dropped off again as the boy reached his full height, it left him gangly and sallow-skinned. A horrifying explosion of acne came and largely went, a photo from his first year at University showed the pockmark scars it had left behind. The last picture was a graduation portrait, and, despite the best efforts of the studio photographer, it was not a result that could ever be said to be pleasing to the eye.

I looked up, the photo in my hand and a question on my lips. "Your brother?" I guessed, amazed two siblings could differ so much.

"Me," he replied. He slid the photo out of my hands and dragged the box over to his side of the desk, his fingers drumming lightly on the table.

"What I am about to tell you is not sanctioned by the British Medical Society. It is not covered by your health plan. You will not find it mentioned in the pages of the Lancet, you won't find it in any pages anywhere. If this bothers you, then I suggest you leave now."

I sat still, my heart pounding, aware of how dry my throat had become.

"I was that ill-made man in the photos, Ms Thompson. I had done, just as you must have done, all that I could with what I had: body building, sun lamps, the most expensive beauty products. To little noticeable effect. Until I volunteered to be a guinea pig for a rather experimental treatment.

"I imagine you're thinking reconstructive surgery? A wonder drug? Skin transplants? It was none of these things. It was a virus."

"A virus?" I echoed. "What sort of a virus makes someone more attractive?"

He gave me a half smile. "A sexually transmitted one, Ms Thompson."

I turned this over in my mind, wondering if it was a sick joke, or the initial twisted gambit in the sort of scandalous doctor-patient relationship you read about in the gutter press.

"My fee for the treatment is fifty-thousand pounds," he continued. "I assume you can afford that?"

I nodded cautiously.

"Very well. I can do the initial inoculation today. For the first month you must restrain your sexual impulses, you must avoid sex at all costs."

I realised he was waiting for me to nod once again, to signal my understanding. What had it been? Nine months? Twelve? Longer? Long enough to feel a sense of disappointment that all he was asking from me was my money. "And after that?" I asked.

"The virus…has a few side effects." He laughed gently at my alarm. "Nothing too serious, nothing that outweighs the benefits. At the end of the month, we'll start you on a course of retrovirals which will prevent it from being transmitted, though I'm glad to say the benefits persist. But I cannot stress how important it is for you to complete the full treatment, Ms Thompson."

I thought for a second, thought about that awkward youth and of the handsome Doctor before me. I thought about what I had seen in the mirror that morning, what I saw in the mirror every morning. Thought of how the reaction of others towards me had driven me into my work, but even my successes were not enough, could never be enough.

I nodded firmly. "Fine."

There was a moment, as I pressed myself against the back of the chair while he tapped the end of the hypodermic, a hypodermic with a disturbingly red tint to the fluid contained within, when I almost said stop, almost told him no. But just one look at his perfect face, his sculpted body, and I forced myself to relax and mutter the mantra I had repeated so many times: "Whatever it takes."

As I was preparing to leave, the ink on the cheque still wet, I thought back to the photos he had shown me and realised how stupid I'd been. "The Class of '82" it had said on the graduation photo. That would make him…what? Around 50? I doubted he was a day over 30. Thirty-five, tops. I stifled a despairing laugh and sped through the waiting room, my eyes flitting over the other patients, wondering which one was going to be scammed next.

~ * ~

The Doctor had warned me to be patient, that the process was slow, that I'd see only minor improvements in the first month. But every morning I still looked deep into that accursed mirror for signs of a change, for some evidence I wasn't a gullible idiot. When I saw nothing, I thought of cancelling the cheque, though it would surely have gone through by now. How had I been so stupid? Taken in by an easy smile, a chiselled chin and an impossible promise.

Then a receptionist asked if I'd done something with my hair and, as I blinked in surprise and prepared an evasion, she added: "It looks good. You should keep it that way."

In the washroom I stared into the brightly lit mirror. *Was* there a difference? Was my hair a little more vibrant? Not its usual lacklustre self, swallowing expensive conditioners and still appearing lank and dull? And my skin…underneath the layer of foundation and blemish cover, was it, perhaps, a little smoother?

Day by day I checked for changes, hardly believing when I received my first ever wolf whistle. Admittedly, it was from the construction workers on the far side of the street, a distance of twenty yards or more, but still. My hair was definitely bouncier, less flecked with gray; my eyes were clearer, my step lighter. Even my gym sessions seemed less punishing than before and I kept stepping up the intensity until I became aware of faintly hostile looks from some of the supposed men in the room.

A week before my follow up visit to the clinic an odd little man gave me his number. I threw away the business card at the first opportunity, then instantly regretted it. He wasn't exactly my type, possibly wasn't anybody's type, but then it had been so long that perhaps nor was I.

The day of my evening appointment it all seemed like a mirage.

I felt ugly, lumpen, weak. And the dreams I'd been having, the ones of the Doctor and me, his gentle caress… Was it the thought of seeing him again, or the fear I would still be hideously ugly in his glistening eyes?

As I approached the corner of the expensive street on which the Doctor's Surgery stood, I noticed flashing lights, thought them some strange echo of the unfamiliar quickening beat of my heart. Closer still I saw the striped blue and white tape stretched across the road, a small crowd of people peering past the policewoman standing guard. Further up the street there was a brace of white vans, blobby figures in yellow hazmat suits, and a tent which covered the entrance to one of the buildings.

His building.

"What…" I spluttered, faint headed and suddenly weak. A woman with a towel wrapped around her shoulders eagerly turned to answer.

"Some freaky medical guy!" she stage whispered. "Body parts and weird things in jars!"

Her companion turned and shook her head. "Don't be an idiot, Sharon."

Sharon giggled and turned back to the drama playing out before her.

"Curling tongs must have overheated her brain," the other woman said with a shrug. "I heard it's one of the Doc's patients. Must be something contagious; they're trying to track down everyone he's been treating, just in case. 'Ere, you don't look so good, luv. You okay?"

But by then I'd spun round and was going as fast as my heels could take me, heading for noise, darkness and drinks, the stiffer the better.

~ * ~

I stumbled into a bar not unlike this one. Perhaps it *was* this one. They are so hard to tell apart: all loud music, dimly lit, a crowd of young men—and women—on the prowl. A pick-up joint, a meat market.

But that doesn't make me indiscriminate. That first time, my nerves still jangling, I'd been deliriously happy for any attention at all, unexpected though it was. Now I turn away the sharply dressed young men who approach with varying degrees of confidence. Now I rebuff the barman in his tight trousers and casually open shirt who has decided enough time and alcohol have flown to chance a second sortie. I scan the room for rarer prey.

And then I spot him, standing awkwardly in the corner, morosely sipping his over-priced bottled beer. I almost gasp with heady anticipation.

I saunter across, a smile that has him glancing over his shoulder to see who is attracting my attention and then a blush as he realises it's him.

"Well hullo!" I coo, placing a casual hand on his arm. He looks unsure whether to shake it off or to stay very, very still and hope it goes away. "Are you here all on your lonesome?"

"What do you…what do you want with me?" he asks, tremulous and uncertain as I lick my perfect lips.

The beast makes *its* urgent desire all too obvious, what all viruses want: to spread, to multiply. I'm merely along for the ride.

"I want…" I draw my flawless fingers down the side of his pockmarked cheek, across the coarse hair of his chin, brush his all-too prominent Adam's apple.

"I want to make you *beautiful.*"

Originally published in: WeirdBook Issue #34, Feb 2017

~ * ~ * ~

Liam Hogan is an award-winning short story writer, with stories in Best of British Science Fiction and in Best of British Fantasy (NewCon Press). He's been published by *Analog*, *Nature Futures*, and Flame Tree Press. He helps host the live literary event Liars' League, volunteers at the creative writing charity Ministry of Stories, and lives and avoids work in London.

More details at www.happyendingnotguaranteed.blogspot.co.uk

A Gift for Our Friends

Jean Martin

We buried five of them in the churchyard at Saint Ludmilla's, in Mariupol. A priest blessed the graves. We had made coffins, out of packing crates, to protect them from the sun. We did not nail the coffins shut, and we did not bury them too far down. It would be easy for them to rise.

We were not sure our plan would work. But, after nearly a year, we were desperate.

When the Russians came, to liberate us from democracy and freedom, we fought them, street to street, house to house.

My mother and I hid in our basement, safe from the Russian shells. We made Molotov cocktails for our visitors.

They kept coming and coming. Putin cleared out his prisons; sent killers and rapists to invade our country.

That was when I remembered what my grandmother told me.

When I was a little girl, my mother worked nights, and I stayed with my grandmother. We watched movies on television. English horror pictures, with Christopher Lee, playing vampires dressed in a tailcoat and evening cape.

Eventually, the vampire would bite the pretty girl, and she would become a vampire too.

"That is not how it happens," my grandmother told me. "If a vampire bites you, he drinks your blood, and you die. But you don't become like him."

"It is when you bury a bad man in sacred ground," she said. "That is an offense to God. Then a devil enters the corpse. It walks, and drinks blood."

I was frightened, of course, but my grandmother shook her head and said, "You die. He lives. That is the way of the world."

My mother was angry at grandmother for teaching me superstition. But granny said she had seen it happen, when she was a girl, during Stalin's last days, the village constable had died from too much vodka. He beat people for no reason. He took what wasn't his.

One night, when he was drunk, he threw his baby son against the wall, and broke his neck.

But, when the constable died, his wife had insisted the priest bury him in the churchyard with prayers to a God he cursed and mocked all his life.

Afterward, grandmother said, he walked the village at night. He prowled outside his wife's house, rattling the windows and calling to her, until her brothers dug up the body, cut out his heart and cut his head off, so he would not walk again.

"Vampires feed off their own, when they can," my grandmother told me. "Their kin or their friends."

My grandmother's stories frightened me, until I got older and found real things to be afraid of, like no food at the grocery, or no money to pay rent.

Then the Russians came. We were desperate to defend our country. I remembered the stories, and I had an idea.

I talked to my friends.

None of us really believed it would work. But we were willing to try anything.

We spoke with people we knew. They looked. We looked. We found five, and that would be enough.

They were dead Russian soldiers. Their bodies still in good condition, with all their limbs, heads, faces and teeth. Teeth were essential.

One had been killed after he shot a nun. Another had sent a grenade down a subway tunnel full of women and children. There was one who had nine cut off fingers in his pockets. Two had raped a woman and were looting her house, when she shot them.

They were not good soldiers, or good men.

They were right for our purposes. They would be a gift for our Russian liberators.

We buried the Russians in consecrated ground. If what my grandmother told me was true, demons would enter their bodies, and they would be vampires.

You say there are no demons.

Do you watch the news at night?

There are devils in this world. There are plenty of them. They kill women and children for the pleasure of hearing them scream. They destroy for the love of destruction. They came to our country, saying they were saving us from Nazis, who were not here.

After we buried the Russians in consecrated ground, we stayed indoors, barricaded in our homes, while their comrades roamed our streets. Some of them on patrol. Some of them drunk and looking to destroy just a little more of Ukraine.

There was a man found near the churchyard at Saint Ludmilla, with his throat torn open. We heard the Russians thought he was killed by feral dogs.

A colonel was killed inside the entry of an apartment building. He kept two young women there, for entertainment purposes. His throat was torn open too. They were talking about wolves after that.

Wolves do not have hands. They can't open doors.

Nine Russians were killed in a bar. The barkeep was found hiding in a closet, soaked in holy water. He said two Russian soldiers had come in and attacked the patrons. He knew the two men. They had been regulars at the bar, but he hadn't seen them for more than a month. Their friends said they'd been going to visit a woman they knew, when they disappeared.

The barkeep swore it was like the stories his grandfather had told him. The two men attacked their old comrades. Their strength was inhuman. They tore the men's throats open with their teeth and gulped their blood, the way they used to gulp his liquor.

The Russians said we were superstitious, because our media wasn't properly scripted. (Scripted is pronounced censored in Russian.)

But we began hearing reports of the same things happening in other towns they occupied.

My cousin, Timofei, in Donetsk, saw a Russian break into his neighbors' house. The soldier planned to rape their twelve-year-old daughter. But the neighbor stabbed him in the back with a carving knife.

Timofei found a packing crate, and a priest. They buried the body in the cemetery beside the Church of the Holy Family. The grave was blessed. But it was not too deep.

Timofei said he didn't believe the stories either.

Now he does.

There is a very grand hotel next to the Holy Family Church. The Russians use it as their headquarters. So far four of them have been found dead, with their throats torn open.

The Russian media are talking about terrorists now.

None of us are allowed out at night, without a special pass. That privilege is limited to our *liberators.*

Many of us don't want to go out at night. We are happy to leave the streets to our Russian friends and their former comrades in arms.

Before the Russians came, I did not believe my grandmother's stories. Now I know she was right. There are devils in this world.

She saw them. I have seen them.

We have set them to destroy each other.

They die, we live. That is the way of the world.

~ * ~ * ~

Jean Martin has a BS degree in Journalism from Ohio University and has been laughing about it for longer than she cares to admit. She lives, at present, in McKeesport, Pennsylvania, with an orange tabby cat named Samwise, who likes bagpipe music.

Unsanctioned Transfiguration

Sam Crain

To the Council of Magicians, An Appeal:

First, I must plead: I am guilty of unauthorized magic—specifically, of unsanctioned transfiguration. I humbly lay the facts of the case before this Academic Council, in hopes I be reinstated. I must also note: this letter contains more of *pathos* than we are trained to. I undertake to submit myself to correction in form.

Blood has its components, as you masters teach in Elements of Chemistry during the first year of study. Platelets, plasma, red cells, white cells. Platelets for clotting. Plasma for water and basis. Red cells to breathe with. White cells for healing. It's the white cells that make pus: we know this.

But even though we all have these, that's not to say one person's blood can be interchanged for another's, a beautiful lesson written in our biology. Blood comes in types.

However, testing for type is an ongoing field of inquiry. And trial and error is extraordinarily dangerous. While the masters work on the problem, their adepts developed their compromise: a blood-replacing potion. Badly named, for it's not a true replacement at all—but it's simple to make except when we run out of coconuts, which provide the potion's base liquid. And it is usable across types.

Yet there is another drawback: the potion nauseates its drinkers, mildly for most but—not for all.

My sweetest friend, he took sudden injury on a research trip—on a dare. We are of different blood types, to my grief.

It was my fault he got hurt, I, the careful one! If I had taken better care, he would have been safe. I take responsibility for my failure. Thomas took risks, not I! The number of times I salved his burns or pulled thorns out of him as we came up together, it scarcely bears remembering. But a mutual rival had mocked me for my cautious ways, dared us to go out to a nigh-unreachable promontory where a rare spell-flower grew. Thomas had wanted to hit him and I held him back. We went. Thomas, with earnest, misplaced faith, was sure we could handle it. It was miserable going—half a day's walk over boggy hills, up and down, one after another until we were both soaked to the knees. Then clambering, already weary, along a ragged, stony coastline. Had we not been on a dare, it might have been beautiful, that part. But nothing is beautiful after that long in wet socks. The promontory—too narrow to quite merit the term peninsula—was sharp black rock in cracked slabs, lapped by an inexorable sea. The spell-flower grows in a tidal pool at its tip. We were just too tired after the bog and the coast, but Thomas would never suggest stopping, and I was still too stung by the tauntings of an idiot. (I submit myself a bigger fool than he is, even.) Thomas slipped on wet stone and went down hard, out-of-reach. I heard the bone of his leg crack, saw it jutting suddenly through his skin, heard his screams and the thud as he struck unforgiving, slippery rock and slid toward the water.

He lost blood fast—far too fast, as I got him stretched out, cut away his clothes. I could taste his blood at the back of my throat, sharp as regret.

I held the vial of potion to his lips with one hand and clutched a bandage to his leg with the other. (For I had brought a vial in case of dire accident—the last evidence of my former self.)

He'd barely swallowed before it came back up. The thick potion coated me, and spasms of vomiting drove yet more blood from Thomas's leg before I tugged his bandage tighter.

Mere words were no good, nor panic neither. I got a grip on myself and reached for my *want*—the origin and essence of magic.

To cast spontaneously violates your teachings, I admit. Spells—and their consequences—must be considered from all angles and directions, meditated upon. A poet once called poetry 'emotion recollected in tranquility' and so are spells meant to be of thoughts: there is a corollary of sorts there, a beautifully true one.

But there was no time. No time.

I conjured a bowl and opened a vessel of my own with a cutting spell, watched my blood gather in the bowl's bottom.

Thomas was groaning but the nausea had passed its crisis point, for I did not attempt the dose again. Instead, I summoned every scrap and fleck of concentration I could muster and cast a fresh spell: a transfiguration. The blood in the bowl stayed as red, but I hoped—prayed—it was changed in an invisible essential as I directed it into Thomas's vein. *Be his blood, not mine.* He had lost too much. I had to give it back.

All of this happened in minutes but the spaces between seconds had stretched out leaving vast valleys between, before a shiver of pink had returned to Thomas's cheeks. I was able to rebandage the wound tightly with a thick pad to catch the blood until it could clot.

There was no fever when I touched his forehead, which was a relief, but that could not break apart the stones of dread settled into my stomach. I had used unauthorized magic—a new spell, called from nothing at a minute's notice. If he died, so was my life forfeit.

Perhaps I could have let our folk think it was merely that the replacing potion had done its work—but for two things: if Thomas ever had need of the potion again, he would need to be told—it was dangerous. Also, just as importantly, his was not the only life this new transfiguration could save. And last, my life is forfeit without him in any case, for I love him well.

I washed Thomas's sick from my robe and my hands and drank the few sips of potion left in the discarded mug. I was weary from fear, exertion, loss of blood, as I knelt before Thomas's pallet of ferns, watching him. In my mind's eye, I saw twin scenes: a man some long time hence using my new spell and then drinking potion, revived and reviving almost simultaneously. Beside this graven image I saw myself, the Council's backs ritually turned against me, my Adept emblem torn from my neck, the embroidery ripped from my robe-hems as I was made to go. Thomas remained, his eyes mother-of-pearl with sadness. I knew—and I still know—what I have earnt.

I bore him home the following morning, and I made my confession. You turned your backs and stripped away my emblem and stitchery as I foresaw, in keeping with tradition. I can say only that I acted for the best to save my friend—and then in hopes of likewise benefiting still others. I revere our teachings and beg this Council to grant my return.

Let me come home.

Robin, formerly a Magic Adept

~ * ~ * ~

Sam Crain is a fiction-writer and a PhD in English Literature.

You can find her on Facebook at SamCrainWritesLonghand.

Blood & Beauty

Brian MacDonald

"Hello, Rory."

The greeting, so unexpected from the patron sitting in a dark corner of the bar, sent shivers up Rory's back. She knew that voice. She knew that person.

Thanatos Laetissimus.

With his signature top hat and ringleader coat.

Sitting in her bar.

"How?" Rory mumbled, "How are you…"

"Here?" Thanatos purred with a cheery smile. "Out of the hospital? Alive? Strikingly handsome?"

"Any of it."

"Well, the good looks are both easy to explain and also a bit more complicated. My parents were both quite handsome, so I had great genetics to go from to develop these stunning cheekbones…"

"I could care less about that," Rory snapped, pulling herself out of her fear and discomfort. There was no time for that. She needed real information.

"No niceties for an old friend?" Thanatos tut-tutted with a sad shake of his head. "Well then…I suppose I could tell you how I survived you dropping a flaming carnival on top of me."

"Your zombie carnival."

"My carnival of unliving individuals, yes."

"No thanks," Rory had heard enough. "Get out of the bar. Now. Or Francis will throw you out."

"Ah. Yes. Your husband," Thanatos nodded. "Sadly, I fear he will be busy tonight. You see, the new beer all the college co-eds are trying here tonight? It's mine."

"Fine." Rory snatched the two ice-cold beers off her serving tray and slammed them on the table in front of him. "Drink up. Then get the hell out."

"Well…I could do that," Thanatos took a slow sip of the beer closest to him, "My beer has a lovely taste. It's a blonde ale with just a touch of grapefruit…"

"Delightful."

"And, some of my own special ingredients"

"What did you do?"

"Why don't you have a seat?" Thanatos smiled knowingly. "We have much to talk about."

~ * ~

The day had started out as normal for Francis as it could. He woke at the crack of noon to his phone blaring Elvis' "Suspicious Minds."

Great.

It was Connie.

At work.

What did the old man want?

"Phone," Rory mumbled. Then, with a sharp yank, she pulled the sheets to her side and curled up to sleep.

"On it." Francis rolled over and slapped blindly until he found the phone. He flipped it open and answered it with a yawn. "Yeah. Whattayawant?"

"Why the hell aren't ya here, ya damn idiot?" a voice with a thick Irish brogue snapped.

"Ummm…it's noon, Connie. I work nights. So does Rory."

"But we have the new beer rollout today."

"Uh-huh."

"With one-dollar bottles."

"Oh."

"On a goddamn Friday."

"Awww…crap," Francis rubbed his eyes and fought off a yawn. "The college kids are gonna be nuts…"

"So, I need yer goddamn butt here. Now," Connie snarled. He was worried. Or excited. It was hard to tell most times. "And grab your pretty wife too. We're gonna need all the help we can get to hand these things out."

"Gimme fifteen. No. Make it twenty minutes," Francis sighed.

"Why?"

"We need showers and coffee…"

"Ya got ten minutes. I'll have a pot on when ya get here."

~ * ~

Fifteen minutes and a decidedly fast and not-fun shared shower later, Francis and Rory sat at the bar of The Two Kings nursing mugs of steaming hot coffee. It was not good coffee. Connie bought the cheapest stuff available and then, somehow, over-watered and burnt it to the point of making it taste like watery mud.

Connie, the impossibly thin white-haired owner of Two Kings, drank the beverage like it was made of money.

He was that cheap.

Or he really liked crappy coffee.

Nobody could tell.

"So," Connie took a long sip of his coffee. Was he actually savoring it? "Teddy's going to work the door. He's got a scanner…"

"Why does he need a scanner to take money from co-eds?" Rory questioned as she poured more milk and sugar into her brownish mud water.

"People had to sign up for the dollar beers," Connie answered with a shrug. "I guess there's some legal reason…"

"To lose money?" Francis followed Rory's lead with the coffee. Maybe sugar would help? "I mean…this beer company…"

"Laughing Banshee."

"Yeah, Connie. Laughing Banshee," Francis nodded. "They're gonna take a bath here. One-dollar beers? There's no way to make money off that."

"It's advertising."

"Advertising. Here? No offense, man, but Two Kings is a dive."

"An Elvis-inspired Irish pub…"

"Okay. It's an old Irish bar with lots of Elvis bric-a-brac tacked to the walls…"

"Hey! That's *memorabilia*!" Connie jumped up to point at the walls covered in Concert posters, photos, and newspaper clippings. They were all in poor condition from their years at the bar and only getting worse. Concert posters hung browned and curled from accidental beer spills. Haphazardly placed photos dulled in the sunlight. Off-center hole-covered clippings stuck, having been placed and replaced by one drunk patron after another. And Connie's favorite piece, the velvet Elvis hanging behind the bar? The dark cloth painting of the icon somehow looked less like his skyrocketing prime and more like his fat, sweaty, drug-addled self.

"It's memorabilia if you take care of it," Rory corrected. "Which you don't."

"Pshaw!" Connie spat. "They're well-loved. Like Elvis hisself!"

"If you call how he ended his career well-loved," Francis smirked with a wink to his wife.

"And howsabout my statue of The King?" Connie wandered down the bar to the end to snatch up a slightly chipped bust of Elvis in his classic white spangly jumpsuit with a red scarf. "Bought it in Graceland me self!"

"You never made it to Graceland, you old coot," Rory chuckled.

"Yeah," Francis nodded with a frown, "You found that one second-hand in some yard sale."

"Well…the kids don't know it. And the guy making the beer? He said this place was perfect for his new beer. He said it was… *charmingly rustic*."

"He did not," Rory shook her head.

"Was he drinking his own stuff before he got here?" Francis chuckled.

"No, he wasn't drinking ya damn jackass!" Connie spat and threw a nearby damp bar towel at Francis. "And coffee chat is done. Get going! The bar isn't gonna get any prettier on its own!"

"It's not gonna get prettier without a bulldozer…" Francis smirked.

"Shaddup!"

~ * ~

The college kids hit the bar hard.

Apparently, the genius who planned the event decided he wanted to start at four o'clock that Friday. Rollouts usually happened at six or later. It made more sense. People would be able to come after work for a drink and try something new. They could also go out a little later with a date or in a group and enjoy the new beer. Either way, there would be enough beer to go around for the people who bought it to enjoy in moderation.

But four o'clock?

On a Friday?

For one dollar?

There was only one reason for that…to get college kids drunk.

So…the beer guy was some sort of genius capable of convincing co-eds to buy more of his beer at a higher price after one wild bender at the bar or he was a moron who had no idea what he was doing.

Either way, Francis was going to be up to his eyeballs in drunk, stupid kids. And, then the after-work crowd was going to pile in.

~ * ~

The crush of barely legal Barnum students flooded Two Kings at four on the dot. It was amazing how punctual kids could be when there were cheap beers to be had. They had lined up outside the bar an hour early just to be the first to try Laughing Banshee.

Francis leaned against a wall, watching person after person flash a green wristband at Connie and receive their first ice-cold beer.

"Here's yer free one!"

"Drink up while they're cold and free!"

The beers weren't really free. The kids had paid for the first one when they signed up for the wristband, but that didn't stop Connie.

The old man cracked a joke for every beer he passed out.

They weren't good jokes, but he said them with a cranky smirk. That was the best the scruffy old gent could do. And, given his typical mood when dealing with the co-eds, a smile from him would probably have scared them from coming back for more beers.

About thirty minutes into the parade of bad one-liners and beer hand-outs, Francis saw a regular. Jeff. The shaggy-haired kid had been at the bar every Thursday since October last year. He was a decent guy. Liked the Mets, but he was a New Yorker so Francis gave him a pass. If he'd been a Yankees fan Francis may have shown him the door.

"Hey. Jeff."

"Oh," the student nodded in his direction, "Hey Francis. Wassup?"

"Not much. Just holding up the wall," Francis shrugged. "So, what's the deal with the new beer?"

"Besides it being cheap?"

"Yeah. Cheap beer is great and all, but I know you drink the good stuff. Heinekens cost a bit more."

"Honestly?" Jeff shrugged his shoulders and took a pull of his beer, "It's supposed to be healthy. I mean, healthy for beer, ya know?"

"Dude," Francis frowned, "What does that even mean?"

"It means that it's got stuff in it."

"Stuff?"

"From what I read," Jeff nodded and took another swig before speaking, "It's got something in it that helps your blood filter the alcohol."

"Really? Why?"

"I guess you get the effects of the alcohol but without the hangover if you over-imbibe."

"And you signed up online for it because…"

"So they have the right to contact you and use anything you say in their marketing."

"So…" Francis chewed his lip in thought, "if this works, they have hundreds of happy college kids blasting reviews about it on all their social media accounts…"

"Pretty much," Jeff said with a nod. "And the beer people own anything we write or say."

"Damn," Francis let out a low whistle. "That's pretty slick."

"Yeah." Jeff finished his beer with another long swig. "Too bad I don't have any social media accounts." Then with a wink, he muscled back into line for his next beer.

~ * ~

"Okay." Rory cautiously sat across from Thanatos Laetissimus, never taking her eyes off his hands and face. "Talk."

"I knew you would see it my way," Thanatos winked and took a long slow pull of the beer in front of him.

"What do you want, wizard?"

"I'm actually a sorcerer, dear woman," he corrected with a sympathetic smile. "I didn't have to chase scraps of magic and old dusty books. I was born with it. It's in my blood, as it were." Then, with a nod of self-recognition, he smiled brightly. "Oh, that was a good one. *It's in my blood*, just like my blood is in…"

"The beer," Rory snapped with an eyeroll. "Yes. You're positively droll."

"You needn't be rude, dear."

"You're dosing everyone in the bar with your blood, and I'm the rude one?"

"Dosing them?" Thanatos clutched his chest in mock indignation. "You make it sound like I'm slipping something in their drinks to snatch them home for my horrible use…"

"You aren't?"

"Oh, no! Absolutely not! I'm going to make them kill you."

~ * ~

Francis noticed something was different.

He couldn't put his finger on it, but there was something.

The bar was full. The after-work crowd had shown up and joined in with the co-eds.

People were drinking and talking.

Laughter was exploding from one part of the room and then another.

Some were even dancing to the booming techno remix of Elvis' *Rubberneckin'*.

But.

Something was…wrong.

Francis could almost smell it.

There.

Under the booze and sweat.

There was something else.

Anxiety?

Fear?

Aggression?

There was something.

He didn't know why, but there was something.

Francis cracked his knuckles as he scanned the room for trouble.

Nothing.

Just drinking and laughing and dancing.

But where was Rory?

~ * ~

"They're going to kill me?" Rory sat back with a thump.

"Well, you and Francis," Thanatos smiled sadly and took another quick sip of his beer.

"How? Why?"

"Why? Really?" the sorcerer frowned "You destroyed my Carnival of the FunUsual and nearly burnt me to death in the process. Did you think I would just get over that? Maybe become best of friends?"

"Honestly? I was kinda hoping you'd just go the hell away."

"Oh, I did. I went away. I went away to heal. And do you know how many blood baths I needed to take to heal my burns?" Thanatos rolled up the sleeves of his shirt to show his arms. They were pink and hairless as the day he was born. "Do you know how many homeless people died for those baths?"

"Oh my…" Rory fought off the horrible image of everyone who must have suffered.

"I bathed in the blood of dirty, disgusting street people to get back to you," the sorcerer leaned in with a sneer. "But? You know what? I had a lot of time to think. There isn't much else to do when you're magically regrowing skin in a tub of blood."

Thanatos sat back with a thoughtful smile.

"I got to think about you. And your idiot husband, Francis. And I thought *They destroyed everything I worked so hard on. Everything I loved. I should find out what they love. And I should have it destroy them.*"

"You're insane," Rory mumbled as she tried to process Thanatos' disturbing ramble.

"Possibly," the sorcerer nodded thoughtfully. "But, back to my story. Where were we? Oh yes, *Revenge*! With beer!"

He took another sip from his beer and emptied it.

"I thought long and hard about how to destroy you. I found your house. I found your car. And then I found here." Thanatos smiled and pointed at the bar where Connie was happily handing out beers. "The Two Kings. Your day job. You two aren't even full-time troublemakers, are you? I was defeated by part-time heroes."

"We prefer *Private Investigators of the Magical and Weird*," Rory corrected. "That job doesn't pay the bills though. This does."

"Fair enough," the sorcerer waved his hand dismissively.

"But it did give me a thought while I was bathing," he bit his lip thoughtfully. "What if I put my blood in a beer? If I used other people's blood to control dead people, could I use my blood to control living people?"

"Can you?"

"You tell me," Thanatos smiled knowingly. "I'll wait."

~ * ~

Rory was a Druid. And not one of the new-fangled spiritualists who whispered to crystals and felt like they communed with nature through their herb garden. They were lovely people capable of living their way and making the world a little better with their beliefs and actions. No. She was a fully-blooded, born and raised Druid from the oldest, most powerful family of Druids ever to walk the earth. But they were all dead and gone. And she was the last one left in the world, as far as she knew.

Thanatos knew this.

Well, Rory assumed he knew she was gifted. Magic users could always recognize each other eventually. There really was no way to hide abilities, especially if you used them in front of another user. Which she had, before.

He knew Rory could see Magic.

There was no point in hiding it.

She wondered what else he knew about her abilities.

Rory took a chance and closed her eyes. She figured Thanatos would have killed her earlier if he had wanted to. He knew where she and Francis lived. He must have had the chance.

No.

He wanted her to see.

He wanted to gloat.

Rory took a deep breath. She waited a full four seconds before slowly releasing the air through her nose. She repeated this, calming her heart and focusing her mind. Then, as centered as she would get, Rory opened her eyes a crack and viewed the world through the haze of her eyelashes.

At first, she could only see the sorcerer sitting across from her with a wide, knowing smile. And then, one by one, the thin and wispy golden threads appeared in the air. The threads connected everything with everything. They floated, traces of paths between people, objects, and places, stuck in the Veil between here and the realms of Magic and the Dead forevermore.

The threads typically appeared haphazardly. They rarely looked organized or even remotely planned. In cases where the same person or persons did the same activities in the same areas, the threads would seem thicker and brighter.

But the threads around Thanatos?

They were whisper-thin but bright.

They were knotted tightly to him.

And they led all through the bar.

In every direction.

And more appeared as Rory watched.

"You can see, can't you? My magic? You can see it," Thanatos purred with pride.

"Yes."

"And you can see what happens whenever someone drinks my beer."

"You control them," Rory hissed through a tightening jaw.

"No. I own them," the sorcerer corrected. "My blood gives me control. But, their signatures for permission? They didn't just give me permission to use their words or their likenesses. They gave me permission to use them."

"And now, my dear Rory?" Thanatos snapped his fingers. "Now, I shall."

~ * ~

Francis felt the change in the room before it happened.

Actually, he smelled it.

The sweet smell of cheap beer and good times shifted to something acrid.

Something nasty.

The punch from Jeff whizzed past his ear and struck the wall behind him.

"What the hell?" Francis dodged to his right and got his hands up to protect himself. His job in the bar was to keep it safe and calm. It wasn't to brawl with patrons. Especially not friendly ones who had been showing up every week for years.

Jeff growled. His eyes looked glazed, but not from beer.

Francis had seen that look.

He knew that look.

It was rage.

Dark, deep, murderous rage.

Jeff threw another punch, this time with everything he had in his little Mets-loving body. He was faster than Francis expected.

But not, thankfully, fast enough to make contact.

Francis stepped to his left and caught the swinging fist and the arm attached to it. He wasn't sure what was wrong with Jeff, but he wasn't going to let it continue. He pulled the patron toward him and quickly stepped one foot behind him. Then, with an open-handed push, Francis tripped Jeff to the ground.

"Dude," Francis growled, "Stay down. You don't wanna do this."

"Yes, I do." Jeff smiled widely as he brushed his shaggy hair out of his eyes. He stood up and spread his arms wide. "We all do."

Francis stepped back and looked at Jeff's eyes. They were still glazed.

Then he noticed the kids near Jeff.

Their eyes were glazed.

Francis shifted his eyes slowly, taking in as much of the bar as he could.

Everyone's eyes were glazed.

And he couldn't see Rory.

~ * ~

"Rory? Honey?" Francis' voice cracked a little as he barked for her attention. "Where are you? I think I might have to fight the whole bar…"

Rory snapped out of her magic viewing. There was nothing more she needed to know. And Francis needed her.

"I'm over here!" the Druid moved to stand and wave until Thanatos placed a hand on her shoulder. Rory's skin froze and then filled with fire. She fought off the urge to turn and punch him directly in the mouth. He would have liked tasting his own blood.

"I have it, dear," the sorcerer smiled sympathetically.

He snapped his fingers.

Feet shuffled.

Lots of them.

Bodies moved.

All together.

Rory could feel them move toward her.

And then all six feet five inches of her husband showed up across the bar from her, surrounded and pushed forward by a throng of glazed college kids.

He was a large man.

He wasn't easy to move when he didn't want to.

And they moved him through the bar like a tidal wave slapping a lost surfboard to shore.

"Hey. Dudes. Watch the threads," Francis barked with a forced laugh as he stumbled to her table and slammed to a stop, "This Metallica shirt is a classic. I didn't get my *Ride the Lightning* tee from Target, ya know?"

"I'm sure the college children appreciate your musical gatekeeping, Francis," Thanatos chuckled with an eyeroll.

"Gatekeeping my ass," Francis said with a growl. "I'm just telling them to appreciate a classic. They can like whatever they like."

"Oh, I see the difference…"

"Says the guy who likes 'creepy ice cream man' carnival music," Francis snapped. Then, with a quick turn, he leaned down to Rory and kissed her on the head. "You okay, babe?"

"I'm fine, love," Rory smiled knowingly, "Just trying to figure out how to deal with this situation…"

"Yeah. You wanna get on that?" Francis cracked his knuckles. "I'm wearing my best ass-kicking pants and all, but this seems like a lot. Even for me. And I really like a bunch of the kids in here…"

"If I may?" Thanatos shrugged. "I do apologize for breaking in on your sweet conversation."

"Go pound sand," Francis grumbled.

"That said? I believe I can solve your problem."

"By killing yourself and ending this madness?" Rory smiled coldly. "I thought you'd never suggest that, but we do appreciate the offer."

"Oh, Rory, dear" Thanatos waved her away with a chuckle, "You are such a kidder!"

The sorcerer reached into his jacket pocket and pulled out a scroll and pen. He rolled the paper open on the table and held it down with the bar's salt and pepper shakers. Then with practiced flair, he held out the pen to Rory.

"Just sign here, Rory, and it all stops."

"If I sign it, what happens?" Rory took the pen and considered the scroll. It was written in an old, dead magical language. If she had time, she was sure she could figure out what it said.

"If you sign it? You belong to me," the sorcerer smiled widely, "And I let everyone else go. I don't need anyone else."

"And Francis?"

"He's nothing," Thanatos shrugged. "He can go about living his miserable life without you."

~ * ~

"Give me a minute to think?" Rory sighed sadly.

"Rory! Don't" Francis surged toward her but was grabbed

roughly by the college kids. "Don't do it, babe."

"I just…just need a minute…" Rory picked up the beer nearest her and sipped it absent-mindedly.

"Rory, dear?" Thanatos nodded, "You do realize you just gave me power over you?"

"Why not?" Rory dropped her head and closed her eyes. She muttered old curses and promises under her breath. Tears welled in her eyes.

"Rory! Honey!" Francis roared "It's not worth it!"

"Yes, it is." Rory opened her eyes a bit and stared through the tears covering her eyelashes.

C'mon.

Be there.

And there it was.

The golden thread connecting her to Thanatos.

"Francis! Now!"

Her husband surged forward again, but this time the college kids didn't hold him back as well. This time he threw elbows, kicked knees …anything to keep moving toward Thanatos.

"What're you idiots doing?" Thanatos frowned with annoyance and snapped his fingers again. The college students flooded forward to grab at and hit Francis.

"This." Rory grabbed the thread connecting her to Thanatos. "You may have me, but now I have you!"

"So what? What can you possibly do to me before they kill Francis?"

"Me? Nothing," Rory shrugged. "But them?"

Rory slammed the glass beer bottle on the table and shattered it.

And then she slashed her arm with it and took a lick of her own blood.

"But them? The old ones I worship? To protect my Francis, I just promised them Blood and Beauty."

"So what? They're your gods and that's your promise."

"And you're connected to me now…"

"Oh no."

"Oh, yes," Rory smiled through blood-stained teeth, "And they would have words with you about overdue payments…"

~ * ~

"What the?" Thanatos mumbled. "What the hell?"

Sweat beaded up on his brow and began to run down his face. He closed his eyes and clenched his jaw.

"No," he snapped. "No. It's mine! Those people are mine!"

"What's the matter?" Rory smiled and took another sip of her beer. It wasn't too bad. Kinda like a Blue Moon but with an earthy background note. Of course, that note was creepy sorcerer blood, but that didn't matter so much right now.

"You bitch! They're taking my power!"

"You didn't pay for it, did you? You thought you just had it in your blood, right?"

"It's mine!" The sorcerer pulled off his hat and flapped it at his face. The breeze didn't seem to comfort his pale flushed face.

"Yeah. About that…" Francis pulled his arms away from the college kids. They were all standing still, staring off in no particular direction. "You killed all those people. Used their blood. Right? So, that was their power…"

"The old gods demand Blood and Beauty," Rory sat back and took another sip of her beer. "You used one for power. And then you tithed neither to them."

"They aren't my gods!" Thanatos pulled off his ringmaster coat. Sweat poured down his face. He looked like he'd just run a marathon.

"But they were always yours," Rory corrected. "The old gods are always here. They are everywhere. They are older than anything you understand. They are older and more primal than anything you ever believed in. And those things you do believe in? Whatever you believe in? They know the old gods. And they fear them. You just didn't know. And the old gods didn't care enough to notice you."

"Oh god," the sorcerer mumbled, tears running down his face. He ripped open his shirt. The baby-smooth pink skin he had on his arms and should have had on his chest wasn't there. At least it wasn't there anymore. "What are they doing?"

Now?

Now his chest was sunburned crimson.

And it was getting darker.

A blister rose.

And then another.

Thanatos screamed in pain and shock and horror.

"Looks like old gods are doing a repo on all the blood magic you did…even the healing," Francis nodded with as much empathy as he could muster for the sorcerer who had tried to take his Rory from him. He didn't have much.

"No…no…no…" Thanatos stammered as he stared numbly at his hands as they changed. Pink to Red. Red to Crimson. Crimson to Blistering and Blackened.

"Damn," Francis smirked. "That's gonna leave a mark."

Thanatos pushed the table from him and sprinted for the door.

He slammed through college kids, screaming in pain with each one he hit, and out the door within a minute.

~ * ~

Rory sat at the bar with Francis. Things quieted greatly after Thanatos disappeared from the bar. A few people wondered why things had gotten so aggressive, but everyone agreed the beer was somehow at fault. They also agreed it was crap.

Most of the patrons left.

Crap beer wasn't worth the throngs of people.

Connie, for his part, pivoted to make sure everyone who stayed got better beers. At full price.

"You know what I really need now?" Rory sighed as she rubbed her newly bandaged arm.

"I dunno," Francis shrugged, "An exorcism?"

"No, silly" Rory smiled. "A drink."

"That's fair. Waddaya want? Beer? Whiskey?"

"Honestly?" Rory smirked.

"Don't say it…"

"A Bloody Mary."

~ * ~ * ~

Brian MacDonald writes in the earnest hope his words can bring joy and comfort like the books of his youth brought him. Twenty-plus years of teaching Intensive Special Education in Massachusetts have informed his worldview and taught him to take nothing for granted as well as to see the beauty in the chaos swirling in our minute-to-minute struggles in life.

Brian would like to state that he disagrees with Conan. While he agrees crushing one's enemies and hearing the lamentation of their loved ones is indeed enjoyable, Brian is absolutely certain "Home-made Calzone" night at the MacDonald house with his wife, sons, and reruns of Leverage is the best thing in life.

Brian has been published by WolfSinger Publications, House of Loki, Enrapturing Tales, and Black Ink Fiction. You can find out more about Francis and Rory and all his other characters on his Facebook page: Brian MacDonald—Storytelling Scallywag or by searching #francisandrory

The Cyclist of the Full-Moon

Lindsay Oliver

Gregor schooled his features into an expression of polite indifference, tamping down the fury that burned within him. He'd been a fool to come out this close to the full moon. At least the cyclist had stopped. As she dismounted from her bike, he examined her potential threat level, a task made easier by her form-fitting cycle shorts and top. She was young, well-muscled, and not carrying any obvious weapons. The tension eased from Gregor's arms and legs as he considered his options. Neither flight nor fight was appealing. If he fled and she pursued, he'd have little chance of getting away. If he stood and fought, he'd need to knock her out with one swift blow. A prolonged encounter was too risky. He'd inflict too much damage. It had happened before. He still saw them sometimes, the ones he'd scratched, or worse, bitten.

The cyclist kicked the bike stand into place, pulled off her bike helmet, shook out her long blond hair and turned to Gregor, her hand extended. "I'm Lydia. I'm so, so sorry. You're not hurt, are you?"

As Gregor shrank back, she stooped to pick up the shopping scattered at his feet. "Let me just get this picked up for you."

Gregor crouched beside her, muscles tense, ready to spring.

"It's okay. I know how hard it is for you. What are you doing out this late? She's beyond gibbous."

Gregor glanced up and cursed the waxing moon, a pale almost-disc in the winter sky. He glanced back at the smiling girl beside him and decided to risk it. "How did you know?"

"I didn't. Not at first. But the way you shrank back, the hunted look in your eyes." She placed the last of the groceries in Gregor's bag. "My father was the same. We kept him safe as long as possible."

Gregor swallowed. His hand itched, and his arm ached. He longed to reach out, offer her the small comfort of physical contact, a hand on her arm. Why was that denied to him?

"Quick, tell me your name. People are staring. We need to look like we're friends or relatives, avert suspicion."

"Gregor," he whispered before straightening his aching limbs.

"Here let me, Uncle Gregor." She grabbed the shopping bags and placed them in her bike basket. "I'll walk you home. That's too much for you to carry. It's a bad time to be out alone."

Gregor didn't understand why Lydia would suggest such a thing. He'd been delayed too long. He'd never make it home in time. Walking side by side was too much of a risk for him, for her. He was about to grab the shopping and flee when she manoeuvred the bike between them, creating just enough of a gap. She was close enough his nostrils still filled with the scent of her shampoo, but, not so close the heat of her body reached him. He should make it home without attacking her.

They walked along together in silence and arrived at his door. Lydia moved around him with the practiced care of one used to avoiding contact with his kind.

As she turned to go, he held up his bag of groceries. "Thank you. I'm not sure how I would make it through till she wanes without these supplies."

"No worries. Don't leave it so late next time. Stay safe. See you on the other side."

~ * ~

When Lydia's knock came, Gregor was sitting at the kitchen table with his medical supplies spread out before him. He pushed himself to his feet and padded to the door. As he peered through the peephole, he steadied himself with an arm braced against the wall. For a moment, he considered not letting her in. Few people reacted well to the sight of him post-transformation. He'd tidied himself up as much as possible, but the flat was a mess, with ripped clothes and food scattered everywhere. The coppery tang of blood still filled the air.

Even through the distorted lens of the peephole, Lydia's smile looked genuine enough for Gregor to relent and let her in. When he led the way into the kitchen, she followed at a sensible distance. She was careful and cautious, rather than skittish and wary. *This might work.* Gregor lowered himself into a chair and watched as she cleaned up his mess.

~ * ~

By the time Lydia came round again, Gregor's wounds had almost all healed. She brought food and replenished his first aid kit. Once everything was squared away, Gregor made tea and opened a packet of digestive biscuits. When he was sure Lydia was situated on the couch with tea and biscuits in easy reach, he plopped down in the armchair opposite her.

"You don't have to do this."

"I know, I don't have to." Lydia took a sip of tea and flashed Gregor a brilliant smile. "I do it because I want to."

"Tell me about your dad."

Lydia set her mug down on the coffee table, leaned forward, and covered her face with her hands.

"Sorry, I didn't mean to intrude. Forget I asked."

Lydia let her hands drop from her face. There were unshed tears in her eyes. "No, it's fine. I want to talk about him, it's only that most people…"

"…most people assume you're glad he's gone."

Lydia jumped up from the couch and paced to the window. "Exactly."

Gregor longed to go to her, place a comforting arm around her shoulder, tell her he understood. How much of that longing came from the man, and how much from the wolf he couldn't be sure. So, he curled his hands into fists and kept to his place on the armchair.

"It's just so unfair." Lydia turned from the window; her face streaked with tears. "They're happy to use your strength in the mines and on construction sites, but then they trap you inside like animals."

Most of the time, Gregor ignored the bars on the windows, or at least looked past them to his small patch of garden. With their shadow cutting across Lydia's tear-stained face, ignoring the bars was not an option.

"Come away from the window. You don't want to be seen there."

Lydia shrugged. "What's the difference? I'm already here. In the system. Non-infected female nine-seven-six-N-I-eight-nine, entered infected domicile eight-T-F-V-, twelve forty-three, or some such. They'll not send anyone to rescue me, not when there's just a sliver of a crescent in the sky."

"Come away anyway." Gregor reached towards Lydia. "My neighbours know me for what I am, and they'll take any excuse to break down my door."

Lydia returned to her place on the couch and, before he could stop her, grasped Gregor's hand in both of hers.

Gregor let his hand linger in Lydia's grasp longer than was wise, relishing the feel of her soft, smooth skin against his own.

As he pulled away, he looked into Lydia's eyes. "Never do that again."

Lydia slumped back against the couch. "I'm sorry. Dumb move." She jumped up from the couch and bolted for the door. "Don't worry. It won't be happening again."

~ * ~

Gregor wasn't expecting to see Lydia again, but she arrived on a Saturday afternoon. The sun was bright and the moon new and absent from the sky. She'd brought a picnic, and as they set off for the park, Gregor spirits lifted as they hadn't done in years. He didn't feel free, but he remembered being free.

They found a spot near the river, under the shade of a beech tree, away from the crowds. Gregor spread out the blanket, and Lydia emptied her picnic basket of Tupperware® boxes of sandwiches and cakes. She'd packed plenty of food, and Gregor smiled at the sight of it all. It had been years since he'd eaten a cucumber sandwich. He wasn't sure he'd ever eaten one with the crusts cut off and cut into triangles. No one had taken so much care of him before.

When they had both eaten their fill, Gregor leaned back against the tree. Lydia lay flat on the ground, her head pillowed by Gregor's discarded sweatshirt. A cooling breeze played against Gregor's cheeks, and he dozed, as the bees droned around a nearby buddleia.

"He wasn't a bit like you." Lydia's words startled Gregor.

"How so?"

"Not nearly as cautious, took risks all the time, stayed out late, almost missed curfew loads of times."

"I nearly missed curfew that first time we met."

"Yeah, but only because I crashed into you."

"Well, yes, there is that."

The pair lapsed into silence. Gregor stared through the green canopy of beech leaves, up into the cloudless sky. If only it could always be like this: no clouds for the moon to hide behind, no moon to hide from, her face turned away from him and all those like him who bore her curse.

"How did you lose him?" It was the one question Gregor wanted to ask the most, yet the one he dreaded asking or having answered. Long ago, he'd accepted that he'd die before his time. He'd slip up, stay out too late, get caught out after curfew, get too close to a jogger pungent with sweat. But would it be the mob that finished him, or an overzealous officer of the law?

"It was me. I did it. I killed him."

Gregor sat up straight and stared down at Lydia in disbelief. "You?"

Lydia propped herself up on her elbows, turned her face towards Gregor and smiled her brilliant smile. "He asked me to, begged me. After he turned my younger brother, he couldn't live with himself." Lydia sprang to her feet and held out a hand to Gregor. When he grasped it, she pulled him to his feet. They stood so close her breath was warm on his neck and carried with it the faint sweet smell of chocolate from the brownies they'd shared.

Before he could fathom whether he wanted to kiss her or destroy her, Lydia whispered in his ear, "How many did you turn, Gregor? How many lives have you ruined?" Then she placed a hand on his chest and gave him a gentle push. "Come on. Let's get this cleared away. Get you back before curfew."

~ * ~

The evening of the next full moon, Gregor knew better than to open the door to Lydia, but he did it anyway. Lydia slipped past him, not even bothering to keep a careful distance.

"What are you doing here?"

"You know why I'm here." Lydia stood by the window.

Saliva pooled in Gregor's mouth, and he swallowed twice before he spoke. "You need to leave. Please Lydia. Go now."

"Don't worry. I'll leave. You're coming with me. We're going for a walk to the park."

This was madness. "We can't. I can't leave this close to curfew. I'll never get back in time."

"You don't need to worry. I'll watch over you, not let you harm anyone. Come on. We best get going. Or we'll be locked in here together. You wouldn't want that, now would you, Gregor?"

The blood pounded in Gregor's head. His joints ached. He needed the door to close, to lock. Why had he left it open? Why was she still here? He mustn't be alone with her. If he took one step closer, the wolf within would spring. He didn't dare get close enough to manhandle her out of his house.

What choice did he have? He bounded through the open door and out into the night. He loped along at a steady pace, dropping to all fours when he reached the darkened park. It had been years since he'd done this, transformed in the open. He gave himself over to the wolf and howled. The answering howls, when they came, were faint and at a far distance. He'd be hunting alone tonight. If he was lucky, he'd make his kill, transform back, find his last stash of old clothes, and slink back home without being caught.

Then he caught the scent on the breeze. It was female, young, healthy. It was Lydia. He should flee, find other prey, but his legs refused to obey him. The crunch of bike tyres on gravel told him she was close. His nose had led him to the bin shelter, and now he jumped up onto it. Her bike crunched to a stop, and she stood bathed in moonlight, smiling up at him. As he crouched, ready to spring, he caught sight of a flash of silver. So, this was what his end would be. He landed in front of her, reared up on his hind legs, and placed his front paws on her shoulders as she plunged the silver blade under his ribs and up into his heart. At last, he was embracing her.

~ * ~

A slight young woman stood alone in the park. Her clothes were soaked in blood. Her smile was full, her eyes wide. She wiped her silver blade clean on the grass by the gravel path, sheathed her knife, mounted her bike, and cycled away under a full moon.

~ * ~ * ~

Lindsay Oliver writes poetry, short stories, and longer fiction. Lindsay's poetry has been published online and in print. She takes part in open mics and poetry slams. Most recently, Lindsay's poem "How to be a feminist poet" won first prize in the Glasgow Women's Library Calm Slam.

Blood of Heaven

DJ Tyrer

Esdrell wasn't certain if they had been right to accept the mission, but the swordswoman had long ago found morals and money seldom ever neatly aligned. Still, there was a difference between selling her blade to kill in battle for some cause she couldn't care less about and kidnapping an unarmed and terrified woman.

Tracking Jezelda had been the most difficult aspect of the job, as she had fled across the wilderness, somehow surviving without being killed and eaten by the beasts that lurked there or captured by bandits. Then she had travelled from city to city down the river to Pathos where Esdrell and the little alien wizard, N'Kaz, had finally caught up with her. Her capture had been all too easy, the woman naively seeing Esdrell as no threat due to their shared sex, and their escape in a stolen skiff had added only the slightest frisson of excitement to their venture.

Jezelda was now bound in the bottom of the boat Esdrell was busy rowing along the river, whilst N'Kaz sat impassively opposite her, concealed by his heavy black robes, his head bowed towards the woman, who had ceased to struggle against her bonds.

The bloated red sun was dropping below the horizon. Not long now, and they would hand Jezelda over to their employer.

"What is it?" Esdrell asked the diminutive wizard, noting his apparent interest in their prisoner.

Grey, rubbery tentacles twitched out from beneath the hood of his robes and she felt his voice insinuate itself into her mind.

"There is something about her. This woman has power."

Esdrell ceased rowing. "Is that why you insisted we take this job?"

She had only agreed to take Yagdriel's money because N'Kaz had desired they should.

"No. I was intrigued why a Haemovore was so desperate for this one woman's blood."

"Wait, hold up," Esdrell said as they continued to drift, "a

Haemovore? As in, a blood-drinker?"

N'Kaz nodded his hooded head. "They float through the darkness between the worlds as seeds and filter down through the air to the ground below to feed."

Esdrell laid the paddle down in the bottom of the boat, then looked up at the darkening sky. "Yagdriel came from up there, like you?"

Again, N'Kaz nodded.

"He looked so human."

"Haemovores take on a form analogous to that of the locally dominant race and possess mental powers that can conceal their true nature from their prey."

"You mean me?"

"Yes."

"But, not you?"

"No."

"You knew what we were dealing with, and you didn't tell me?"

"It didn't seem necessary at the time."

"I would never have agreed to hunt Jezelda down for him!"

"Because he would feast on her blood?" The alien wizard's tentacles quivered. "What was it you thought Yagdriel would do with her?"

It was a question she didn't want to answer.

"You said to take the job."

"Yes. I was intrigued. Now, I see some hint of what he desires."

N'Kaz was silent for a moment, then said, "If you're not going to row, please, remove her gag."

Esdrell snorted, but did so.

Jezelda looked up at them with wide, frightened eyes.

"Why does the Haemovore want you?" N'Kaz asked. Although the words were directed to Jezelda's mind, he allowed Esdrell to hear them, too.

"I…I don't know what a Haemovore is," the woman whimpered.

Esdrell laughed. "I've met enough liars in my time to know one when I see one. Tell the truth. You were fleeing, don't deny it. Were you fleeing the Haemovore? What did it want with you?"

The woman sobbed. "I don't know. Not exactly."

"Please, tell us," N'Kaz said. "We may be able to help you."

She nodded. "I was the wife of a farmer on the eastern fringes of the Hills of Ghor. It was a hard life, but a happy one." Her face clouded at the memory.

"Then, one day, *it* happened."

"What happened?" Esdrell asked, leaning closer.

Jezelda's reply was to smack her on the side of her head with the paddle, sending Esdrell sprawling backwards to slump over the edge of the boat, one hand trailing in the river.

The woman dropped the paddle and prepared to jump into the water, but instead fell backwards with a sigh into the bottom of the boat.

Esdrell raised her head to see N'Kaz returning one of his white-metal wands to the depths of his sleeve. Apparently its beam had sent Jezelda into a swoon.

Rubbing the side of her head, Esdrell looked down at her and wished the beam had stunned Jezelda as painfully as the blow from the paddle had her. A couple of her teeth had been loosened by the blow and she spat blood over the side before crouching down to rebind the woman. How she had managed to get free without them noticing, Esdrell didn't know. Clearly, her life in the vicinity of the hills of Ghor had taught her to be resourceful; they would need to be more cautious with her.

Esdrell resumed rowing whilst waiting for Jezelda to awaken from her faint; it seemed they were still travelling back along the river to meet Yagdriel.

After a while, Jezelda regained consciousness and they resumed their conversation, though she was more sullen this time.

"Then," Esdrell said, reminding her, "one day, *it* happened. *What* happened?"

Jezelda pulled against the ropes, but finding they wouldn't loosen, sighed, and spoke.

"I was weeding our vegetable plot, when the light of the sun seemed to grow brighter and there was a sound like the roaring of a martichoras, followed by a loud crash and a flash of flame a short distance from me.

"I was knocked off my feet and, when I stood, once more, I approached the fiery hole that appeared in the middle of our patch of rutabagas."

"Something fell from the sky," N'Kaz stated.

Jezelda shrugged. "Down from the sky or up from the ground, I don't know. All I saw was a burning pit where, before, there had been vegetables."

"What happened, then?" Esdrell asked.

"I approached it, to see what lay inside. There was nothing but a liquid, like golden water pooling in the bottom of the hole."

"You touched it?" N'Kaz asked.

She nodded. "Yes. I touched the golden water, and it flowed up my fingers to where, earlier in the day, I'd cut the back of my hand on a steely thorn."

"It flowed into you?" N'Kaz asked.

She nodded, again.

"It is in you."

"Yes. I think so, at least."

"And, the Haemovore?"

"I…I think that must be what attacked us. It was the next night. It broke down the door of our home and killed my husband as he fought to protect us. Then, it killed our daughter before I could get her out. It looked like a man, tall and gaunt, yet it stood over her and touched its long fingers to her body and they adhered like suckers and drained her life from her."

She sobbed. "I watched in horror, unable to intervene. Then, it turned and came for me, and I fled. I fled outside and ran to our barn, took our horse and rode it bareback in the direction of Vize, though I only made it as far as the village of Salfetter.

"It pursued me with unnatural haste and I knew it meant to kill me, as it had killed those I loved."

"I managed to fight it off with a burning torch and galloped away into the wilds. When the horse grew tired, I set it free and continued on foot until I reached the river and was able to beg passage on a boat. The rest you know."

Esdrell nodded, then looked at N'Kaz. "What is in her?"

"I do not know. However, it would seem the power I can sense entered into her blood and the Haemovore seeks to drink it. It may be such blood would empower it in some way, or it is possible it is no more than the equivalent of a fine wine to it. But, either way, it wants to drain her of her blood."

"And, it hired us to bring her to it?" Esdrell said. She spat in anger.

N'Kaz nodded his hood. "Yes. And, it would seem we are almost there. Come, let us take her to it and see what shall transpire."

"Wait," Esdrell said. "You mean, you intend to hand her over to it, even if her blood could give it greater power." She shook her head. "Who can say what it will then do?"

"That," N'Kaz said, "is what intrigues me."

They drew up at a jetty and Esdrell helped Jezelda out of the boat. There was an old and weather-beaten hut close by.

"It's too dark to proceed, now," N'Kaz said. "We will rest here in the hut and resume our journey in the morning."

"Please," Jezelda begged, "don't hand me over to that monster. I don't want to die."

Esdrell gave a shrug. "It seems your fate is still in question, Now, get in the hut."

~ * ~

They were woken by a loud sound as the door of the hut was torn free of its hinges.

Esdrell had rolled into a ready crouch and grabbed for her sword, even before she was awake.

Yagdriel was standing in the doorway, his true form no longer hidden by a glamour.

Esdrell recoiled in spite of herself. The Haemovore had a human shape, but was taller and thinner with longer limbs, and its fingers ended in suckers that twitched towards the bound and cowering woman in the corner of the hut and opened and closed as if already sucking her life away.

N'Kaz was standing as casually as the little robed figure ever did and was pointing a wand at the Haemovore. Esdrell rose to stand beside him, sword in hand.

"You have her," Yagdriel said in a wet voice. "You shall have the agreed reward when she is mine. Give her to me!"

"No," Esdrell said. "I know what you are and what you want."

"No? No?" Yagdriel laughed. "No! If you know what I am, you should know better than to come between a Haemovore and its prey!"

He opened a mouth fool of needle teeth.

"I was never that smart," Esdrell said, suppressing a shudder.

"I am not of this world. Your paltry blade doesn't scare me."

He reached out for Jezelda and Esdrell slashed, removing the suckers of that hand.

Yagdriel howled in pain and anger.

"Refined steel," she said. "A trick of the ancients. Better than mere iron."

The Haemovore snarled. "I shall taste your blood, then drain hers."

It lunged for her and seized her by the throat with its good hand and lowered its head to bite her neck.

N'Kaz raised his wand. A beam of silvery light shot from it and struck Yagdriel, who released Esdrell, throwing her to the ground.

Yagdriel turned and opened its mouth and a high-pitched shriek came from it, enveloping N'Kaz and sending him flying backwards, through the wall in a shower of splinters, and out into the night.

Esdrell groped for her sword as the Haemovore leaned towards Jezelda and reached out with its sucker fingers.

"What is it about her blood?" she gasped.

"Full of fire and life," Yagdriel said with a laugh. "Should taste most delicious."

The suckers touched the woman's skin.

Esdrell lunged, but she was still groggy from her fall, and Yagdriel swatted her clumsy blow aside with its injured hand. Her sword flew from her grasp and struck Jezelda's arm, slicing her skin and releasing her blood in a wild spray of deepest crimson and brightest gold.

Yagdriel shrieked and recoiled from her as a wave of energy exploded free from her body. The walls and roof of the hut were blown away, exposing them to the open sky. The glow from the spurting blood lit the area like the dawn.

Esdrell had no idea what was happening, but, although disorientated, she didn't pause. She seized up her sword and swung it in a wide arc, slicing the Haemovore's head from its shoulders.

It shrieked and fountained blood of its own, dark and horribly viscous, then fell to the ground, its head rolling away. Dead.

She turned back to Jezelda, who had collapsed to the ground, the bright spray of blood still spurting from her arm, her skin paling even as Esdrell watched.

She tried to reach her and press her hands to the wound, halt the flow, but it was like trying to draw close to a raging fire and she couldn't do it.

Esdrell screamed in anger and fear. Jezelda was going to die, regardless.

There was a sudden rumbling and the ground shook, causing

her to fall to her hands and knees.

"N'Kaz, where are you? What's happening?"

"I don't know," she heard his voice in her mind. It sounded weak and far away and that scared her.

She looked about. As the last of Jezelda's blood escaped her body, things like crystals were exploding from the earth and growing larger and larger till they towered over her, glowing brightly from within.

Esdrell shook her head in confusion.

Then, the rumbling ceased and the glow lessened to a bearable level.

A number of blocks of crystal stood along the riverbank.

N'Kaz walked over to her and helped her stand.

"*That* was in her blood?" she said, incredulously.

"Apparently so," the little wizard said.

She shook her head in disbelief. Then, she looked down at Jezelda and felt tears spring to her eyes. The woman was pale and lifeless.

"We killed her," she said. "We're to blame."

N'Kaz made no reply and gave no hint of anything she could call an emotion.

She sucked in a breath, uncertain whether she would shriek at him or start bawling, but let it out in surprise when she heard a soft sound close by.

Esdrell turned to see a black void, like a rectangular doorway, had opened in the side of one of the crystal blocks. As she watched, a figure stepped out.

He was almost, but not quite human in shape and a little shorter than she was. His skin was translucent like glass and within she saw organs that looked like cut jewels rather than flesh and blood.

She gaped at him.

The figure opened his mouth and spoke a buzz of sounds that might have been words, but which meant nothing to her.

"I shall translate," N'Kaz said. She supposed he could touch the figure's mind as easily as hers.

"What is he? Where did he come from?"

N'Kaz was silent for a moment, then spoke. "It seems that, like myself and the Haemovore, they come from the heavens. Their home world was destroyed and they sent out… I suppose you could say, the building blocks of life and their civilisation."

"In the form of the golden liquid?" she asked.

"Yes. It was within a vessel that broke apart when it came to earth here. When Jezelda touched the liquid, it entered her body and all the…information…was then carried within her. The Haemovore could sense the power in her blood from a distance away and began to stalk her. Had it drained her, the…information her blood carried, their civilisation, would have been destroyed."

"But, when I cut her, it was released…"

N'Kaz nodded. "Yes. And took root, as it were."

"A new city," she breathed. Then, she looked at the figure. "A new people."

"It will cause a stir along the river," N'Kaz said, without any hint of whether he meant the words literally or sardonically.

She looked at the dead woman. "Jezelda…"

The figure said something in its buzzing tongue.

"Hmm, it seems you will not have to mope any longer," N'Kaz said.

She looked at him in confusion.

The figure produced a rod of crystal and pointed it at the dead woman. Light flowed from its tip and into her flesh, which slowly resumed a healthy colouration.

There was a sudden loud gasp of indrawn breath and Jezelda sat bolt upright, her eyes wide with terror and confusion.

"It seems they are grateful for the part she played in restoring them to existence," N'Kaz said, "and, as she was touched by their nature, they were able to restore her to health."

Esdrell dropped down beside the woman and hugged her. "You're okay. You're going to be okay."

"What…?"

"I'll explain everything…" Esdrell turned her head towards N'Kaz. "Just as soon as it's all been explained to me."

~ * ~ * ~

DJ Tyrer dwells on the northern shore of the Thames estuary, close to the world's longest pleasure pier in the decaying seaside resort of Southend-on-Sea, and is the person behind *Atlantean Publishing.* They studied history at the University of Wales at Aberystwyth and have worked in the fields of education and public relations. When not writing fiction, DJ enjoys roleplaying, wargaming, and the arcane art of conlanging. Their fiction has been widely published in anthologies and magazines around the world, such as *Tales of the Black Arts* (Hazardous Press), *Pagan (Zimbell House),* and *Us/Them* and *Crunchy With Ketchup* (both Wolfsinger Publications), and issues of *Broadswords and Blasters*, *BFS Horizons*, *Journ-E*, and *Tales from the Magician's Skull*, and in addition, DJ has a novella available in paperback and on the Kindle, *The Yellow House* (Dunhams Manor). Other stories featuring Esdrell and N'Kaz have appeared in *Swords Against Cthulhu III* and *Swords and Sorcery Magazine.*

The Witch Bottle

Tim Newton Anderson

To the unenlightened eye, the Witch Bottle just looked like an old glass object with some odds and ends inside. However, Rupert Bonneville's eye was anything but unenlightened.

"Provenance," he said. "That is what we must consider. You can tell me anything about the history of this item, but if you have no, ah, documentary evidence, it is worth nothing. Provenance is everything. We must know where things came from. It's like ancestry—it divides the elite from the hoi poloi. I could claim to be descended from Henry VIII but unless I have the documents to prove it, the assertion is worth nothing."

Bonneville was out on one of his regular scouting missions for his Chelsea Embankment antique shop. The flood of antique shows on television had vastly increased the demand for his goods, but it had also ramped up people's determination to get a good price for the things they wanted to sell him. Everyone thought they were an expert and the tat that had been hidden in their attic for a generation must be worth a fortune. He lamented the days you could buy a Chippendale for a fiver from some old lady out in the sticks.

As if he had read Rupert's mind the man said: "I've seen one of these on Antiques Roadshow. They said they could fetch hundreds."

The man was not the usual isolated farmer or house clearance dealer Rupert normally dealt with, or a charity shop volunteer who priced things by usefulness rather than intrinsic value. He was a builder who had come across the bottle when demolishing a dilapidated cottage in the Fens to make room for a new dormer village. His pin-striped suit was better quality than the dress down outfit Rupert had chosen to hide his prosperity, and he had the toned body of someone who could afford lots of sessions at the gym. His shaved head gave him a thuggish look, but Rupert suspected there was a shrewd mind inside of it. Rupert's wavy blond hair and broad smile probably reminded the builder of every bank manager, council executive and lawyer he had outmanoeuvred. He was also relaxed and at home in his plush office, where he had summoned Rupert after hearing of his visit to some of his tenants. The Witch Bottle would not be cheap, cheap, but perhaps it could be bought for as little as possible. He had already offered Rupert various items of architectural salvage and it was clear he knew their value to the last farthing, but this was outside of the builder's area of expertise.

"The bottle seems of the right age, mid seventeenth century, but the contents…"

Rupert let the man—Bill Watson—digest this thought before continuing.

"As you know," a nod of the head to acknowledge a degree of expertise with just enough condescension to suggest Watson didn't know *everything*, "Witch Bottles were common in East Anglia, filled with blood, urine and pins and other items designed to ward off supernatural attacks. This certainly seems to contain pins and nails and some dried substance that could well have been blood, urine and hair. But how do we tell if this is not a more modern forgery placed there as a joke? Or, more importantly, if it was done by some superstitious peasant rather than a witch or wise woman helping a client? The latter would make it much more valuable; do you see? The difference between a few pounds and a few thousand. Provenance."

"The cottage had been in the same family for five hundred years," Watson said. "They'd done a few improvements like connecting mains water and putting in an inside toilet and bathroom, but they had a septic tank for waste and weren't even on mains electricity, let alone gas. That bottle's probably been there since the Leman family first built it in fifteen-eighty."

"So we know whose home it was, but not who created the bottle, do you see?"

Rupert decided to play his trump card.

"I can offer you fifteen pounds for it—final offer—but if you want more I'll have to walk away. Feel free to see if you can find someone who knows less about these things to take it off your hands." He started to rise in his chair.

"All right," Watson said. "Better than nothing, I suppose."

He handed over the bottle in exchange for the money and Rupert shook his hand and left. Once outside he took a deep breath and smiled more genuinely.

Provenance, he thought. *History, heritage.* There were lots of experts who would examine the bottle if it came up for auction and test it to see if its age was as advertised. But they hardly ever examined the evidence of origin as closely, especially if you had many genuine documents of provenance to draw attention away from the carefully faked ones. He could get documents certifying the ownership of the house and adjoining smallholding, and birth, death and marriage records from the local church. And the name Leman rang a bell. Some neighbour of the family? A distant relative, perhaps.

As well as cold calling on likely prospects, Rupert relied on a network of experts to help him source objects. One of them was Maggie Hermitage—a white witch who lived further into the fens at Great Marshway. Behind all of the flim flam that attracted the gullible to buy her readings and potions, Maggie was a qualified historian who was an expert in her field. It was just that esoterica was more profitable than academia—especially as she could play an old hag convincingly with a lot of theatrical make up and a grey wig that hid her red hair.

Rupert didn't believe in witchcraft, or anything supernatural. For him the value of the past was counted solely in the amount of money it could make him in the present. Lots of people had told him Maggie was the real deal and said how much her spells and nostrums had helped them with everything from bad skin to attracting a lover. However, his only use for her skills was in tracing the back story of something he had found and transforming it from old rubbish to valuable antique. If other people wanted to believe all that stuff, more fool them.

"You are correct about the name Leman," she said as she handed him a cup of tea and slice of home-made rhubarb and ginger cake in her living room. Unlike the small study where she entertained clients that was crowded with mystical paraphernalia, her lounge was modern and comfortable. The furniture was stylish and instead of crystal balls and dreamcatchers, there were family photographs and a vase of flowers on her bureau. She was an attractive woman, Rupert thought, and it was a shame she had to dress up as a crone most of the time. He had sometimes wondered what she would look like dancing naked round a sabbat fire. That was one part of witchcraft that would appeal to him.

"Mary Leman was the first wife of Thomas Oliver." she said. "They emigrated from here to Salem, but had to come back after she was accused of witchcraft. She then died in questionable circumstances, and Oliver returned to America where his second wife was also accused of sorcery and hanged in Salem. This was a bit later than the peak years of witchcraft trials in this country, but they were still going strong in New England."

Rupert was well aware of the activities of local boy Matthew Hopkins—the self-styled Witchfinder General—who had made East Anglia the capital of witch hunting. He and his associates were responsible for more than 200 women being hung or burned for witchcraft and the majority were from his home region. As a local boy himself, Rupert had taken a great interest in the stories when he was a child. His family had lived on the edge of the Fens for centuries and celebrated their roots. Rupert had not been able to wait until he could pull them up and set off for the bright lights of London. One thing he had learned, though, was how to spot genuine antiques. Generations of the Bonneville family had made their living by travelling round the region buying goods from the gullible and finding the right expert to sell them to. Other dealers said they had the magic touch. They could even sniff out the good stuff in antique shops—each had their own areas of expertise and may not properly value something outside of their field. The Bonneville's never had a shop—too much overhead and too much dead money in stock. They bought, then they sold. As quickly as possible.

"So this bottle could have been created by Mary Leman?" he asked.

"Your guess is as good as mine," Maggie said. "I'm betting you will find a way to prove that, though. At least enough to hike the price considerably. If it was, it didn't work. They are supposed to reflect back any spells on the person who cast them if they are buried. Or if that doesn't work, burned or shattered. If Mary or her family thought it would protect them, they were wrong. There's a record of a Mary Oliver being burned for witchcraft at about the right time, but given her husband's later history, I suspect he was the witch rather than either of his wives. It was always women who got the blame—typical misogyny."

"A load of warlocks then," Rupert joked.

"Feel free to laugh," Maggie said, "but it was no joke to the women who were tortured and killed because they were outspoken or got in the way of some man's desire for their property, or simply didn't get on with their neighbours. I bet if you look hard enough, there are people in every family round here who were either the victims or the perpetrators of the crimes against these women."

Rupert wisely wiped the smile off his face. She may dress up in her Halloween costume for the punters, but she took her trade very, very seriously. He wasn't worried she would cast a spell on him, but he didn't want to lose her expertise. That was also the reason he had never acted on his attraction for her. In a choice between business and pleasure, business won out every time.

He was a bit nervous of the Witch Bottle, though. There had been stories about them from elderly relatives when he was growing up. All of them knew someone who had been cursed in some way after getting on the wrong side of the local wise woman. Their punishment ranged from boils to cattle keeling over. He also knew many of those wise women had been Maggie's ancestors. There had been several Witch Bottles buried on the family farm to protect the family. Not that they worked—he was the last one living. Accident and illness had carried off the rest of them and there had been a few years when he was up every other weekend for a funeral. After each death he had surreptitiously unearthed the Witch Bottles, invented a background story and the documents to 'prove' it, and sold them for a good price.

He made some trips to the local church and the archive centre in Norwich before returning to London, armed with a briefcase full of paperwork that could be presented in a way that would boost the Witch Bottle's value fifty-fold. He lost no time in submitting it to a specialist auction. The Church visit had increased his unease and made him determined to sell the Witch Bottle as soon as he could.

The priest had changed again since the last funeral he had attended there. A woman, this time. She had four churches in her parish which had expanded as the number of parishioners had shrunk. Rupert had nothing against women vicars per se, he just wouldn't want one officiating at any ceremony of his. The middle-aged woman had seemed pleased to see him—probably because she earned as much money from amateur genealogists and brass rubbing enthusiasts as she did from the collection plate. She had been happy to show him the area of the churchyard where the unconsecrated graves were—witches were not allowed on hallowed ground—with a few remarks about how they would move them into the main area if they could get a grant from some feminist group to do so. She toddled off back to the church to unearth the relevant tomes from the archive with the details he needed.

He quickly found the grave he was looking for—Mary Oliver, ne Leman. He also found one for a Margaret Hermitage. This must be one of Maggie's ancestors.

He wasn't sure why, but he decided to visit the area where his own relatives were buried. He hadn't been there since his sister had been interred—the last of the line apart from himself. He had bought a pre-paid cremation plan for himself as her death had absorbed the last of the family's money. The previous vicar had tried to get more money out of him, but Rupert had pleaded poverty and negotiated a discount.

There were lots of Bonneville gravestones, becoming more and more weatherworn as he walked down the line like a general inspecting troops on parade. Quite a few Ruperts as it was a family name. He should have been surprised to see a few mentions of the Hermitage name, but this was West Norfolk and everyone was related to everyone else in some way. He was more shocked to see some Olivers. By the dates, probably sisters or descendants of Thomas Oliver. So he had witch blood in him as well. He gave a slight shudder and could swear he felt a twitch from the shoulder bag in which he had placed the Witch Bottle.

He saw the vicar walking towards him across the church yard and quickly moved to intercept her and grasp the bundle of photocopies in her hand. He was so disturbed by his discoveries, he just pulled a handful of notes from his wallet and gave them to her in exchange. He would regret it when he realised how much he had overpaid, but he just wanted to get back to his shop and leave the past behind.

The auction was not for a few days yet, and he had put the Witch Bottle in his shop window for a sum larger than the valuation the auction house had given. If he could sell it himself and save the commission, all to the good. It would be some compensation for the over-generous payment to the vicar. He should be feeling good about it, but he wasn't. He had sold things which were both physically uglier and with darker pasts, but this gave him a feeling of unease. Perhaps it was the slightly sickly green tinge of the glass, or the rust-coloured bodily fluids in the bottom. Or perhaps it was because it brought to mind a horrible time in the history of his home and family. It was created a long time ago, but for once he saw an intruder from the past as a haunting rather than a profit.

It was sitting there in pride of place, glittering in the sun, when Bill Watson stormed in.

"You shyster," he shouted. "You said that bottle was next to worthless and now it's in the Sotheby's catalogue for hundreds of pounds."

Rupert came from behind the counter. He didn't want Watson breaking any of his stock. He held his hands up in an attempt to calm the builder. He was wearing a white tee shirt and jeans, and Thomas could see the muscles beneath the cloth. He now wished he had gone to the extra expense of having a panic button put in as the man who had installed his burglar alarm had suggested.

"Provenance," Rupert said. "I said it wasn't worth anything much without provenance. It took me a lot of work to be able to prove it's the genuine article. Time and money, and time *is* money, don't you see? If you had put it in an auction without that you would probably have less than I gave you for it."

Watson walked over to the window, still fuming, and grabbed the Witch Bottle from the display. He shook it angrily towards Rupert.

"Nobody cons me," he shouted. "I didn't get where I am today by letting people make a fool out of me. You're not going to make a profit at my expense."

He hurled the bottle to the floor where it shattered. Pins and nails ricocheted across the shop and the brown substance inside oozed onto the tiles. The glass shards shone like diamonds. Rupert could have sworn a brown gas escaped from the bottle as it broke, but surely that was imagination.

At first Rupert thought the tightening in his chest was simply shock at his lost profits. Then his face slumped on the right side and his arm became stiff. He lost strength in his legs and fell to the floor. He felt as if his blood had frozen in his veins.

Five hundred years ago Mary Oliver had created the bottle to protect her from the magical attacks of her husband Thomas. It hadn't been strong enough to save her from the spells that doomed her and her successor to death at the hands of the witch hunters. But it had endured long and became stronger and stronger. And if it hadn't saved her, at least now she had revenge on her husband's descendant.

Rupert tried to croak out a plea for help to Bill Watson, but the builder just spat at him and walked out of the shop. By the time the next customer came in an hour later, Rupert Bonneville was beyond help.

~ * ~ * ~

Tim Newton Anderson is a former senior daily newspaper journalist and PR manager who has recently started writing fiction. In the past nine months he has had 21 stories accepted in publications including: *Parsec Magazine*, *Tales of the Shadowmen*, *Emanations*, *Zoetic Press non binary review*, *SF Writers Guild*, *Dark Horses Magazine*, *Crowvus*, *Trees Anthology*, *Magic Portals Anthology*, *Planet Bizarro*, *Thuggish Itch*, *Suffolk Writes*, *Dark Lane Books*, *Fall Into Fantasy*, *Black Scat Review*, *MX Book of New Sherlock Holmes*, *Bewildering Stories*, *Feast of Laughter*, and Touchpoint Press.

A member of the London Institute of 'Pataphysics, when not writing Tim sings, plays guitar and blues harmonica and used to run a cabaret night.

I Am Awake

Mariah Southworth

The first moments of consciousness are hardly that—as in, you don't really realize you're conscious. You just sit there, floating, vaguely registering the gentle bumps of the large disks you share space with knocking into you on their way passed. Then you move your fins in an odd way, actually notice the feel of the gentle current against your skin, and you are awake! *I* am awake. Awake in a wide, smooth tunnel, suspended in a thick liquid.

All around me are fat bodied, red disks with a slight dip in the center, bobbing along in the current. With consciousness comes the awareness of an empty ache inside of myself. I shoot forward, latch onto one of the disks and sink my teeth into its flesh. It gives with a pop, filling my mouth with delicious salt and iron.

I eat until the ache is gone, then I nestle into what's left of the disk and rest, letting the current carry us away.

Something is tickling me, and suddenly I am awake. With a start I look around and realize I am no longer alone on my dinner-turned-raft. Amorphous, blob-like things have latched onto it, dozens of them. I watch, mesmerized, as the one nearest me flattens, and a pale ooze crawls out from underneath its form. The ooze quickly turns red, and the blob sucks it back up, leaving behind a deep scar in the disk we both rest on. The blobs are eating my raft!

A light, feather touch makes me turn as one of the blobs settles onto my own body, and I glimpse myself for the first time. Long and dark, with fins and spines running all down my sides. This is the first time I have ever seen myself, and I stare, leaving the blob be. It flattens itself.

Pain! Searing, burning, pain! With instincts quicker than thought, I lunge for the creature and suck it up, burning ooze and all. One chomp ends its life. I quickly swim away, leaving the half-eaten disk to the blobs. *What was that?* I wonder with disgust. It hadn't tasted good at all, too sour. I take a bite out of a passing disk, not out of hunger, but to get the taste of the creature out of my mouth.

Then, as I swallow. I wonder, *What am I?*

~ * ~

I eat, I swim, I grow and explore. I know what I am now; a long flat creature, lined with fins and spines, all leading to a wide mouth filled with row upon row of teeth. My world is one of tunnels and currents. Some currents are lazy, others are so fast I find myself whipped about against the smooth walls and carried away to distant reaches. There are vast chambers where the walls pulse, so wide I cannot see the far end, and small, intimate rooms where the currents swirl. All manner of things live in the tunnels, more than just the delicious disks and the sour blobs. My favorite are the huge white slimes who hunt in packs, searching for the spiny clusters and sharp-angled creatures that lurk in the currents.

The slimes spear these monsters with forked lances, then fall upon their prey and consume them. The slimes sometimes try to spear me, but their lances will not stick, and so they leave me alone. Do they think like I do? It's hard to say. I have swum all over these tunnels, to the narrowest crevices where strange light shines through, to the largest chambers where the drumbeat of the walls turn the current into an impossible whirlpool, and I have never seen anything like myself.

~ * ~

I am bigger now, grown long and sleek on my delicious disks. I don't fit inside the smaller tunnels anymore, and when I try to squeeze through I roughen up the walls. Waxy plates in the currents stick to the rough parts. They make the tunnels even narrower, and I have to clear them out to get through. I eat the red disks by the dozen now. Once I could curl up in the dip of one and sleep, with plenty of space all around. Now one disk is a single mouthful.

~ * ~

I am afraid.

My world has shrunk, pressing in around me. I can barely see the white slimes anymore. In fact, I cannot help but eat them when I open my mouth. I drink it all now, delicious disks, the sour blobs, the white slimes and the monsters they hunt.

I'm trapped in one of the larger chambers. Not *the* largest, with its pulsing walls and violent currents. By the time I realized my peril, I was too far away. It was all I could do to squeeze in here. And here I am. Too large to leave; and getting larger.

What will I do? I eat, though it seems the disks are fewer now. And I grow. And I despair of what will happen when I crush against the walls. Even now, I fill the whole chamber. The current has stopped. No more liquid, no more disks.

Nothing.

~ * ~

Dr. Fujita paused, scalpel halfway through its incision. She looked up at the man standing across from her over the table. "Did you see that?" she asked her assistant.

The technician, Palmer, blinked at her. "See what?" he asked.

Dr. Fujita shook her head. They were both at the tail end of a nine-hour shift, and tired. Dr. Fujita had *thought* she'd seen something grab the end of her scalpel before retreating back inside the body, something like a tiny mouth. "Nothing," she said, continuing with the autopsy. The patient—or rather, cadaver—had been admitted to the hospital for severe anemia several days ago, then discharged. Today he had returned via ambulance due to a stroke but had died before reaching the hospital. It was a bit of a mystery, considering he'd had no family or personal history of stroke, or anemia, for that matter. Dr. Fujita needed to find out why it had happened.

Gathering her wits about her, the doctor finished exposing the left carotid.

"What the Hell?!" Palmer jumped back as something came boiling out of the corpse. Dr. Fujita froze. She only had a second to look at the thing, but its image was burned into her brain. As long as her pinky finger, with mottled black and red, slug-like skin. Spines and paper-thin fins ran all down its body, and as she stared at it, it opened a wide, flat mouth full of red needles.

Then it was gone, scuttling off the body and down onto the table. Too late, Dr. Fujita stabbed at it with her scalpel, missing wildly. It hit the floor, and Palmer went chasing it across the room, stomping with his foot.

"Damn, its gone," he said, running up against the shining wall of storage drawers. "A centipede? How the hell did a centipede get in there?"

"Look at this," Dr. Fujita said.

Palmer came back over, and she showed him the ragged hole in the wall of the artery. "Is that how it got in?" he asked.

Dr. Fujita shook her head. "It doesn't terminate. No, I think it was trying to chew its way out."

They stared down at the body for a long moment. "God damn," Palmer said at last.

Easy for him to say, Dr, Fujita thought. *He doesn't have to write the report.*

~ * ~ * ~

Mariah Southworth is a writer of horror, fantasy, and science fiction from the northwestern United States. Her short stories have appeared in Humans Wanted, from CuppaTea Publications, Bubble off Plumb, from Feral Cat Publishers, Monsters in Space from Dragons Roost Press, and Supernatural Horror Short stories from Flame Tree Publishing. Her self-published children's books, Lydia No Lying, Twenty-Four Scary Stories for Scary Poems for Scary Kids, and I Am A… are available on Amazon.com.

For more about Mariah Southworth, visit her website: www.mariahsouthworth.com.

Blood Token

Deby Fredericks

Deep in concentration, Secori stirred the hot cauldron with a bundle of chrysanthemum sprigs. Ten times to the left, ten to the right, twice around the outside, and repeat the pattern. In her native goblin tongue she chanted, "Begone, begone, begone."

Early evening was best for brewing potions. During the day, Secori had to stay at the counter, selling potions to her regular customers. After she closed the shop and refreshed herself with a meal, she could devote her full attention to the exacting craft.

Simmering bubbles swelled and popped. She leaned over to take in the scent. This draught was nearly perfect. It only needed her customer to provide the key ingredient.

"Criya," she called to her familiar. A blackbird flitted down to the corner of the table. Its blood red eye fixed on her. "Go look for Hesperion, will you?"

"But of course." Glossy black feathers gleamed as the blackbird spread its wings in a courtly bow. A flick of feathers took it under the faded green canopy and upward, out of sight.

Secori stirred and chanted. "Begone, begone, begone."

The canopy, which blocked prying eyes from above, rustled in a lazy breeze. The courtyard was also enclosed by a high wooden fence with a sturdy gate. Brewing potions was a secretive business. Secori hoped Hesperion would be there soon. The wood elf had never been late before, but things were tense in the city. The humans who ruled Toberlyn kept imposing more laws. Goblins and city born elves couldn't move around as easily as they once had. Woodland elves were best not seen at all.

After giving the draught a final stir, Secori lifted it over to a cloth pad on the table. The hot brazier made sweat trickle down her back. She flapped her tunic to cool herself while she waited.

Her workbench was in the center of a cobbled court, behind the potion shop. She always did her brewing outdoors, in case an error caused the cauldron to spew noxious vapors. There was the tripod brazier, cheerfully glowing. A basket of charcoal rested on the ground beneath it. Beside the brazier was the mixing table. Shelves below it held small cauldrons for individual potions, along with assorted clay jars of ingredients and the little tin cups she used for measuring. The cooling cabinet, with its veil of netting, stood two steps behind her.

A musical chirp announced Criya's return. Her familiar lit on the back gate. With a nod of thanks, Secori hurried over to lift the bar. A hooded and cloaked figure glanced behind himself before he slipped through. She barred the gate as Hesperion prowled toward the workbench.

"Is it ready?" he asked.

"Not until you bleed for me," Secori answered casually.

"Always the pain." With a wry smile, her customer threw back his hood.

"Pain is the coin humans pay us with," Secori replied.

The two of them were close in height—half the size of a human—but otherwise opposites. The wood elf was deeply tanned, with bright green eyes. Thick red hair had been tamed into short braids like a workman's. The rough garments he wore as a disguise could not conceal the grace of his movements. Secori had gray-green skin, a deeply hooked nose, and jutting fangs. Her protruding eyes were bright red and slit like a frog's. Thinning black hair was done in a long braid. On her forehead was her clan tattoo, a short, wide T with a circle beneath each arm.

One thing overcame their outward differences: humans were no friends to either of them.

"Then I'll pay back some of it." Hesperion turned up a shirt sleeve and held out his left arm. Secori leaned closer, inspecting the row of three pale pink slashes. She breathed lightly and scented no hint of infection. While she was at it, she let him see her sniffing for any other surprises. Elves and humans liked to hide things, but a goblin's nose never lied.

"They're well healed." Secori plucked a thin blade and two small clay pots from under her counter. Dipping her knobby fingers into the first pot, she cleaned the blade carefully. She capped it and opened the other, which held healing ointment. "If you need any more of this draught, I'd suggest using the other arm."

Hesperion nodded but said nothing. Secori asked no more. She pulled out a small bowl, this one made from a clam shell with preservation runes drawn in the bottom. Setting it under his arm, she made a quick stab parallel to the others. A rivulet of bright crimson trickled down into the clam shell.

You could always tell elven blood. It was brighter than human, almost golden. Goblin blood, by contrast, was darker and murky. Secori kept her blade in his skin. When the stream thinned out, she twisted slightly to draw more blood. Hesperion hid his wince.

Many people, especially humans, talked about Goblin potioners as if they were some kind of vampire, reveling in bloodshed. The reality was more prosaic. Secori had lost track of how many customers tried to fool her with blood other than their own. That was why she made them come and bleed in person.

A line of crimson crept up the side of the clam shell. When she had enough, Secori pressed a square of cloth to the cut. Setting the knife aside, she dipped her fingers into the ointment and lifted the cloth long enough to cover the wound thoroughly. Hesperion had come to her for this draught before. He held the cloth while she moved his cauldron back over the brazier. It immediately began to simmer again.

She told him, "Sit and rest, if you want to."

"No need."

Holding the clam shell over the cauldron, she dipped in her knife blade and let a single drop fall into the cauldron. After seven drops in all, she leaned closer to sniff the rising steam. Satisfied, she moved the clam shell over to the cooling shelf and turned back to resume stirring the cauldron with the bundle of sprigs.

"Begone forever, begone," she chanted in goblin.

Hesperion checked under the bandage and pressed it down again. "Why do you need so much?" Still concentrating, Secori glanced a question. "You took a lot more this time, and only used a few drops."

Secori considered her reply as she completed the stirring pattern and moved the cauldron back over to the table to cool.

"Why do you need so much flea killer?" she asked with an ironic smile. This draught might repel fleas, but they both knew that wasn't what he would use it for. Human settlers were encroaching into the elven forests. The wood elves weren't strong enough to resist with arms, so they sought other means.

Hesperion glanced away. Secori could see the reminder was hurtful. She softened her tone.

"The blood of every creature has its own properties. Elf blood makes a good longevity potion. You'd be amazed how many humans want it." Even if they wouldn't admit they came to her, a lowly goblin, for the service.

"It would be better used to improve their wisdom," Hesperion replied bitterly.

"The best use," Secori said quietly, "is for invisibility potions."

The wood elf thought about that as he peeked at his arm again. Setting the bandage aside, he pulled his sleeve down to cover the vivid red line of the cut. With real concern, he asked, "Why do you need so much invisibility potion?"

"The humans." Secori began to put her jars away. "They don't want us little folk coming and going."

"Human-only laws," Hesperion growled. "There's a new one, I heard. Something about owning property?"

"It's a curfew, and we aren't allowed to gather in numbers. Property ownership was last year. If they don't like us goblins, maybe they should have stayed in their mountains and left us alone." Secori shrugged fatalistically. "I've seen this before, Hesperion. It always builds to the same thing."

He nodded solemnly and asked no more. Secori chanted a rhyme to cool the potion. She tried to focus on that, and not on the past. Memories tried to erupt all the same. Screams and smashing, a haze of blood and dust and smoke. Playing dead while a mob rampaged in the streets. She didn't have nightmares as often these days, but the tang of blood and death tinged the air more and more.

Secori took out a clay bottle, set a funnel in it, and carefully ladled Hesperion's draught into it. She scraped out every drop she could get from the cauldron and stopped the jar with a thick cork. Chanting "Hold, hold, hold," she tied a black cord over and around the cork. Finally, she pushed it over the table to him.

"Be careful going out," she told him. "You aren't a goblin, but it might be better if you aren't seen."

Hesperion raised his hood. "Good luck, goblin witch."

"And you, wood elf."

~ * ~

Daylight still lingered after Hesperion departed. Secori wanted to get started on the invisibility potion right away, but it was no good starting a complex draught with a dirty workbench. She sealed Hesperion's blood in a small jar, then tossed the bandage and chrysanthemum sprigs into the brazier. While they burned, she scrubbed down the cauldron, utensils and table.

Criya lit on his favorite corner of the table. He folded his black wings neatly and focused a ruby red eye on her. Most people couldn't understand familiars, but it was better if they thought Criya was only a pet. When they were alone like this, he always had plenty to say.

"Do you really think it's that bad?" his sweet voice piped.

"I don't know what the humans are planning," she answered, "but I can smell it coming. All these laws that pack us into smaller areas. The rules about what work we can do. Sure, they want us to clean their houses and gather crops from the fields. But to have to look at us, any other time?"

"The young ones are angry," Criya said. "They say the elves have it right, and goblins should stand up for themselves."

"That's because they're young and stupid." Secori shook her head. "It never works out for us to resist. We get lynched. Sometimes just one or two, sometimes whole districts are put to the torch. The city guards can never seem to figure out who did it."

"I remember," Criya hopped closer to her. "It's how we met, after all."

"I remember, too." Secori gazed at her familiar fondly. "The youth are foolish, but that doesn't mean they're wrong. We have to do something, and it can't be what the humans expect. That's why I need Hesperion's blood so much."

Criya cocked his head sharply. "Someone's out in the street. I'll take a look."

The small bird flew up over the shop roof, black wings nearly invisible in the dusk. Secori scented the breeze. Nobody should be moving around in the goblin's quarter, not this close to curfew. She caught the faintest whiff of floral perfume—not something a goblin could afford to wear, but she knew who did.

Quickly she shoved the jar of elf blood to the back of the cooling cabinet and grumbled the goblin words to seal it. Then she hurried toward the shop. Criya glided back down to her shoulder.

"Human, male. Fancy dress. Masked."

"That's what I was afraid of," Secori murmured.

As she stepped inside, a commanding knock shook the shop door. Never mind she had the closed sign out. Only a human would be moving around after curfew. Fortunately, Secori was prepared.

An old dress, styled for a human girl, hung by the back door. It was threadbare but good enough to conceal her sweat-stained tunic. Criya fluttered to the top of a shelf as she swung the garment on. She buttoned up the front while hurrying around the tall bookshelf that hid the back door from the front of the shop.

The knock sounded again, impatiently. A quick word from Secori lit the candles around the shop. There was a tin mug on the counter with an assortment of hair sticks in it. She chose one with three green beads in the shape of frogs, and used it to coil her long braid into a prim bun. A shadowy figure was visible through the front window.

Taking a deep breath, she turned the bolt. Almost before it was free, the door shoved open. Secori went staggering, perhaps also due to the powerful floral scent the human brought in with him. He shut the door quietly, looking behind himself in almost the same way Hesperion had. That was not reassuring.

"Good evening to you." Secori switched to the humans' tongue. She backed a few steps away and curtseyed, hiding her expression.

The human didn't answer right away. A black cloth mask concealed most of his face, but she saw pale blue eyes scanning her shop. The human studied the cluttered shelves, the dusty corners, and the cobwebs around a window with a small corner broken out. An embroidered handkerchief rose to his nose. That was the source of the floral perfume.

If that was how he wanted it… Secori seized her own moment to study her unwanted customer. The human was big, of course, twice her height, with yellow hair combed back into a tail. His beard was short and pointed, in the current style. As Criya had said, he was finely dressed, with loose black trousers tucked into soft boots and a long sleeveless green coat over a bright gold tunic. Unfortunately, he wore no signet or other hint of his identity.

Despite the curfew, the wealthy class had no intention of giving up their pleasures in the goblin gambling houses. They wore these masks as a supposed effort at discretion. The man looked like something out of a drama. If it hadn't been so alarming, she would have laughed at how ridiculous he was.

"What brings you to my shop at this hour? Is there an illness? You need medicine?" Secori spoke in the bland singsong she always used with human customers. He paused in his scornful assessment of her store.

"You are Secori, the master potioner?" His words radiated skepticism.

"Yes, noble lord." Secori curtseyed again obsequiously. She was fishing for information about his rank. He didn't deny the epithet, but neither did he preen the way a commoner would have. That said …something.

"Humph, well," he sniffed, and brought the scented handkerchief up to his nose again. "They say you are the one I need."

"That is my great honor." Secori had developed a tight-lipped smile that kept her fangs hidden. She used it now. "Will you sit for a consultation?"

Three candles in a wall rack illuminated a small wooden table tucked between the tall shelves. A chair and a stool sat beside it. The man gazed down at her, then seemed to flinch from contact with her bright red, bulging eyes.

"Tea, noble lord?" Secori offered.

"Hells, no." The human strutted over to the table. With a frowning glance, he inspected the chair and swiped at the seat with his handkerchief.

He sneered at common hospitality. And yet, he was here in her shop. Secori was not sad about his refusal. It allowed her a moment to analyze his cologne. Rose with a hint of citrus and spice. Such combinations were a favorite in the royal court, up in their castle, high above the slums. She wondered, was he so offended by a bit of dust, or did he think he was clever, and the handkerchief would disguise his personal scent?

She drew a slate and chalk from the shelf and seated herself on the stool. This placed them nearly at eye level. Criya flew to the top of a bookshelf, out of the human's view. With one ruby eye on the customer, he preened the cobwebs out of his glossy black feathers.

"Tell me your need, noble lord." Secori gestured to take in the contents of her shop. "I have many remedies here, but from your caution, I assume you are looking for something…out of the ordinary."

"This is a delicate matter. We require the utmost discretion." The human leaned a little closer for emphasis.

"Please, noble lord." Secori glanced down, softening the rebuke. "If this was an ordinary request, you would come during the day and not be masked."

He snapped back, offended, but then breathed a curt laugh. "So true."

"You haven't been to me before," she said. "Allow me to explain my limits." The human frowned, but before he could interrupt, Secori held up a long green finger. "Firstly. This is a healing shop. I do not make poisons, ever."

He almost chuckled at that. Imagine, a goblin claiming not to be a criminal! Secori raised another bony finger.

"Secondly, I cannot turn anything into gold. Potions have an expiration, you understand? What seemed to be gold would not remain so. It would be embarrassing to be caught in a counterfeit, I'm sure you agree."

"I'm not worried about gold." The human sounded amused. "You, however, might benefit from some. This place needs brightening up."

Secori ignored this attempt to lure her away from her standards. She couldn't fix up her shop, because a goblin wasn't allowed to have nice things. No matter how small it was, the humans would find a way to wreck it. She raised a third finger.

"Lastly, I do not make so-called love potions." Secori grimaced, allowing her fangs to show briefly. "Nor anything else that might control the thoughts and actions of another. It's a sickening idea, but so many people think they want that. Again, the potion wears off and the victim is rightfully angry."

"Yes, yes. Anything else, master potioner?" The human breathed through his handkerchief, feigning boredom, but Secori sensed he was about to get down to business.

"I will inform you if necessary." She dropped back into her singsong voice.

The human folded his handkerchief and tucked it inside his jacket. Not quickly enough, though. Secori glimpsed the heraldry embroidered there. It was all she could do to not jump off the stool. The background was blue and white chevrons, with a red eagle outspread. He was from the humans' royal family! And a big secret?

This got worse and worse.

The human brought his hand back out with a small leather pouch. It hit the tabletop with a heavy clink and the distinct whiff of gold.

"This is to be a gift," he informed her, "for King Joseph himself."

Secori made no move to touch the pouch. "You honor me indeed."

"It is also a medicine," the human went on, deepening his voice into loving concern. "His majesty doesn't sleep well at all, I'm afraid. We are quite concerned."

"Surely there are healers in the castle," Secori evaded. Whatever mischief this was, there were a hundred ways for it to go wrong. Some political rival—or this man, if he got caught—would be quick enough to blame those dirty goblins.

"The apothecary has weak potions, fit for children." The human brushed her words aside. "A king carries great burdens. His majesty is growing despondent and confused with lack of sleep."

More like erratic and temperamental, from the rumors Secori had heard.

"I only wish to bring him some relief," the human coaxed. "I long to offer his majesty a deep and dreamless sleep."

He spoke with such conviction, Secori almost wished she could believe him. As it was, her anger surged. How dare this human think she was so stupid! She set her chalk down with a click.

"Deep and dreamless sleep?" she quoted, forgetting for a moment to look down, not make him gaze into her red eyes. "I have said I do not make poisons."

"Oh no! That's not what I wanted at all." Irritation flared for a moment, that she dared to call him out. He quickly covered it with the appearance of deep shock. "I owe the king so much. My position, my very life. I only want to give him the gift of sleep."

"I am not the right person to help you." Flames leapt in Secori's memory, a portent of the consequences if she accepted this commission. "If the court should learn King Joseph was taking a draught brewed by goblins? Think of the scandal."

"Who can tell one potion from another?" Clearly this man was not accustomed to being told no. He was still certain she could be bought.

"The palace apothecary will know it was not of his crafting."

Secori added a jealous apothecary to the growing list of things that could go horribly wrong.

"Nobody will know of it." The human's pretense fell away. With hard blue eyes he asked, "Where are your priorities? Don't you want the king to be well?"

Their gazes met and held, crimson against blue. Her hands fluttered in agitation, and she couldn't keep her fangs hidden. Secori couldn't seem to get a full breath. It was a mistake to resist, to show the fury a goblin had to keep hidden. But they both knew a goblin couldn't refuse a human. The human would always win.

"I do know a very good sleeping draught." Secori bit off each word, emphasizing her anger. "Anyone who drinks it will enjoy a deep and dreamless sleep."

"Oh, excellent!" The human gave a dramatic, relieved sigh. "I was wondering about your loyalty."

A smug gesture indicated she should take up the pouch. She did not.

"Money is not what I require." Secori struggled to resume her bland singsong. "There is the matter of blood."

"Ugh, blood?" Every wild story this human had heard about goblin magic was visible in his eyes. He drew out his handkerchief again. "Barbaric..."

"Blood, yes." Secori held back her anger. "A draught such as this is a collaboration between myself and the buyer. It is not my desire to make this thing. If you want it, you must provide some of the materials."

"Come now..."

Steadily, she met his irritable gaze. "The potion will not work unless you work for it."

The human puffed a little breath and shifted in his seat. Was he uncomfortable? Good.

"For this draught, I require three materials," Secori went on. "I need sap, or blood, from a poppy plant. You have some in the castle gardens, I believe?" The human appeared relieved, but then wary. He hadn't told her of any connection to the royal household. Secori hoped that wouldn't be a problem. "Bring me several large, thick leaves to press for the sap."

"Easily done," the human said.

"If the draught is to be as powerful as you wish, I will need the blood of a powerful creature. Dragon blood would be best." She reached to the shelf again and held up one of her tin measuring cups. "This much, at least."

"Dragon?" he sputtered. "They only live in the western mountains."

"Dragons are a menace to the people. A noble lord should confront them. Perhaps you might invite your friends for a hunting expedition." If he had any friends, which she doubted. Secori placed the tin cup on the table beside the coin pouch. "It will be great sport, I'm sure."

"How long will that take, while the king suffers?" The human played up his compassionate indignation.

"You ask for a difficult thing." When the human was still restless, she relented. "Failing that, some other strong creature might work. An elephant, or a rhinoceros." He gazed at her impatiently. "At the very least, bring me the blood of a bear, or a wild bull."

The human's expression cleared. Secori fully expected he would bring her blood from a common cow. It pleased her to imagine his surprise when she rejected the inferior material.

"I also require ten drops of blood from the one who wants this crafted," Secori finished.

"Human blood?" he half-accused.

"Excuse me if I misunderstand," she said. "You are an intermediary, correct?"

"I beg your pardon?" The human drew so much indignation about him, she knew she had guessed right.

"You are from the royal household, yes? Your patron sent you to acquire the sleeping draught. I will not ask who!" She quickly raised a hand. "The draught requires blood from whoever commissioned it. Whether it's you or someone else, I must have ten drops of blood."

That was excessive, but she expected him to short her, so she raised the amount.

"You ask much," the human turned serious again. This time Secori would not back down. If something went awry, the potion would be analyzed. Probably by a jealous royal apothecary. Whoever put blood into it would be identified—and it wasn't going to be her.

"The potion will not work without blood," she answered. Then she rationalized, as he had to her. "Surely, if someone goes out hunting dragons, it wouldn't be too surprising that they were injured."

"Hmmm..." The human seemed to be coming around. Then he balked. "No, but really. Blood?" The face mask did little to hide his disgust.

She answered in a bland singsong, "Where are your priorities?"

That annoyed him, but he again sighed dramatically. "I suppose a few drops are not too much to ask."

From the human's crafty expression, he had some plan to trick her. Secori assumed he wasn't going to bring his patron's blood, but someone else's. In that case, the potion wouldn't work. Which meant less risk to Secori, and it would serve him right.

She reached out slowly, rested her long green fingers on the money pouch, and slid it back over to him. "Send me this when you deliver the materials." It was a final safeguard. The last thing she needed was to be accused of cheating a human. "You need not come in person. Send them with a trusted servant, during my shop hours. Remember, freshest blood is best."

"How soon can it be ready?" He tucked the pouch back into his jacket, eager to leave now that he had forced her to accept the commission. He left the tin cup on the table.

"This will be a delicate task. I need at least a week to brew it properly, and I cannot begin until you provide the materials. Also, what fruits does his majesty favor?"

Halfway to the door, he paused and frowned at her.

"It has to taste good, or he'll never drink it," Secori said.

"Peaches if you can get them. Or blackberries," he answered. Opening the door, he peered out, and was gone.

"Ass." Secori followed, allowing her full fangs to show in a grim snarl. In the dark of night, the human strutted away, back to whatever gaming room he had snuck out of to barge in on her.

She locked the door and slumped against the hard boards. Laughter rolled up her spine, bitter and furious. It ended with something like a sob.

Criya was back on her shoulder. "You can't trust him."

"I don't," she snarled. Criya fluttered up with a startled chirp as she tore off the suffocating dress and stormed back to hang it up. Her long braid tumbled down her back when she yanked the beaded stick out.

"Should I follow him?" Criya perched near the broken window.

"No need." Secori didn't mean to snap at him. "I want nothing to do with human politics. Anyway, you saw how he acted. 'Blood?'" she squealed in imitation of the human's dismay. "Chances are, he won't even turn up with the materials. I refuse to worry about it."

"But you should," Criya twittered.

"I know," she groaned. "Why can't the humans leave me alone?"

It was hard to feel bad about King Joseph. He hadn't been openly hostile to her people, but he wasn't their friend, either. If he was, he wouldn't have signed the decrees that trapped them in the slums with little hope of escape.

This was the disaster Secori had been scenting these past few weeks. She was certain of it. Humans-only laws were bad enough, but if something happened to the king and word got out a goblin brewed the potion, Toberlyn would explode. Her people would be slaughtered in the streets. Everyone would blame her, even though it was a human's fault.

"What will you do?" Criya asked.

"Stop them. There must be a way."

Temptation flared in Secori's heart, as sudden and fierce as a volcanic blast. Yes, she was a healer, using her skill to save lives. But surely it wouldn't be so different to brew up a curse, instead.

The humans deserved it. They were the oppressors, tearing goblin families apart with travel bans and stealing their hard-earned coin with endless taxes. Maybe the youth were right, and it was time to fight back.

This nobleman thought he could use her as a vessel for his ambition. She would use him, instead. Let loose a contagion, or… She didn't know.

Criya cocked his head, studying Secori's face. "Can you be more specific?"

His worry pulled her out of that volcanic fever. She took a deep breath, denying her darkest desires.

"No." Secori shook her head. "My best hope is that he doesn't come back."

Whoever he really was, that human was from the nobility. They were used to having things handed to them on demand. Maybe cutting some plants or cutting himself would just be too much effort. Criya gave a skeptical chirp.

"Meanwhile," Secori said firmly, "I'm going to keep on doing what I have been doing. I'm going to brew more invisibility potions."

~ * ~

She didn't try to start brewing that night. In such a dark mood, she would only spoil it. After a restless night, Secori woke with a clear understanding she needed help if she was going to save her people.

The next day, she closed shop at noon and packed a few things in a basket. Smells of salt water and fish guts rose to meet her as she walked downhill to the fish market. Fishing was one of the few jobs the humans hadn't tried to take away yet, probably because it was so dangerous. A human guard insisted on searching her basket, even after she told him she was delivering salve to a customer.

Berubi was one of the oldest goblins in Toberlyn. A fisherman's widow, and a good sailor herself, she mostly circulated between pubs along the wharf. Goblins couldn't choose a leader. If they ever did, the humans would make up an excuse to arrest them. Still, the goblins all knew it was Berubi who organized the fishing fleet and made sure the profits were shared fairly.

When Secori found her, Berubi was knee deep in stinking bilge water, helping one of the younger fishermen unclog a hand pump. Secori caught her eye and nodded at a nearby pub. A few minutes later, the older goblin woman walked in, set her filthy boots on a mat by the door, and came to join Secori. On her shoulder, Criya gave a saucy whistle of greeting.

"Umph," Berubi grumbled, rubbing stiff hands together. Secori passed over a jar of her favorite salve. "Ah, there's the thing. Don't know what I'd do without you, Secori."

"Stand around in a bilge, apparently." Secori smiled. It was good to relax, meeting a friend's eyes without shame. While the other woman rubbed salve over her knuckles, Secori set a plain clay jar on the table between them.

"What's that?" Berubi asked.

"Invisibility potion," Secori spoke softly. The older woman's startled gaze jumped to her face. "I don't like what I scent in the air. You know what I mean."

They were both of an age to remember the last major purge. "Yes, I smell it too," Berubi murmured.

"I've been storing this up," Secori said. "For families with children, I thought, but you're the one to pass it out. You know who needs it the most."

"I hope you aren't suggesting we all rob the humans," Berubi joked. Secori grimaced; thieving was exactly what the humans would expect of them.

"Our fishing boats go out every morning, don't they?" she asked.

"Ah." Berubi's expression cleared, but worry still lined her gray toned face. "That bad?"

"I had a visit from a human wanting a sketchy potion," Secori told her. Criya added his own opinion in a razzing chirp. "This could bite me, hard. Even without that, look at the laws they're putting in. We aren't safe here."

Berubi snorted as she tightened the lid on her jar of salve. "You sound like my nephew. 'Make the humans pay.'"

"I don't want to fight them," Secori assured her, "but that doesn't mean we have to sit and wait for the worst to happen. We need to move our people, slowly."

"Invisible refugees on the fishing boats," Berubi nodded slowly. "They go out before dawn, so no one should notice them riding lower than usual. It would only take a few minutes to put in somewhere secluded, let them off, and go about fishing just as ever."

"That's what I was thinking. We should save who we can." Before Secori was forced to make a potion that would ignite the flames of hatred.

"We can't just dump them in the middle of nowhere. I'll have the crews look out for safe places." Berubi's red eyes glinted with the challenge, but then she sighed. "If only there was another way. Humans and goblins haven't been at war for a century. They don't need to keep punishing us."

"I wish we could change their hearts," Secori agreed. Criya tweeted his opinion of that.

"Things haven't been the same since old Queen Edna died," Berubi said. "That was decades ago, and her bloodline is getting worse as we go."

"Queen Edna?" Secori went still as those words penetrated her mind. There was something about that, a memory she had locked away with other agonies of the past.

"Thank you for this," Berubi was saying. At Secori's expression, she trailed off. "What is it?"

Carefully, thinking her way through it, Secori asked, "When the boats go out again, can anyone get me mermaid scales or hair? Scales would be better."

"Mermaid scales in a potion? Say no more." Berubi leaned a little back from the table. "Merfolk do like to trade for jewelry made on land. Can't work metal under the sea, you know. I'll give our people your potion if they give me a trinket for trade."

"As long as they keep it quiet. I'll leave this to you." Secori rose, with Criya on her shoulder giving one of his little bows.

"Rascal," Berubi chuckled.

~ * ~

Nothing caught a guard's eye like a nervous goblin, so Secori strolled sedately back to her shop. For the rest of the day, she tried not to fidget in front of the customers. Ideas burned in her brain. She jotted the best ones on a slate. From time to time she sent Criya poking through the upper shelves, looking for a small box she knew must be there.

At last, with a gusty sigh, she locked the shop door and climbed a ladder to where Criya was perched. There it was; a plain wooden box half buried under old ledgers. Secori took it down and immediately moved the ladder back to where it had been. At the consultation table, she brushed off the dust.

"Is this it?" Criya had settled on the chair back opposite her.

It was a puzzle box, with no obvious closure. Her grandmother's clan tattoo was carved into the lid, a wide T with two circles under its arms. She pressed it to her forehead, where her own tattoo would match. A tiny click sounded in her ears.

"Yes!" The scent of blood rose to Secori's nostrils as she opened it. (Human, female.) Her pulse pounded in her ears.

Inside was an oiled cloth tied with twine. Unwrapping it revealed a smaller cloth pad, completely darkened and crusted with old blood. Grandmother had preserved it, all those years ago. Criya eyed the parcel doubtfully. In a low voice, Secori explained.

"My grandmother, Nacosi, was also a master potioner. When Queen Edna had trouble with her birthing, they called her to the castle. Nacosi's draughts saved the queen's life and delivered King Joseph's father into this world. The human healers were jealous. They made her clean up the bloody bandages." Secori bared her fangs in a smile. "Their spite allowed Nacosi to capture a blood token. She passed it to me before she died."

That had been well before the purge Secori so narrowly escaped. She was amazed, looking back, that she had been able to save it when so much else was destroyed.

"What will you do with it?" Criya cocked his head. He was a potioner's familiar. Surely he had some idea. He just wanted Secori to say the words.

"The blood of a queen holds power, and birthing blood has even greater potency. Now that power comes to me." Secori sagged a bit, overcome by emotions she couldn't name.

"For vengeance?" Criya pressed.

"In a way." Secori rewrapped the blood token and replaced it in the box. "Queen Edna was kind to our people. She wanted mercy to follow victory, Nacosi said." She pressed the box to her forehead and listened for the click. "Edna's descendants may choose to forget, but I think she would approve of my plan."

Maybe Secori would be lucky. The human noble might not bring her any dragon's blood. Berubi's fishermen might not be able to trade for mermaid scales. But if they did, Secori had the weapon she needed for a much larger reckoning.

~ * ~

A potion's base could support many different enchantments. She started one by cutting up peaches and boiling them down to syrup. The pulp was quite tasty when Secori spread it on toast. Criya also asked her to leave a dollop out in the yard so he could snack on the maggots. Secori also sent a jar of preserves down to Berubi in the fish market, and received back a very thin packet of iridescent scales. She stored them in the puzzle box along with the blood token.

Days passed. Secori sold many potions to help settle stomachs or bring down fevers, but she didn't make any more remedies. Invisibility potions were all she brewed. The draught was complex. Not only would the user vanish from sight, thanks to the elf blood, but she also worked in dandelion sap and thistledown to muffle any sounds of movement. Extra ingredients lengthened the brewing time, and she had to concentrate while chanting, "Unseen, unheard, unknown." Her headaches were worth it, knowing how many lives depended on her craftsmanship.

Rumors began to circulate that Prince Justin had gone on a hunting holiday. There was no mention of any injuries, but one morning a human maid came to Secori's shop. In her basket, several fresh poppy leaves covered a small jar of blood (bear, yearling male), a blood-stained handkerchief, and a heavy pouch that smelled of gold. The maid loitered, uncomfortable in such a lowly shop.

"Return in five days, before the close of business," Secori told her. The girl was relieved to go.

"Are you really going to brew this?" Criya asked as she stored the materials.

"It seems so." Secori was saddened, but not surprised, to scent a family relationship between Queen Edna's blood and what was on the handkerchief. So it was someone in King Joseph's own family who wanted him dead? Her majesty would have been very disappointed.

Secori turned over the closed sign and locked the shop door.

~ * ~

This potion would be a masterwork, and she wished no one would ever know about it. A good deal of time in her shop had been devoted to planning how she could weave the blood, poppy and scales into the perfect vessel for her revenge. At least she had built her stamina with all the invisibility potions she had been making.

The blood would be at the bottom of it, adding power and stability. That was key. Secori added the bear's blood to the peach syrup and brought it to a boil, summoning the animal's strength to power her draught. Then she took it off the fire and slipped in the dark packet of Queen Edna's blood token. She steeped the brew and stirred it every second hour, ten times left and ten times right, while chanting, "bound with my blood, your heart bound to me." When no crusted blood was visible on the bandage or at the bottom of the cauldron, she left the draught to infuse overnight.

Next came the hidden viper's bite—the mermaid scales. Again Secori brought the brew to a boil, this time drawing in the merfolk's legendary siren power. Stories of their alluring song usually dealt with cruel fates of human men, though Secori knew it held equal power over all races and genders. As before, she brought the potion to a boil and let it steep.

"Hear my song, dream my dream," she chanted. While she stirred it, she dredged up her oldest and ugliest memories to build the illusion the draught would wrap around its victim. The sessions left Secori trembling with exhaustion. Criya chirped and scolded until she ate something. When she slept, she suffered nightmares of her own.

The following day, Secori was reluctant to return to her workbench. She delayed by moving the cooling shelf over. She had put it where it was to cover a loose cobble that always tripped her. Now she dug the stone out and murmured a goblin funeral while she buried what was left of Queen Edna's blood token and the mermaid scales. Criya chittered his approval. Secori scattered a bit of soil to help disguise the loose stone, and pushed the shelf back over it.

By then she was ready to take the final step—the poppy leaves and the handkerchief. This was the surface layer of the sleeping draught. She wanted it to be bold and bright. When another apothecary examined the draught, Secori wanted them to detect the poppy leaves first. If they persisted, they would discover the human's blood. That should link the potion to whoever had paid her to make the draught. She didn't want them to sense a mermaid, or Queen Edna, and certainly not herself.

It was such a relief to finish that she opened her shop back up while the draught steeped one more time. Business was brisk, since she'd been closed for three days. There was some kind of cough going around. She sold out most of her remedies for sore throats. All the while, she caught up on the goblins' news. There were rumors of families disappearing. It was good to know Berubi was helping their people.

"Look at all the laws," she told her customers. "Maybe it's not a bad idea to leave Toberlyn."

Not everyone wanted to hear it. Some goblins wanted to believe if they followed the rules, the humans would see they were loyal. Secori hoped, deeply and truly, that they were right.

She herself could not have faith in the oppressors. Throughout the fourth day, she sold much of her remaining stock. In the evening she went up and down ladders, picking what to take with her. Some of the rarest ingredients went into Nacosi's puzzle box. That joined her personal recipe book and the last month of her business ledger in a battered old leather satchel. The pouch of gold was buried in the bottom of her pack under toiletries, clothes and food.

The fifth day passed in carefully concealed anxiety. What if the maid never came to take the wretched sleeping draught? What if, instead, whoever was up in the palace sent a troop of guards to seize the draught and accuse her of plotting against the king? No matter how often she reminded herself someone had shed their own blood to make the draught, her fears hovered like a storm cloud in the rafters.

Criya went out through the broken window to hunt insects. Just before noon, she heard the scrape of his tiny claws. "Human coming," he cheeped.

Secori was ready when the human maid entered the shop with her covered basket. "I placed an order," she declared, as snobbishly as any noble.

"Here it is, mistress." Secori set a slender bottle on the counter. A ray of sunlight made the peach syrup flare reddish-gold. Such a small thing to hold the vengeance of the goblin people.

"Very well." The woman tucked the bottle into her basket and hurried out the door.

Secori had to sit on her stool for a moment until her heart stopped pounding in her ears. Then she sent Criya with a note to Berubi. Before long, a couple of goblin boys came through the back gate to collect the rest of the invisibility potion. Secori kept shop as normal for the rest of the day. Finally, she was able to lock the front door. Wasting no time, she shouldered her waypack and picked up her satchel. At the back door, she paused.

With the candles extinguished, the cluttered shop was full of shadows. Secori had arrived in Toberlyn with nothing but a small blackbird and Nacosi's puzzle box. Despite everything the humans did, she had built a life here. It hurt to leave so much behind. But Berubi had told her to bring only what she could carry. Secori was leaving nearly as empty-handed as when she came.

Predictably, Criya interrupted her thoughts. "Is this truly your revenge?"

"Mine is a healing practice," Secori reminded him. "I do not make poisons, ever."

"You might as well have."

"Maybe. But after everything they've done to us, there has to be an answer."

Secori was well aware she had broken her own rules. Her draught would control the feelings of others, and it was the next worse thing to poison. Yet, a close relative had shed his own blood to give King Joseph "deep and dreamless sleep." She couldn't stop that, only use it.

Because she had Queen Edna's birthing blood, her draught would snare every one of the queen's bloodline. No matter where they were or what they were doing, when King Joseph drank that sleeping draught, Toberlyn's entire royal family would fall into deep slumber. And because of the mermaid scales, they would all dream.

In the dream, they would be goblins. Small and ugly, cowering before giant humans. Beaten and kicked. Strangled by malicious laws. Nothing could wake them until they suffered through her darkest memories.

They would lay on hard cobbles, covering a satchel of potion books with their own bodies and pretending to be dead. Horse hooves would hammer around them. Flames would crackle, smoke would blind them. On every side they would hear cries for mercy cut off, and the uproarious glee of human murderers as they 'cleaned their village' by eliminating the filthy goblins. This was the nightmare she had woven for them.

The sleeping draught, Secori's masterwork, held this hidden trap. She didn't know when the trap would spring, but she wanted to be far away when it did.

Criya chirped, and she gently rubbed his head. What she had left out was her escape by crawling into scorching ashes, where she found a little blackbird, all but dead from the smoke. The humans wouldn't see how Criya gave Secori something to care for, after everyone she loved was dead and ruined.

When they all woke, the noble and privileged humans, what would they do? Secori couldn't predict it. Her hope was Queen Edna's blood would awaken within them. They would feel compassion and remorse; and take back the cruel laws they bound onto goblin kind.

"Bad dreams aren't much of a revenge," Criya said.

"You don't think so?" Secori asked wearily.

Maybe a change of heart was too much to hope for. The other humans wouldn't like it. There would be arguments and back-biting. Even civil war, if the royal family didn't all draw the same lesson from their nightmare. That was revenge, if you had to have it.

Unfortunately, it was just as likely the humans would be enraged. Their fury might explode into the violence she feared so much.

Regardless, Secori had to leave Toberlyn. When the whole royal family fell asleep at once, there were going to be questions. No amount of precautions would protect her. They would only delay the hunt. She hoped her fellow goblins would take the danger seriously; and leave before it was too late.

Secori moved through the cobbled yard, set the key on her workbench, and continued out the back gate. One of the pubs in the fish market had a room where she could stay overnight. In the dark before dawn, she would test out her own potion and board a fishing boat to escape from Toberlyn.

~ * ~ * ~

Deby Fredericks has been a writer all her life but thought of it as just a fun hobby until the late 1990s. She made her first sale, a children's poem, in 2000.

Fredericks has had short work published in *Andromeda Spaceways*, selected anthologies, and small magazines. Most recently, she self-publishes her fantasy novellas and novelettes, bringing her to 15 books in all. Her latest project is The Minstrels of Skaythe series.

Learn more from her web site: www.debyfredericks.com.

Ben was Struck by Lightning

Michael Paige

On those cold, cloudy days, I still think of what happened.

It was January 24, 1989. George H. W. Bush was president of the United States, Theodore Bundy had been given the electric chair, and the entire western Nebraska region was being pummeled by the worst thunderstorms I'd ever seen.

Ben and I watched as the next of the storms beat toward us, the winds rustling with whispers of despair. It was the next half of a storm that hit just a day earlier, leaving trees with their tops stripped off and patches of our crops all twisted up in the fields. It was vicious, and Act Two was well on its way. We were thirteen back then.

The farm was twenty miles from the nearest city, overlooking up to twenty acres of plowed prairie. We were maize farmers, pure-breeding strains of corn for cents on the dollar—great big stalks that shivered in the half-light breeze.

Living in tornado country, our family was always prepared for the worst weather conditions: a storm shelter in the basement, weeks' worth of supplies, and a lightning rod on the roof to prevent a house fire.

We ate a hot supper at five, picking silently at our plates while our mother was asking who, between us, was responsible for leaving the shed door open to flap and swing in the wind. She'd known one of us had used it but couldn't tell who—one of the many benefits of being twins.

Ben and I were born minutes apart, and aside from a few freckles here and there, looked exactly alike, from our style of clothes to our hair. We got away with most things that way, though sometimes one of our particular *looks* ended up killing our alibis.

After supper, Dad had us out in the field with him to harvest the damaged crops before the next onslaught. We grew stalks in clusters of three, running down the center of thirty-inch-wide beds. Most of the battered stalks had a chance of straightening themselves up again, but the brittle, broken stems were dead, with no prospect of bouncing back. Dad called it a green snap.

The black exhaust of clouds rolled closer and was nearly on top of us by the time it finished eating up the rest of the sky. Wind was kicking up with angry gusto.

We headed for the house. My father was the first one inside, and Ben was just a few paces in front of me.

That's when it came—a sudden prickly feeling that fell over the air like an invisible net, tingling the back of my neck and vibrating my molars. Something covered my tongue—an acrid, sharp taste, like rolling a penny around your mouth. A sort of fuzziness.

In a fraction of a second, I saw movement, like a bright spider web igniting from nothing and arcing downward in front of me, right where Ben was walking.

Everything went white.

A rapid series of snaps and bangs slapped the air, and then, all at once, *BOOM*—a gunshot of pure pressure. My vision shut off, taking ten seconds to return.

Ben was flat on his back, as if he'd been socked in the face, his right hand clutching at nothing whatsoever.

"Ben!" I shouted, ears still ringing as I stumbled toward him.

His face was pale, and wisps of smoke were drifting off him. I could smell a burned, sulphury scent in the air, which I prayed was just his clothes, not his skin.

Hearing the crack, my father raced out of the house and shoved me aside much harder than I'm sure he realized.

He slapped Ben's cheeks lightly, planted an ear firmly on his chest, and then began pumping it for CPR.

Rain started to fall.

Ben wasn't moving. His mouth was open, his eyes were fixed on the weeping sky, and his lips were as white as a mackerel.

Dad kept pumping. Ten. Twenty. Thirty chest compressions.

I was sobbing. *"Don't go, Ben! Please, please don't go!"* I begged, wishing it with every particle and fiber of my being as I stared at my twin. *"You can't go! You can't!"*

My heart went cold.

I looked up at the gray blotch of sky and then at the weathervane atop our roof—handcrafted from iron with a walking cat motif, its spindle squeaking in the airy swoosh as the gray cat spun atop its bar, twirling mindlessly and forever.

~ * ~

Ben survived that day and, despite the storm, made it to the hospital, where he'd spend the next several days in the trauma center. Parts of his clothes had completely melted, clinging to his skin like hot candle wax. Surface-level burns marked his back, starting from his left shoulder and streaking across his spine all the way down his right leg—a twisted grid showing the exact path the lightning took through his body. The bottom of his right shoe and sock even had a dark, round hole through them.

Dr. Sullivan called the marks lightning flowers. He said he'd seen them before—but not quite like this—from an electrician who once got zapped from a high-voltage switchgear. He said it was nothing short of a miracle Ben had survived, considering the tens or hundreds of thousands of volts he'd been shot with.

"He's okay, though, right? Our son will be okay?" My mother asked with bleak, pleading eyes that wished none of this had happened, while my father held a silent, white-knuckled clasp over his own legs.

"Yes, I believe so," Doctor Sullivan replied, smiling through his white bushy beard, as mall Santas do during the holidays.

"But he isn't out of the woods yet. Shocks like this tend to harm the nervous system, attacking the brain and peripheral nerves even after the burns heal. The injury, however subtle, will continue to show itself neurologically and could lead anywhere from chronic pain to short-term memory loss. But whatever may pop up for him in the future, we'll be ready for it."

After the trauma center, they transferred him to the burn ICU and, after that, to the acute rehabilitation unit. He needed a walker to get anywhere, and the third-degree burns running down his back needed to be scrubbed and redressed daily.

Before long, Ben's name started making rounds in the newspapers as word of the incident spread. Several articles read *Farm Boy Survives Lightning Strike.* Ben even had an interview with one reporter: a gray-stubbled man who asked to see Ben while his stalky partner was filming. His hair looked neither washed nor combed. "So, I guess the big question right now is how you're feeling?"

"Good, I guess," Ben replied.

"Do you remember the first thing that was on your mind after it happened?"

"Waking up in a white room and staring at the ceiling, like—Where am I?"

"Do you have any way of describing how it felt to be…struck?"

He thought about it and said, "Like I'd been smit."

"Smit?" the reporter asked, confused.

"Yeah, like from the Bible—the passage that said God chose to smite the city of Sodom."

That got a laugh around the room.

Two weeks later, Ben came back home.

~ * ~

We had cake that day, with friends and relatives, and a big colorful sign outside that read "WELCOME HOME!" There was not a single cloud in the sky. Everyone was happy to have Ben back, but I'd wager I was happiest of them all. People all over the world get lonesome, but I think twins feel a special sort—a bone-deep loneliness that *infests* their insides when the other isn't there.

The doctor suggested Ben still use the walker to get around, and although he hated the thing, Mom wasn't taking any chances.

While Ben was recuperating, I covered the slack for chores around the house and the work needed on the fields. Despite what life threw at us, there was always something that needed lifting, scooping, and pushing. The storms had flattened more than half of our crops, so we had to pull double-duty to replenish the stock and keep the family's income afloat. As Dad used to put it, *farmers always bounce back*.

I remember spotting him on the house during those days as he was replacing the lightning rod on the roof with a new one. Why the bolt had targeted Ben instead of the pole, we'd never know, but I know it kept Dad up at night. He sometimes talked to Mom about it and other times just muttered frustrations to himself.

As the rest of the month went by, Ben slowly got his strength back and eventually ditched the walker. Although the burns on his back had healed, you could still see the vague fernlike patterns all fanned out on his skin, left behind by a hungry current.

Ben sometimes complained about a biting pain in his toes, as if his shoes and socks were filling up with hot sand—one of those *neurological* things Dr. Sullivan talked about. Even though the electricity had long passed, the nerves were still misfiring their signals to the brain, still screaming.

Despite the discomfort, Ben still found a way to joke about it, letting static run off in his hair until it fluffed up, and shouting at the dinner table, "My powers have awakened!"

~ * ~

On the warm, cloudless days, we loved to go for a dip in one of the sandpits off the North Platte River. Most other streams around were tainted by runoff or polluted from fertilizers and pesticides, but our lake was the cleanest. Best to avoid the bad brews.

We walked the interstate, hiking through crisscrossing paths and different cattle farms that reeked of livestock ammonia. In fifteen minutes, we were at the lake, encircled by tall cottonwoods. After the trek, it was always a glorious sight.

I was the first one in, along with one of our buddies, Jean. We splashed at and wrangled with each other as we crashed through the sun-warmed surface. Jean then looked over at Ben and hollered at him, "Ben! You see that? What the hell's on your back?"

I looked over too as Ben was tugging his shirt off and over his head, his bare back facing us—those same haggard trails, the ones that had faded a month ago, had reappeared, spreading even more jagged branches down his spine. The lightning flowers had returned. Back from the dead.

~ * ~

Keloids—that was Dr. Sullivan's diagnosis. Thickly raised scars that can sometimes form in the tissue while the body is healing itself, especially after a severe burn. He talked about how they weren't cancerous and how some bodies were more prone to them than others but assured it was not a cause for alarm—unless they became painful. However, what *did* confuse him was how the scars differed from the original path they first left. The branching feathered endings had become more numerous now, spreading out much more than they had before. They still started at his left shoulder, but had now somehow crawled upward and sprouted an entirely new mesh over his right shoulder blade.

"Well, Ben, at least we know one thing for sure—you're just full of surprises!" Dr. Sullivan chuckled, flashing that mall Santa grin.

I'd give anything to say that was where it ended—that Dr. Sullivan was right about the keloids and nothing further came from them, but that's just wishful thinking, and wishes, as Dad put them, weren't worth a warm bucket of spit.

~ * ~

I awoke in the middle of the night, disoriented, my room utterly silent. It was three, maybe four a.m., give or take, and my brain was still swimming with sleep. There was something coming from the hallway—the sound of someone retching their guts out.

I opened the door to the hall bathroom and saw Ben hunched over the toilet. The scars on his back were even darker than the last time I'd seen them.

It smelled like vomit.

"You alive?" I asked.

"Maybe," he answered bleakly, spitting into the bowl and making something like a hiccup sound. "Can you grab me some water, please?"

I brought a glass and left it on the counter for him. When he said he needed nothing else, I headed back to bed, hearing every so often another gag from the bathroom.

The sickness stuck to him for the next few days. Mom said it was either from school or from swimming around that *"filthy"* sand-spit. Ben had perhaps caught some kind of bug.

To make matters worse, Ben started to complain more about the prickly pain in his toes and how it had moved all the way up his left calf, like a tight sock choking the veins. Of all the tormenters in the world, nerve damage must be one of the worst.

The muscles in Ben's legs were getting weaker, and the fever his body was fighting off wasn't letting him keep anything down.

Then, on a cloudy Sunday afternoon, we heard the *thump-thump-thump* of someone plummeting down the stairs. Two steps from the top, Ben's leg had completely given out on him. No broken bones, but it scared us all to death.

Trips to the hospital were becoming the norm for us, and despite the CT scans, MRIs, and different tests they ran on him, the results were inconclusive. Whatever was happening to Ben's nervous system was evading them, and the medical bills were stacking higher.

When your household income was as volatile as ours, every penny counted.

I remember listening to my mother's voice from her bedroom one evening. The door was slightly open. "…We have credit. Take out a loan!"

"…Gonna need to refinance the farm." My father sighed, sounding exhausted. "…Working with what we have."

"It's not enough!" my mother shouted. I heard a few footsteps move toward the door, then it was shut the rest of the way. The crying continued on the other side.

I was crying too.

Any social activity for Ben was confined indoors for the most part, and just so he wouldn't lose his mind, we learned how to play cards. Beggar-my-neighbor, Slap Jack, Rummy. I was lousy at remembering them, but he caught on pretty quick. Ben was always a faster learner than I was.

Sometimes, though, Ben's attention would blank out, and he would stare in front of him with his mouth hanging open, as if a signal had just been cut. Then, just like that, he'd blink and come back, wiping away the drool dribbling down his lip.

One night, we were watching TV together—some game show where kids won prizes and adults (usually their parents) carried out ridiculous tasks. Mom made soup that night as it was easier on Ben's stomach. During one of the bonus rounds, Ben's bowl clattered onto the floor. He'd dropped it from his lap, spilling broth all over the place. His face was drooping, and he seemed tired. "Why did God do that?" his voice came out, shaking. "What did he smite me for?!"

I grabbed his wrist, forcing myself to keep it together. "He didn't! God smites only the wicked, remember? Besides, He probably just mixed us up and smit the wrong one." That got a smile out of him, but I could tell those heavy eyes didn't believe me.

~ * ~

It wasn't long before storm clouds in the west started forming again, swelling up and bruising over like fumes from a great blaze. Winds were on the rise, and as the temperature began to drop, radio stations issued out their dire warnings.

On a dreary day, I was slogging up the driveway after school. Rain was coming down in buckets, heavily pounding the umbrella

Mom had given me.

To my shock, Ben was just outside the house, clothes sagging with rainfall and feet buried in the soil. He was looking up at the sky, letting the droplets pelt him with his mouth hanging open, standing at the exact spot he'd been struck.

At that moment, Mom came running out of the house, shouting and dragging him back inside. But as she grabbed him, I saw something strange.

From the back of Ben's soaked collar, the lightning flowers had moved all the way up his neck, a place they'd never been before, and when she put her hands near them, they shifted, shying away from her touch completely. Before I could get a better look at them, Mom and he were already back inside. When I checked there again, the ferny patterns had retreated to their spots. Mom didn't believe me when I told her and said the last thing we needed right now was tall tales. But I know what I saw.

Ben never told us why he'd chosen to stand out there in the storm or how he'd gone out without his walker, giving little else but a confused look at Mom's hollering, as if his thoughts were all blurred out, beamed away by some far-off satellite.

~ * ~

It was Saturday when the storm reached peak intensity, roaring across the plains with shrilling gales and heavy torrential rain. It wreaked havoc on the county, kicking up dust storms over the roads, pelting towns with hail, and toppling power lines, with furious winds climbing to sixty-five. A real shit show.

It rattled our windows, making the whole house groan as the drafts howled and cranked up another notch.

I paced the kitchen, frequently checking the driveway to see if the family pickup had pulled in yet, but there was still no sign of it.

We had only one truck, and earlier that day, Dad had taken the old Ford to town for a new rear axle. Mom joined him to get some badly needed groceries for the house as neither expected the storm to hit today.

I went upstairs to check on Ben. His door was shut, so I thumped it a few times. "You still alive in there?"

A groggy mumble sounded on the other side, as if I'd just awakened him. There was no further response.

The phone rang downstairs. I felt nervous answering it, but I didn't waste time. It was Dad, telling us to stay safe while they made their way back home. They'd ended up stranded as the road got closed and they had to wait for the squall to subside. "If the storm persists, take Ben and wait in the basement. We'll be home soon," he assured me before ending the call.

As I hung the phone up, I heard a strange noise from outside, the squeal of something being swung around repeatedly. The shed door.

Shit, I cussed. I remembered closing it earlier but found a chunk of warped wood at its base, which was making it hard to keep shut. I rushed outside on impulse to close it.

The air outside slapped me and was churning everything up in a mad frenzy. The stalks in the field writhed like fans at a concert while the trees nearby were all doing a jig. Thunder bellowed in the distance.

I made a mad dash for the shed's swinging door before the gales could swipe it away. Slamming it shut, I turned toward the house, set on sprinting back.

Rain was starting to fall.

Then I saw it—an image that made my brain feel as though it had detached and been taken in the squall. Ben was climbing out of his second-story window and onto the roof, slipping a bit in the process.

"Ben!" I shouted, my voice nothing but a murmur to the wailing breeze. "The hell are you doing?!"

He didn't answer or even look in my direction, even as another gust nearly swept him off his feet. He started a slow climb up the shingles and toward the peak of the house.

I broke for the door with panic-fueled nitro, racing through the kitchen and then up the stairs. His door wouldn't budge, and after a few useless tugs at the handle, I slipped into my room and forced my own window open.

Cold air blasted into the room and spattered rain onto the windowsill. My whole body was shaking. I had no real plan, not even thinking to grab Dad's ladder from the garage. All that mattered at that moment was getting Ben down from the roof and back inside.

I hopped up, stepping out and onto the wet shingles. What started as mild rain was now a full-on downpour. Moving cautiously,

I climbed up the roof, using my hands and knees as anchors as it steepened.

The wind howled, the sound of rain hitting the tiles like roaring applause in my ears. I bent low and held on as an especially fierce gust ripped through me. Everything was wet and freezing. I wiped the drizzle from my eyes and called out for Ben. Nothing but rainfall answered. I couldn't see him anywhere.

The sky rumbled above through a deathly shade of gray. Every instinct inside me screamed to get off the roof and get to safety, but I wasn't about to turn back now. Not without my twin brother.

I reached the top of the ridge and hoisted myself over. Ben was just ahead of me, curled over at the very edge of the house. He was clutching the lightning rod, practically folded against it. *Idiot*, I seethed, *You God damn idiot!*

I shuffled toward him, staying as low to the roof as I could, the gray cat on the weathervane spinning faster than ever. Everything flashed—a stray bolt, like a barbed, silvery vein, streaked across the clouds, followed by the loudest *Crrrack* I'd ever heard.

My ears buzzed. I thought for a moment I'd gone deaf. Still, I kept moving, hell-bent on getting to him right away. Nothing else mattered.

"Ben!" I screamed at him, forcing it out of my throat with an agonizing throb. He remained curled there, unmoving even as the wind grabbed at his clothes. I was nearly on him, and just as I pulled a bit closer, I stopped.

It was true, after all. My brain had really gone away, yanked right out of my skull by the hissing gales. Even now, it's difficult for me to piece everything together. My dribbled eyes pulled wide, my world filling with things it shouldn't.

There were heaps of it, all tangled together in long, ropey strands. Pale-bodied shapes as skinny as centipedes snaked out of his mouth, his ears, even his eyes, smothering his face in its mesh. The only part of Ben I could see, the single eye within its clusters, stared out with blank indifference, vomit still dripping from his chin.

The thing that had coiled and branched and shifted under his skin—the lightning flowers—had come out to taste the wet air, gleaming with sky water and dark veins that pulsed actively. It extended from him, straddling the lightning rod in gray, wormy knots until its larger, Y-shaped tips stretched even higher, reaching toward the sky like white, knobby fingers begging to be struck.

A familiar sensation fell over me, the prickliness shaking the air, a mounting pressure drawing up breath to silence the world. My tongue felt frizzy. The hairs on my arm went rigid.

The bolt struck, firing down in a brilliant arc of chaos. My vision went negative. The metal pole flashed white and then bright blue. I slipped from the ridge. Thunder punched my skull and battered my ears. Shingles rolled beneath me. I reached for the rain gutter, but it was too late for me to grab it.

When I finally stopped falling, everything went away.

~ * ~

The world came back in brief fragments. Car doors closing. Voices speaking in hurried gibberish. Lights meshing together like gelatin. Ears ringing.

I woke to an awful clamminess. The walls were white, and at first, all I could make out was the white sheet sprawled over me. A hospital room. I could tell time had passed, but I had no idea how much. Blurry silhouettes that had turned out to be my parents were in the room as well, thanking God I was waking up.

I'd fallen from the roof, breaking my leg in several places, and shattering the wrist I fell on. They didn't want to pelt me with too many questions at once, but I could tell they *needed* to know exactly what had happened.

"Where is Ben?" I asked. "Is he okay?"

Mom stood up and left the room, unable to keep herself together. That was enough to answer my question. He hadn't survived this time around. Gone. For the first time in my life, I felt very much alone.

The miraculous story of the farmer boy who survived a lightning strike had just as quickly become a tragedy, dulled down to two stupid boys playing on the roof during a thunderstorm. But that was not what had happened. Not at all.

I remember the faces at Ben's funeral, all ashen and saggy with grief as they hugged me and shared their condolences. Flowers everywhere. Nothing on that day felt real, even as I watched the casket disappear into the earth, taking my reflection with it into the hollow cavity.

My wrist and legs healed up just fine, but the ringing in my ears hadn't gone away. Dr. Sullivan called it tinnitus and said it should go away on its own. Maybe it would, but I no longer trust his conclusions. To this day, I can still hear that lingering hum.

Jean and the others checked on me often, trying everything they could to help, but I wasn't ready to let them. Even now, I'm still lost. A twin only half dead, amputated like a lost limb. Green snapped. What I would give to have been the one in Ben's spot that day, the one who was smit. But it was not God who did the smiting. It was something else. Something I can't stop seeing in dark corners.

I hold the responsibility to live for both of us, to carry on my brother's presence before the brightest light I'd ever seen took him away from me. Pain continues to live in my chest, sometimes intense, sometimes subtle. That wild, crippling loneliness that *infests* all severed twins—I keep thinking about that word.

I've been doing some reading lately, more than I ever have before. There are these things called Leucochloridium paradoxum. Small worms that hide in bird droppings for a snail to gobble up their eggs. Once inside Mr. Snail, the worm hatches and claims its new home, eating up all the nutrients it needs. The worm matures. When the time is right, they take control of Mr. Snail's brain, manipulating him to leave the shade and wander up to the treetops. The worm then pushes up into his eyestalks, pulsating brightly in green, yellow, and red, practically screaming, *"Eat me! Eat me!"* to any hungry bird nearby. The bird, mistaking Mr. Snail for a caterpillar, either gobbles him up or plucks out his eyes. Neither matters to the worm, as long as its cycle continues. The parasite lives, and the host is left behind. Evil things, aren't they?

I don't want to keep seeing them, but I can't stop it. They're still there, squirming and digging and writhing around my thoughts. They came down from the sky, rode the lightning like a railway to their next host, and when they finished feeding, reached back up to the clouds with white, milky hands, pleading for The Lightning Mother to bring them back home. To continue the cycle.

What would have happened if the first bolt killed Ben? Would they have just dried up and died with him that day? A failed landing—something I'm sure happens a lot. But Ben survived, and so did they.

Where they go, I'll never know, but I'd wager on how they'll be back, and I've been waiting for another of those articles to appear, that another person out there survived a strike. Maybe just an incident the person will recover and walk away from, or maybe something far worse, something as horrible as what happened to our family. I can never bring my brother back, but I will do whatever it takes to show the world what really happened.

That is my promise to him, one that I repeat to myself on those cold, cloudy days.

Originally published in The Horror Zine Magazine Summer 2023.

~ * ~ * ~

Michael's work has been included in several literary magazines such as *The Furious Gazelle*, *The Scarlet Leaf Review*, *MetaStellar*, *Midnight Magazine*, *The Horror Zine*, as well as printed & digital anthologies for Savage Realms Press, Crimson Pinnacle Press, Ill-Advised Records, Gravelight Press, October Nights Press, Media Macabre, Little Red Bird Publishing, Chilling Tales for Dark Nights, Culture Cult, Skywatcher Press, Jayhenge Publishing, Wicked Shadow Press, Moonday Mag, Eerie River Publishing, Dragon Soul Press, a charity anthology for Great Lakes Horror Anthology (GLAHW), and most recently, WolfSinger Publication.

Sanguinary Kin

Chris Horrell

I groan when I feel her weight on top of me. She kicks the cross, perfectly centered on my chest, out of my hands. It falls beside me into the dirt, and I wake up. Rather, I'm forced awake by the wicked magic that binds me. "How did you get out," I ask as I stare into her cold blue eyes.

"Don't look so depressed about it, James. The cross the Union Soldiers used was made of iron. It rusted enough to break apart," Virginia Chester says with a sharp-toothed smile.

I spit and kick the dirt. I hate the name James. My parents called me Thebiti, but Virginia would never allow it, and it's not worth the fight.

I climb out of the grave and examine my surroundings. The white church looks much the same as the night of our capture and interments, its black windows watching me in the night, studying how far I've fallen, but the trees in the little graveyard have grown mightily. Where they once stood fifty feet above me, now the live oaks tower at a much greater height. Their arms are sprawling, large and low, across the churchyard, graced with Spanish moss that shines silver in the moonlight. I walk over the dirt road running beside the graveyard and look down to examine the strange tracks. "What year is it?" I ask.

"Why don't you go look for yourself, boy? It's posted on the church sign," she says with a snarl, busying herself with picking worms off her long scarlet gown.

I start walking down the long church drive bordered by dogwood trees on both sides without giving a retort. *Not worth the beatin'*, I say to myself in consolation. I straighten my coat as I go. It has rotted away slightly while I've been underground, but it has held together well for the most part.

Upon reaching the sign, all thoughts of self-deprecation leave, and I find myself staring open-mouthed at the date written thereupon. It says, "2023." *Has it been one hundred and sixty years*? I think to myself before I hear a distracting roar behind me and turn to watch as two yellow orbs approach with rapid speed. I jump with the agility of a young panther behind the sign, attempting to take cover, but the machine passes me by. I can say with certainty that if my heart had been able to beat, it would have been racing, but the fear passes as I connect the treaded marks in the dirt with the mechanical carriage I had just witnessed.

"James, get back here. We've work to do." Virginia calls to me. I attempt to stay rooted to the ground beside the church sign, but I cannot resist her call. The magic she wields as my creator unto death forces me to rise and march. As I walk back to her, I notice the corn fields that carry deep into the night beyond the trees lining the road and think back to how things once were.

One hundred and sixty years ago, this was the eastern end of the massive Clear Run Plantation in North Carolina, and those fields were cotton. I was born into slavery in the year of our Lord 1840, and Virginia Chester is my legal owner. It was odd in those days for a single woman to own so much land and hold so much wealth, but I never thought of it at the time. I was too busy trying to avoid the whip of the plantation managers to care much about the mysterious owner who only came out at night. *Had I given it some thought, I certainly would have been more careful*, I think, as I reached Virginia's side.

"We're goin' to the house. Hopefully, some of my family still run the place, and we need food. So when we get there, I expect you to fetch a child from the quarters for me," Virginia says. I visibly wince at the thought of it, and Virginia's eyes, as in tune with the dark as a wolf's, catch my discomfort. "Oh, James. Just think," she says with a sneer. "If you hadn't tried to escape that night in eighteen sixty-two, you'd have been in Glory over a hundred years now instead of here with me."

"It's my ever-present thought, mistress," I say earnestly.

As we walk along the dirt road heading west past the church, the tall trees blot out what moonlight there is, sending a shiver of dread running down my spine. However, while I'm uncomfortable along the road, I fear the house more than all the darkness. "Pitiful excuse for a vampire," Virginia says, watching my face, and as much as I hate her, I figure she's right.

The two-mile walk to the massive plantation home is much shorter than I hoped, and presently, I am confronted with its sickening facade. After all this time, it still stands, lording its massive ivory face over me out of the darkness of the night. Though this place is the only home I've ever known, it certainly doesn't feel like it. There are too many ghosts that sweep across the expansive property.

"Ah, good to be home at last," Virginia says, giddy with anticipation.

"How do we even know your family still owns it after all this time," I ask, hoping the thought will cause her pain.

"Don't worry 'bout that boy. The Chesters are a proud people, and any living relatives of mine would have gladly taken up the mantle," she says before continuing. "Why don't you head up to the house and investigate?"

"You know I can't go in without being invited," I say, wanting to escape the chore.

"I'm aware of this curse's rules, boy. Now go. Look in a window if you must," she says.

The curse propels me forward until I reach the house. I can smell the family within before I see them, and the smell of warm flesh is intoxicating. I push the urge to attack away from my mind, but the battle is fierce. Walking by the kitchen window, I see "Chester" written on a curious-looking piece of wood above a door frame. I curse and kick the dirt, hating that the old crow was correct. My mood remains sour until I reach the living room, where my breath catches in my throat with the surprise laden upon me.

I stared, flabbergasted, at the Chester family before me. I see a white father, a black mother, and three mulatto children, none greater than ten years old. *We won*, I think, leaping for joy and running back to Virginia with a broad, teeth-baring smile I haven't used since I was a boy.

"What are you so happy about," Virginia asks with a look of confusion.

"We…we won," I say between fits of laughter.

"What," Virginia spits back.

"Well, not we; I won. See for yourself if you want. A male from your family married a black woman, and they have children. I bet there ain't even quarters anymore," I say, spinning around to see the land where the slave quarters once were was now only a grassy field. I roar with laughter again until I feel Virginia's hands close around my throat and turn my body to face hers.

"Silence," she screams into my face. My mouth closes against my will as if my muscles no longer belong to me.

Virginia drops me to the ground, and I watch as she begins to pace, trampling the long summer grass underfoot. "How could things have devolved this far," she muttered to herself. I sit silently, still unable to speak, until she turns to me. "James, you know how important my bloodline is to me," she says as if she were a lost little girl. "That bein' said. We must protect and conserve it from bein' degraded."

"And how do you intend on doin' that," I ask, my tongue finally freed from bondage.

"In due time, boy, but now we must feed," she says, confidence filling her voice again.

My heart sinks into my shoes, and Virginia once again notices the disturbance on my face. "Don't tell me you're still withholding," she growls.

"It's the one thing you cannot force me to do," I say in an almost inaudible whisper.

"That may be true, but I've never seen one of our kind that doesn't."

"I have a feelin' my resistance is the only thing that keeps me from becomin' as dark as you," I say, willing to accept whatever beating will come, but Virginia only smiles.

"Oh, poor James turned against his will and still resistin' his darker urges. Tell me why you insist on hangin' onto that shriveled piece of a soul you have left."

"Because it's mine," I say solemnly before Virginia beckons me to come, and I follow her toward the house.

I watch as she marches across the sweeping lawn, pulling the long folds of her dress up above her ankles. She didn't look a day over five and twenty years with her back turned and the years of cruelty etched on her face hidden from view. "I highly doubt the magic that binds you still considers you the owner of that home," I call.

"Oh, I'm very aware. I can feel it," she scoffs before launching into the air. Her dress billows around her as the red layers of fabric turn black, rendering her invisible against the night sky for a moment. Then I hear a screech that makes even this lifeless version of myself shudder with terror and watch as a great bat flaps its wretched leathery wings toward one of the upstairs windows.

The bat knocks its wings ever so lightly against the house. It takes me a moment to realize precisely what is happening, but when I finally see the child step out onto the widow's walk at the sounds of the bat's incessant tapping, I moan in agony. My cries go unheeded because, in another second, the unsuspecting child is wrapped up in the creature's decrepit wings that carry her to the edge of the forest bordering the field. I run as fast as my weak, unfed form can muster, but I'm too late. By the time I reach the child, Virginia has already silenced her and fed to her black heart's content. I watch in disgust as Virginia raises her blood-stained lips and looks at me. "Would you like the last drops, James," she asks coldly.

I can hear the child's heart struggling, and it seems to make me melt with anguish, but I can also smell the blood that calls to me with a voice of wicked gluttony. "No," I say as emphatically as I can.

"Very well," Virginia replies, and within a few sickening seconds, the child lies dead in front of me. "Put her body deep into the forest," Virginia commands. "We need her father out looking for her at sunset tomorrow." I groan in pain as my body is forcibly bent over, and my hands stretch out to pick up the child. I lay the girl's body under a tree and surround her with the most beautiful tree limbs and stones I can find. It isn't a fitting burial place, but I tell myself it will have to do as I feel Virginia's pull and find myself walking back to her side.

"What was the point of harmin' the child, Virginia," I ask with unbridled anger as I approach and stand towering a foot over her.

"That's Ms. Virginia to you, boy," she snarls, and the blood shines silver on her teeth in the moonlight. "Let's call her a sacrifice for the greater good of the Chester bloodline. Now let's go to ground before the mornin' draws any closer," she said, beckoning me to come with her.

The barn she leads me to is one I'm familiar with, but in the last hundred and sixty years, it has grown into a rotting and dilapidated version of its former self. I watch as she pushes old equipment out of the way and feels the floor with her foot. "Ah, ha," she finally says, pulling open a trap door leading to an underground tunnel. When we reach the end of the tunnel, I see a dirt floor with a pile of discarded trinkets in the corner. I begin to ask Virginia where I am supposed to sleep. "Lie down," she says, cutting me off. I obey because I must, but secretly, I am thankful she did not say to go to sleep, giving me a chance to plan.

~ * ~

I wake up earlier than expected, and Virginia is still fast asleep when I look to my right. I silently leap from my bed and begin rummaging around the small cavern, looking for anything sharp. Eventually, I am able to find a small knife among the rubbish in the corner. "What are you doin', boy?" Virgina calls from behind me, and I fearfully freeze. Instead of answering her, I continue digging through the pile, hoping she will surmise that whatever I'm doing is unimportant. "Fine, take what you want. I have no use for those things, anyway; besides, what I want is hopefully still buried under my house."

Virginia rises from her bed and begins walking toward the tunnel's mouth. I follow without being told because I have what I need. "We're goin' to wait outside the house, and when the father comes out, I am goin' to turn him into one of us," Virginia explains as we walk.

She is focused on the house, her blue eyes full of evil intent, so she does not notice when I remove a long, flat piece of bark from the large pine tree outside the barn. *In my youth, it wouldn't have been big enough to provide such a perfect writing tablet*; I think to myself as I watch Virginia sit down in the tall grass just outside the border of the lawn. She seems to care very little about what I'm doing, so I take the opportunity to sit a few paces behind her and scratch out a note.

I smile when I finish it, glad I took the opportunity to teach myself to read and write on those long nights just after I'd been turned. I am forced into solemnity quickly, however, as the house's front door opens, and the Chester man walks out into the darkness, calling his daughter's name into the night. He sweats almost instantly in the humid night air, and I salivate uncontrollably at the smell. Virginia leans back and breathes in deeply before she leaps off the ground and attacks her progeny.

She overtakes him in seconds and snaps his jaw shut before he can yell. He struggles against her, and though he measures nearly six feet in height with the build of a lumberjack, he's no match for Virginia, who easily drags him into the tall grass. She latches her mouth onto his throat and drinks with gluttonous gulps. The sounds issuing from her throat are disgusting pounding noises as if something trapped inside were banging on the walls, attempting to get out.

I feel the ordeal will never end, but eventually, the man lies still, just as I once did. Virginia then presses a single fang to her wrist and lets a large glob of congealed blood fall into the man's mouth. He shudders, and his eyes flicker open for a second. "What's your name," Virginia asks coldly.

"George Chester," he replies weakly before falling into unconsciousness.

"Only a few hours now," Virginia coos as she looks down lovingly at the corpse in her arms. "Same name as my father.". I stare into her empty eyes, refusing to speak. Virginia's eyes narrow as she looks back, and her face hardens in anger. "Listen, boy. Tonight you'll feed with us. You won't resist enterin' into the fullness of your new state of being any longer," she says.

"You can't force me, Virginia," I say coldly.

"Maybe not, but I'll make that home such a bloodbath you won't be able to fight the temptation," she says. I lean back and close my eyes. Fear is rushing through me like a river about to break its banks.

"Resist the devil, and he will flee," I whisper.

"But I'm not a he," Virginia whispers back with a giggle reminiscent of a girl.

~ * ~

"Come on, George. Walk us into your home," Virginia says as she stands, looking up at her fourth great-grandnephew. I watch as he resists. I'm sure even in his new state, he knows what he will do to his family. He walks in front of Virginia, and I walk behind as she beckons to me. It is very late now, and I look toward the eastern sky as we reach the wide front porch, trying to will the Sun to rise.

With a crash, George knocks the door off his hinges, and we all walk inside. George's wife and their two remaining daughters run into the foyer at the sound. "Kill them," Virginia shrieks and flies toward the cowering family. George reaches out to stop her, but Virginia lazily swats his hand away.

I almost turn to despair, but then I feel the Sun begin to rise with an instinctual fear that boils inside me. I work against my instincts and throw open the living room curtains. Virginia, George, and I scream as the light hits our skin. "Let's go," Virginia yells, running for the door. I follow, but not before dropping the piece of pine bark to the floor. It reads: "Tunnel under the barn. A wooden stake through the heart. Kill us all. He is too far gone." As we run from the house, I pray my grandmother's words are true: *Don't ever mess with a mama bear.*

~ * ~

I feel danger coming and jerk myself out of sleep even though it's still the middle of the day. I hiss and roll to the side to avoid the light coming from the tunnel's mouth. The Chester woman can't see us yet in the darkness, but I can see her and smell her fear. I look over at Virginia, who remains asleep.

I must admit I'm not quite sure why she remains asleep. It's possibly due to the lack of hunger she feels while I, on the other hand, am starving. I lay back down and pretend to be asleep as I watch the woman raise the shaved-down broom handle above her head. I smile at her bravery, and though I want to watch the end of Virginia, my curse will not allow me, and I am forced back into unconsciousness.

~ * ~

I awake with a groan. "She didn't listen," I say out loud before thinking about how foolhardy it was. I roll over and then sit up quickly. I take a moment to ensure my eyes are not playing tricks on me, but there she is. A genuinely dead Virginia lays there with a stake through her heart. I almost leap for joy, but then I see George's intact corpse beside her.

As I pull the stake from Virginia's heart with the sound of soft food being squished between one's fingers, George begins to stir. "Lord, forgive me," I say, and I drive the stake through George's heart with much less hesitation than I would have liked.

I bow my head in sadness as I walk toward the Chester mansion. The lights from the upper windows of the grand home stare back at me like watchful eyes in the darkness. I wonder momentarily if I should embrace the night and let it overtake me, but it seems that there is a small point of light inside me even now.

I knock on the door, and George's wife answers, then attempts to shut the door in fear. “Evening Ma’am,” I say as I hold the stake out to her. “I hate to trouble you, but you need to use this on me as well.” She stares at me as a shocked look crosses her face.

“Why would I kill you? You saved us,” she says as her voice shakes.

“I’ve been a slave for a hundred and eighty-some odd years. You know what I am by now, so you should also know this is the only way out,” I say as she takes the stake.

I walk back down the steps, taking in the beauty of the night for the first time in ages. The moonlight shines down on each extended blade of grass, making them glow like a symphony of lights.

“Where’s George and Tabby,” she asks shakily as she stands before me.

“I’m sorry about your daughter, but she’s gone. Virginia killed her. Virginia killed George as well. She made him like me.” She sobs openly but still manages to honor my request and raise the stake. “You have a kind heart. I’m truly sorry it’s broken,” I say, thinking of my mother and grandmother while I say it.

Then, it all happens in an instant. I feel a momentary pain, and then I’m finally and gratefully free.

~ * ~ * ~

Chris Horrell is an emerging author, and when he isn’t wrangling his three children, you can probably find him reading or writing. Chris holds an undergraduate degree in communication from the University of North Carolina at Pembroke and a Master of Divinity from Southeastern Baptist Theological Seminary.

Chris lives in New Hampshire with his family but is originally from North Carolina, and most of his stories are set there.

Family Tree

Mike Murphy

All Magdalena could think about was the blood.

Amid the blooming flora and happily singing birds of the forest, the middle-aged, bearded Arkon withdrew the ceremonial knife from its worn sheath. "Are you ready?" he asked the young woman with the long hair beside him. The finely honed blade glittered in the sun.

"Is this part…necessary?" she asked nervously.

"The tree must know of your sincerity," he told her, indicating the towering elm with the enormous roots before them.

"It's only that…"

"Speak!" he demanded. "I have *much* to do."

"The money."

"Your fifty gold coins?"

"One hundred," she admitted after a pause, ashamed and blushing slightly.

"Ah, you wish for a *child* as well."

"I am but a poor washer woman, sir."

"I know of your situation."

"It took me years of scrubbing my fingers to the bone to save up that much money. My meager table has not seen meat in *months*."

"Do you wish to withdraw?"

"Oh no, no!" she answered him quickly.

"Then *what*?"

"Is there any…guarantee this will work?"

"I have been the Arkon for nearly six years. I have seen few negative outcomes, but even I cannot predict the tree's mercies."

"But the money—"

"We all must make choices in life, my dear," he said. "Is filling your belly more important to you than a husband and child?"

"Certainly not!"

"If you could have accomplished either of those things on your own, you would not be here today," he summed up. "Are you ready?"

"Will it…hurt?" the fair-skinned woman asked.

"Only for a moment," he told her.

Magdalena nervously extended her ring finger. She could not watch as the robed man sliced a small cut into its tip. She pressed her eyes tight against the sting. Crimson began to appear. "Quickly!" the Arkon ordered. "Before the clotting begins." They hurriedly knelt by the tree. Taking hold of her finger, the man squeezed one, two, three drops of blood onto the roots. Magdalena moaned quietly each time. "It is done," the Arkon said seconds later, and they rose together.

"It is?" she asked, not daring to look at her wounded finger for fear of swooning.

He removed a bandage from the pocket of his scarlet robe and handed it to her. "Wrap this about your finger," he said. "It has medicinal qualities."

She thanked him and did so. "When will I know?" she asked eagerly.

"Your donation will be used to care for the tree so it grows strong. Hopefully, it will look upon you favorably."

~ * ~

Grinning, the Arkon walked into his well-appointed office. Broog, his dim right-hand man, was seated at a table counting coins and making hasty notes on scrolls. The Arkon tossed the satchel containing Magdalena's money at him. It landed with a *clink* on the table. "Another fifty?" Broog asked happily through his broken teeth.

"One hundred," his boss told him.

Broog giggled. "She must be a real *witch*."

"Perhaps acceptable to someone in a lower caste."

"Will anything happen for her?"

"Who cares? We have her money. Soon, we will leave this village for good and live *very* comfortably overseas."

"Does the family tree have any *real* powers?" Broog inquired.

"None," the Arkon said after a chuckle.

"But your predecessors—"

"Were *fools*. None of them saw the tree's potential to be a gold mine."

"No woman has *ever* benefitted from the bleeding ceremony?"

"Of course not!" the bearded man exclaimed. "It's all for show."

"Then why—"

"If these simple-minded ladies want to water an ordinary tree with their blood and pay us for the privilege, so be it," his boss told him. "You don't *really* think—"

"Not for a minute," Broog answered quickly.

"Good. If you did," the Arkon added, "I'd have to rethink our …'business arrangement'."

~ * ~

Gray-haired, elderly Tursa, her tattered pink shawl hanging loosely over her shoulders, was standing behind the front desk of The Crescent Inn that early morning when Magdalena entered. They greeted each other, and the younger woman asked, "Any washing for me?"

"No."

She was surprised. "Have your guests all decided to wear their dirty clothes over and over again?"

"As long as they pay for their lodging," the elderly proprietor said, "what they do with their clothing is none of my concern."

"But surely—"

"They all know your services are available. I have a notice posted in each room," she assured Magdalena. "I can't *make* them contact you."

"Of course not."

"Perhaps tomorrow."

The bell over the door rang. Magdalena looked up, and a god entered the inn—the most handsome man she had ever seen, she had ever *imagined*. He was tall, he was fit, he was strong, and his blue eyes sparkled brilliantly—like twin lakes on a sunny morning. Carrying a sack over one shoulder, he approached Tursa.

"May I help you, sir?" Tursa asked.

He replied in a most-pleasing voice. "Please. My name is Klim. I wrote for a reservation."

"I remember. Two nights. Your room is ready."

"Excellent!" he exclaimed. "Might you help me with something?"

"What is that?"

"I have a case to argue tomorrow."

"You are a barrister?"

"Yes," he answered. "Unfortunately, my court attire became muddied on the way here."

No sooner had he plopped the bag down on the desk than

Magdalena sprang forward saying, "I can help you with that, sir."

"You…can?" he asked, taking in the vision before him.

"Magdalena is the best washer woman for miles around," Tursa informed him. "If anyone can make your attire *sparkle*, she can."

"Magdalena, is it?" Klim asked, turning to her.

"Yes, sir," she replied.

"A *lovely* name," he told the washer woman. "Will you be able to finish the job for tomorrow morning?"

"May I have a look?"

"Of course," he said, and he pulled the sack's drawstring open for her. With her dainty hands, Magdalena rummaged through the soiled items: A shirt, a vest, a pair of trousers, his barrister's wig. Some hosiery began to fall from the sack. Together, they grabbed for it. Their hands touched. "I'm *so* sorry!" he told her. "It was accidental."

"Not a problem, sir."

"Please, my name is…Klim," he said, longing to hear her utter it.

"Not a problem, Klim."

"Since it *wasn't* a problem…"

"Yes?"

"Might I…touch it again?"

Magdalena looked at Tursa, who nodded that she should. "Of course," she replied, putting both her hands in Klim's.

He touched them tenderly. "So delicate," he remarked, "and purer than any snowflake that ever fell from the heavens."

"You flatter me."

"I speak the truth—always."

Tursa cleared her throat. "The garments?" she reminded them.

Taken aback by his uncontrolled display of affection, Klim chuckled. "Oh, yes. Could you make these presentable for court tomorrow?" he asked Magdalena.

"Without fail."

"They will look *better* than new." Tursa handed her guest a sheet of paper detailing Magdalena's fees.

"Very reasonable," he pronounced after scanning it. "I am indebted to you."

"The pleasure is mine," she assured him. "When in the morning will you need your things?"

"Would seven be too early?"

"Not at all. I sometimes hire a boy to run garments to their owners. He can—"

"Could *you* deliver my things?"

"I…suppose I could."

"If there's any additional charge for…"

"No. I will see you in the morning."

"I can think of no better way to begin my day."

~ * ~

Magdalena was scrubbing linens against an old washboard leaning in a bucket of soapy water when Klim entered her small home, surprising her. He was still in his court attire, but he held his white barrister's wig in his left hand.

"I hope I'm not disturbing you," he said.

"Not at all," she told him, removing her hands from the water and wiping them dry on her well-worn apron. "How did you find me?"

"The innkeeper gave me your address. Forgive me for intruding, but I *had* to share the news with someone."

"What news?"

"I won my case!"

"Good for you!"

"My superiors have asked me to move *permanently* to this village. It is near the locations of several pending cases. I'm going to purchase a home soon."

"It will be good to have you as a neighbor."

"And the judge—oh, you *must* hear this! —The judge commented on the immaculate condition of my court attire. He said it showed my sincerity and respect for the law. I gave him your rates. I hope you don't mind."

"Not at all. The more clients, the better."

"I cannot thank you enough, Magdalena. Thank you!" Before Klim knew what he was doing, he pressed his lips to hers and held them there for several seconds.

When it was over, she asked, "Did you just…kiss me?"

"No," he lied, ashamed of his uncontrolled behavior. "No, I…I didn't."

"A shame."

"Why?"

"I was going to ask you to do it again."

~ * ~

It was on a beautiful, sunny day in the village square that Klim proposed to Magdalena, who eagerly accepted. "Oh, my love, you make my heart sing!" he exclaimed for all the villagers to hear. "I have purchased a home for us on Sunflower Way."

"The one with the two spiers?" she asked.

"Yes."

"That must have been *so* expensive."

"Don't you worry your pretty head about *that.* My position is secure. We will live there together in harmony forever. Now let us plan the wedding—the biggest affair this village has *ever* seen."

~ * ~

A few months later, the doctor confirmed Magdalena's pregnancy. As she was heading home, she saw the Arkon in the village square. She called to him, and he stopped. "I haven't seen you in months," he said.

"Eventful, *glorious* months, sir," she replied, beaming.

"How so?"

She showed him her wedding band and told him of the child to be. "Such wonderful news! I'm going home to tell Klim."

"But your house is in the other direction."

"Not any longer. I live on Sunflower Way now."

The Arkon was impressed…and jealous. "That's an…*expensive* part of the village."

"It is a joyous part of village! And to think all this happiness came from a mere one hundred gold coins and a few drops of blood. Oh, may the family tree be blessed for always!"

~ * ~

"She married Klim," Broog told him later, "the village's new barrister."

"How could I have *missed* this news?" the Arkon asked.

"I assumed you heard," he replied. "She got everything she asked for in the bleeding ceremony, didn't she?"

"She did," the Arkon admitted, confused.

"But if there's no truth to—"

"Are you going to start wondering about that stupid tree again?"

"No, but it certainly is a coincidence that—"

"That's all it is: A coincidence." Even as he spoke, he grew unsure. "Even though things were *not* looking good for her before…"

"What are you thinking about?" Broog asked, seeing his boss was pondering something.

"A way to profit from that woman's good fortune. We could be overseas in no time." The Arkon sat at the table and steepled his fingers before his face. "All we need," he told his employee, "is an angle."

~ * ~

"You are confident in your duties, Hannah?" Klim asked his wife's nurse.

"Yes, sir," the young woman replied. "I am to care for the lady and make sure she does not exert herself."

"Exactly. The doctor says she should rest during the remaining months of her pregnancy. When I *must* be at the office, I am putting her care in your hands."

"I…I understand."

"You sound unsure."

"It's…It's not that. I have cared for many in the village."

"Then what?"

"I'm…not sure I should say."

"Please do."

"Some months ago," Hannah explained, pausing briefly and then choosing her words carefully, "I cared for the children of the Arkon."

"And?" Klim prompted her.

"I once heard him talking to his aide, Broog. I…I didn't mean to eavesdrop."

"Tell me!"

"He was speaking meanly of a woman who had paid him one hundred gold coins for the bleeding ceremony. He said her name was…Magdalena."

"*My* Magdalena?"

"I believe so. His description of her matches your wife. He was gloating of how he had stolen her money."

"What is a…a bleeding ceremony?" Klim asked.

"At the edge of the woods, there is a large, old elm known to the locals as the family free. Many believe it has supernatural powers."

"A *tree*?"

"I do not share that belief."

"You said this ceremony involves payment?"

"Yes, sir. A woman gives the Arkon fifty gold coins if she desires a husband; one hundred for a husband *and* a child. The gold is meant to secure the tree's blessings." Hannah found it difficult to utter the next words: "And then there's…the blood."

"Blood?"

"The woman's ring finger is cut with a ceremonial blade. A few drops of her blood are applied to the tree's roots. The blood and the gold, the women believe, will win the tree's favor and grant their wishes."

"Barbaric!" Klim exclaimed. "My wife took part in this?"

"From what I heard, yes."

"The Arkon stole her money!"

"He has done so to many. In public, he speaks of the tree's powers. In private, it is a windfall for him."

"He *will* pay for this!"

~ * ~

In repose on her daybed, Magdalena grew teary eyed. "I did, my sweet," she admitted.

"You thought that a *tree*—"

"I did and do," she told him. "Look at what that investment has wrought: You and soon, our child."

"My dear," Klim explained, starting to pace. "I didn't come to this village to fulfill the promise of a tree. I came of my *own* accord. I never heard of this family tree until a short time ago. It has no power over me."

"Then how did we meet?"

"Chance! Wonderful, *blessed* chance," her husband told her, stopping his pacing. "The Arkon stole your money. He will pay for that."

"Please don't!" she urged him, rising slightly. "To anger the Arkon is to anger the tree. That will ruin everything we share!"

"Nonsense! Nothing bad will happen to you, me, or our child when I confront him."

"Back then," Magdalena said, leaning back and remembering her days before Klim arrived in the village, "a hundred gold coins was an *incredible* amount of money. Does it matter now that we are well off?"

"It is *your* honor," Klim told her, cupping her lovely chin and looking deeply into her eyes. "I will not stand for someone treating you so poorly."

~ * ~

"Klim is waiting to see you," Broog nervously told his boss, who was seated behind his ornate office desk. "He *doesn't* look happy."

"Excellent!" the Arkon exclaimed. "Here I was wondering how to extract some money from him, and he pays me a visit. Show him in."

Broog opened the door to the outer office and called, "The Arkon will see you now, sir." Klim stomped in, fuming.

"So good to meet you, barrister," the Arkon began, rising to his feet. "I usually *personally* welcome all newcomers to our village, but business has been piling—"

"I'm not here to exchange pleasantries," a clearly angry Klim announced.

"Have a seat."

"I prefer to stand."

"As you wish." The Arkon sat back down. Broog stayed in the office, expecting trouble.

"You know my wife, Magdalena?" Klim began.

"Of course—a lovely woman. I understand she is expecting. Congratulations!"

"You have cheated her."

"Me? How?"

"In the bleeding ceremony," Klim stated. "Do you deny she participated in it?"

"No."

"How could anyone believe in such foolishness? A tree that can grant a woman a husband and family! You don't believe it *yourself*, do you?"

"Of course I do. I am the Arkon."

Klim put his hands on the desk. "You are a thief and a scoundrel!"

"How dare you!" the bearded man angrily replied, rising quickly.

"Sir?" Broog asked anxiously.

"Stand your ground."

"You stole money from my wife. I demand its return."

"I stole nothing. Your wife asked for a husband and child. Both wishes have been granted through the good graces of the family tree."

"Rubbish!"

"You insult my beliefs, sir, and those of many villagers."

"I want her money returned!" Klim repeated, spacing his words for emphasis.

"It has already been spent on the care of the tree—fertilizer, pruning, watering, and such."

"I'm sure you have a hundred gold coins lying about here. Give her those!"

"Why should I?" the Arkon asked. "She paid for services rendered and now has what she wished for."

"I'm *not* part of a tree's plan, and neither is our child!" Klim told him, pounding on the desk. "Will you give her the money back?"

"I will not."

"Then I challenge you to a duel."

"What?" the Arkon asked, amused.

"I have two pistols at home. They will do nicely."

"When and where?" the red-robed man inquired, sitting down slowly to look at ease with the challenge.

"Tomorrow at noon…and by this *supposedly* sacred tree. We will invite everyone in the village to witness our battle."

"Agreed."

"Tomorrow then." Klim hurriedly left the office, slamming the door shut behind him.

"What are you thinking?" Broog asked. "A duel?"

"I am an excellent marksman," his superior said.

"What if Klim is a *better* one?"

He rose from behind the desk, looking pleased. "It's *all* coming together."

"What is?"

"How dim can you be? Tomorrow, Klim dies by my hand in a totally legal way. Then, I slowly, but expertly, advance upon the grieving widow and stake my claim to the riches her late husband has no doubt willed her." He smiled, turning over the thought of a luxurious future in his mind. "It's all so simple."

~ * ~

Despite protests from several, particularly Magdalena, the time of the duel arrived. Standing in the clearing near the family tree, the village doctor announced to the many onlookers that both parties had asked him to officiate.

"Gentlemen, you *definitely* wish to go through with this?" he inquired. Both men, pistols in hand, replied with an adamant *yes*. "Please check your weapons." As the combatants did so, the doctor continued: "The rules: You will stand back to back. At my say, you will take ten paces—no more, no less—turn and fire. You each have been given one bullet. Are there any requests before we commence?"

"Just one," the Arkon said.

"Yes?"

"I would like to take my ten paces *toward* the family tree. It has always given me comfort."

"Klim?" the doctor inquired.

"I have no problem with that," Klim answered.

Magdalena, great with child, left the crowd of villagers and ran to Klim. "Husband!" she pleaded, pulling him close.

"Get with the others, dear," he told her.

"But—"

"Go. I will see you after the duel." Magdalena left reluctantly, returning to her place.

"Back to back now," the doctor went on, positioning the duelists properly. "Remember: Ten paces." He paused for a moment, hoping the men would come to their senses, but that was not to be. "Go!" he ordered. "One, two…"

For Magdalena, Broog, and some other spectators, the ten paces seemed to take an eternity. "Ten!" the doctor finally said.

Both men turned as one. A shot rang out. Klim winced as the fired bullet hit him in the shoulder. Seconds after the Arkon smiled, there was the sound of a loud *crack*. A heavy limb fell from the family tree, hitting him on the head. He fell in a heap to the ground.

Magdalena ran to her husband, weeping for his pain. The doctor approached and examined the wound. "Not too serious," he said. "I can take care of it in my office."

"Doctor!" Broog called from under the tree. The doctor, Klim,

Magdalena, and several of the villagers went to see what had happened. The Arkon lay on his back, unconscious—a jagged tree limb beside him. Blood, the same crimson as his robe, was pooling under his head. "He's not moving!" Broog nervously pronounced.

The doctor knelt beside the unconscious bearded man and checked his vital signs. "He breathes not," he announced to many gasps from onlookers. "Klim," he said, rising, "you are the victor. You have killed the Arkon."

"No, I haven't," Klim disagreed. He opened his weapon to reveal his allotted bullet still in its chamber. "My gun never fired."

Magdalena looked first at the Arkon's body and then, at the broken limb above her head. "Then how…" she asked.

"I may have been wrong about the family tree, dearest," her husband said.

"How so?" she inquired.

"I'd say it just took its revenge on the Arkon."

Originally Published in: Fantasia Divinity Magazine Issue 21, Apr 2018

~ * ~ * ~

For years, **Mike Murphy** has written audio plays. He has had over 150 of them produced in the U.S. and overseas, many for Audible.

Mike has won The Columbine Award and a dozen Moondance International Film Festival awards in their TV pilot, audio play, short screenplay, and short story categories. In 2020, his screenplay *Die Laughing* was a semi-finalist in the Unique Voices Screenplay Competition from *Creative Screenwriting Magazine*. The following year, his TV pilot script "The Bullying Squad" was a quarterfinalist in the *Emerging Screenwriters* Genre Screenplay Competition.

Mike's prose has appeared in many publications and more than a dozen anthologies. He is the writer of two short films, *Dark Chocolate* and *Hotline*.

In 2013, Mike won the inaugural Marion Thauer Brown Audio Drama Scriptwriting Competition. In 2020, he came in second. For several of the in-between years, he served as a judge.

Sins of the Forefather

Kay Hanifen

As soon as we turn twenty-seven, everyone in my family contracts a strange malady, one no doctor can fully explain. It starts with fatigue, an exhaustion so profound it becomes difficult to get out of bed. Weakness, muscle spasms, and pain all follow. For most, it stops there. Life is far from easy, but they can still function. The rare, unlucky ones suffer seizures and hallucinations, contorting themselves into impossible positions and claiming to be possessed by demons.

We've been studied by doctors all over the world, but none of them can explain why our bodies suddenly break down on our twenty-seventh birthdays. We've done blood tests, genetic tests, urine tests, EKGs, MRIs, CT scans, and just about everything else they could imagine to fix us, but they all come back frustratingly normal.

It's harder for the women in our family. Half the time, the doctors ask if we're pregnant and the other half, they say we just have anxiety. The truly desperate have turned to faith healing, Hoodoo, crystals, paganism, spiritualism, and just about every wellness guru who has ever tried to make a quick buck off sick people.

Maybe looking for a bloodline curse is also a bit desperate. But family lore says our great times eleven grandfather was Matthew Hopkins, the Witchfinder General who tortured and murdered innocent people across Europe in the 1600's. He died at the ripe old age of twenty-eight during a botched exorcism after more than a year of claiming to be possessed. I wondered, then, if he had captured a true witch, one who cursed him, and all his children after, to suffer from this affliction. At this point, the explanation feels about as logical as a doctor seriously suggesting I was pregnant even after I told him I was a virgin lesbian.

I joined our family's twenty-seven club last year. We celebrated my birthday the day before. My younger family members and I walked all around the city, enjoying museums and shopping. When the sun went down, we hit up a rave, and I savored the ability to drink, dance, and flirt without pain.

But I felt the moment the clock struck midnight. It was like I'd been wearing an empty backpack, and someone just filled it with fifty pounds of rocks. I stumbled out of the club and into the cold night air, my little brother, Max, following close behind.

"Already?" he asked, brows furrowed with concern.

I nodded, my eyes screwing shut as a sudden migraine stabbed like ice picks into my eyes. I pressed my hands to my ears and regretted eating all that greasy food as my stomach roiled with the threat of vomit.

I didn't hear him call a cab, but soon, he was helping me into a car. He let me lay my head in his lap as the cabbie drove us back to the hotel we'd booked for the night.

According to my older family members, the first few days were always the hardest. They felt like the flu, but instead of getting completely better, you would only bounced back about fifty percent. And that fifty percent was about where I had been for the past year.

But yesterday, I had a seizure for the first time. One moment, I was folding laundry and the next, I was on my side, resting my aching head in my girlfriend's lap. But this wasn't like any seizure I'd ever read about. This one came with flashes of images like a half-remembered dream.

I saw a knife slicing into an arm, and the arm welling with blood. Cloaked figures prodding with needles as I stand chained to a wall. A deep lake and a burning funeral pyre.

And then I was back in my apartment with my girlfriend, Talia. We went to the hospital, but as expected, they couldn't find anything unusual. All signs pointed to me being a perfectly healthy adult. But I had a feeling about what I needed to do next.

Within a week, Max, Talia, and I touched down at Heathrow airport. "Remind me of the plan," Max said as we collected our luggage.

I rubbed my forehead, trying to stave off the budding migraine. I barely slept on the plane and felt like I was a few seconds from a meltdown. "I think that, to fix this curse, we need to find the person who cast it. Obviously, they're dead, but I'm hoping that if we retrace our evil Great Grandpappy's steps through his life, we'll find a way to break it."

"Makes perfect sense," Max muttered.

"Hey, you wanted to come along," I snapped, roughly grabbing my bag from the carousel, and ignoring the way my shoulder protested.

He put his hands up in a placating gesture. "Sorry. I was just hoping we'd have a little more to go on."

Talia, ever the practical peacemaker, put an arm around my shoulder. "I think we all just need a good meal and a nap before we get started. I know I do."

I have no idea how I convinced her to come along. Though she knew what she was signing on for when she and I started dating, I doubted she ever expected to fly all the way to England to try to break a family curse that may or may not exist. But here she was.

We grabbed a cab and headed to the hotel. After getting showered and settled in our room, we charged Max with going out to pick up some lunch for us. Talia laid back on the bed with a groan. "I hate flying."

"Me too." I yawned. "I hope Max finds a chippie or something because I'm—"

The world once again became nothing but flashes: shadows and torchlight on the wall, a stylized white chalk horse etched into a hill, the feeling of my thumbs being crushed in a vice, a thatched roof and a cave, a name carved onto a wall.

Agnes.

Her name was Agnes.

I returned to myself with a gasp and before Talia could say anything, I lunged for my phone. With shaking fingers, I looked up the horse in the hill. "There," I said, showing her the picture. "She wants us to go there."

"Who?" Talia asked, her eyes wide with concern.

"Agnes. The witch Matthew Hopkins killed." My head throbbed like twin icepicks trying to lobotomize me. I pressed my hands to my eyes as though that would somehow stop the migraine in its tracks.

"Here," Talia said, handing me some pills and a glass of water.

I took both gratefully as she turned off the lights and texted Max to be quiet when he came in.

While I was asleep, they had rented a car so we could drive straight to the Uffington Horse Figure. I felt better the next day than I had in a very long time, and I took it as a good sign. She seemed to be leading me somewhere. Maybe, somehow, I could appease Agnes's spirit and break the curse, not just for my sake but for Max's. He was twenty-six and would be turning twenty-seven all too soon.

I wondered if the other members of my family afflicted with the seizures had the same visions. If so, did they try to follow the breadcrumbs or were they committed before they had the chance? It seemed as though there was one in every generation who had these seizures.

We didn't drive all the way to the Uffington Horse. As we approached an exit, I felt a jerk in me, like a dog pulling on a leash. "That way," I said.

Talia looked over from the driver's seat. "What?"

"Go there. Just trust me."

Her eyes met with Max's in the rearview mirror. He nodded. "I kind of feel it too. There's something we need to do there."

"Okay," she said, and took the exit. She drove slowly, turning every time I told her to turn until we reached a small forest.

"Stop here," I said, and she was barely parked before I bolted out the door.

"Wait!" Max called after me, but the pull was too strong. I needed to go. I needed to find her.

The sins of the father shall be visited upon the son. For centuries, my bloodline has been cursed because of the monster who destroyed untold lives. I cannot fix what he did, but maybe I can help one suffering soul.

The mouth of the cave was so small and overgrown I almost missed it at first. It was only a tug of that unseen thread that let me find it. Though every part screamed for me to go in, I waited for Max and Talia to catch up.

"What the hell are you doing?" Talia demanded as soon as she caught her breath.

"Agnes is in here," I said. "I'm going to find her."

"Wait," Max said, grabbing my arm. "I'll go with you."

"And I'm not letting you two go wandering in a random cave by yourself," Talia added.

I don't think I could have protested if I wanted to. The pull I felt was like a riptide and there was no fighting against the current. Without even turning on my phone's flashlight, I descended into the darkness.

Though the mouth of the cave was small, the inside opened up to a series of tunnels. In the pitch black, I walked with confidence, only vaguely aware of the voices and flashes of light behind me.

Agnes was waiting.

She'd been waiting for more than three hundred years.

I stopped short when the tunnels widened into a chamber. Max and Talia bumped into me, the light from their phones casting alien shadows on the wall. "Holy shit," Max breathed as his light settled on a far corner.

In it, a skeleton slumped against the wall. Her clothes were partially decayed but appeared to be little more than an underdress, something far too thin for a drafty cave. If the cold didn't get her, then dehydration or starvation would. He left her to die alone in the dark.

I approached as though under a spell.

"Look!" Talia said, pointing her flashlight to the ground where a series of sigils were painted. I stepped away, examining them closely. The tang of iron filled the air. In all these centuries, time had not dried her blood nor the damp wash it away. It looked as fresh as when she had first painted it.

"Wait, don't!" Talia exclaimed too late, far too late.

I touched the blood and saw everything. A young girl watches her mother burned at the stake by a dark figure in a wide-brimmed hat. A black goat whispers to her as she cleans out the barn. She signs her name in a book bound in human skin and dances naked among the rest of the true witches. The man in the wide-brimmed hat returns and her revenge is set into motion. Shouts of accusation and a kidnapping in the dead of night. Torture and tests of witchcraft, and he leaves her beaten and bleeding to die in a cave. She waits until he leaves before sitting up. Using her teeth, she cuts open her wrists and draws the sigils, cursing him and his entire bloodline. And then she bleeds to death.

The memory stopped there, and she looked at me. I realized I was standing above my body while Max turned me sideways, and Talia placed my head in her lap.

"You finally came," Agnes said. "All these years, I've waited for a Hopkins to return."

"I'd like to apologize on behalf of my ancestor," I said, "and I'm asking for you to break the curse."

"Beg," she said.

I blinked. "What?"

"Get on your knees and beg for this curse to be lifted." Her gaze was cold and cruel, contempt radiating off her like heat from a fire.

I did as she ordered, clasping my hands together and saying, "Please, I know Matthew Hopkins has wronged you, but he's long dead. The people who suffer now for his actions have done nothing wrong."

"I cannot lift the curse until it's complete," she said. "Take my hand."

I held it out to her, and she took it, jumping into my body and dragging me along with her. My eyes flew open of their own accord and my body sat up. I tried to move, tried to do anything, but it refused to obey.

"Are you okay?" Talia asked.

Against my will, my lips curled into a smile. "Perfectly fine. The curse has been broken," I said, but I wasn't actually speaking. Someone else was in control of my tongue.

Max's face lit up. "Really? How'd you do it?"

"To be honest," Agnes said in my voice, "I have no idea. But we should probably get out of here."

"Yeah," Talia said, lifting her—me—to my feet. Max took my other side, and they supported me all the way out of the cave.

"*What did you do?*" I screamed in whatever corner of my soul I'd been tucked inside.

"*For the curse to end, I must take full possession of a Hopkins,*" Agnes replied airily. "*If it's any consolation, the curse has been lifted for the rest of your family. They're going to wake up feeling better than ever before.*"

I kicked and screamed and struggled in my own mind, but to no avail as my loved ones led my body out of the caves, not realizing I was still imprisoned in their all-encompassing darkness.

~ * ~ * ~

Kay Hanifen was born on a Friday the 13th and once lived for three months in a haunted castle. So, obviously, she had to become a horror writer. Her work has appeared in over forty anthologies and magazines.

When she's not consuming pop culture with the voraciousness of a vampire at a 24-hour blood bank, you can usually find her with

her two black cats or at: www.kayhanifenauthor.wordpress.com.
Twitter: www.twitter.com/TheUnicornComi1
Instagram: www.instagram.com/katharinehanifen/

Unfinished Business

Joe Stout

"I'm sorry."

The warden nodded toward the dark window and drugs started to flow from the network of tubes running through the wall. As the first drops reached the man strapped to the gurney, he closed his eyes.

In the next room, witnesses seated on cold metal chairs watched the proceedings. One, a Roman collar on his black shirt, crossed himself. Another let a soft smile creep across her face. The reporter made a note in her book. A tear rolled down a gray-haired woman's face as she put her hand to the glass.

On the gurney, John Bennett's eyes opened and he looked over at the warden. "Did it start?"

The warden jumped, looking down at the man. "Close the blinds," he ordered a guard as he reached to switch off the microphone hanging over the prisoner. When that was done, he tapped on a door in the wall. It opened to reveal a dark room, a series of syringes laid out on the table with an IV bag hanging on a small tree.

"Is there a problem?" he asked a man sitting by the tree.

"Shouldn't be," the executioner replied. "I just injected the Pancuronium, I'm about to push the potassium chloride."

"Then why is he still awake?"

"What?" The man stood up, then looked down at the syringes on the table in front of him. Walking to a cabinet, he took out several vials and studied the labels. "Nothing is wrong back here. The drugs are all in date, the tubes were labeled as normal. He should be unconscious and not breathing."

The Warden looked back at the gurney, where the prisoner was watching him. "Not the case."

"Is something blocking the tube?"

"Not that I saw. Everything seems to be flowing freely."

The executioner walked into the chamber and studied the tubing traveling from the portal in the wall to the arm on the gurney.

"Are you in any pain?" he asked Bennett.

"No, sir," the man replied.

The executioner shrugged as he walked back to the warden. "I can't explain it. He should be dead."

"Then why isn't he?" the Warden demanded.

"No telling. We can use the alternate injection site?"

The warden sighed, then nodded. "Wait for my signal."

As the door to the room swung closed, the Warden straightened his tie before walking to the gurney. "Alright, John. Looks like something went wrong with the first injection site. We're going to switch to the backup."

The man on the table nodded. "Fair enough."

"Open the blinds," the Warden ordered as he turned the microphone back on. "Ladies and Gentlemen, there was a problem with the primary injection site. We are switching to the alternate."

He nodded to the dark window again, then watched the prisoner, occasionally moving his eyes to the clock on the wall behind the gurney. A minute passed, then two, then three. John lay on the table, looking up at him. At four minutes, John smiled.

"Warden, anytime you're ready."

"Close the blinds," the Warden snapped, turning the microphone off. This time, he didn't knock as he stormed into the control room. "What the fuck is going on?"

The executioner shrugged. "He's taken ten grams of thiopental, more than triple what the protocol calls for. There is no way he should still be awake. I even pushed the pancuronium and the chloride! He should be stone dead!"

"Well, he ain't!" the warden growled. Going back into the chamber, he reached for a phone on the wall. "Get me the Governor," he ordered.

~ * ~

On the gurney, John smiled up at the ceiling. He'd seen the confusion in the warden's eyes, heard the panic as he talked, first to the executioner and now to the governor. Part of him hoped they'd keep trying. He thought back to what had brought him here, and the secret that was driving them crazy.

~ * ~

"We found an upgrade, a twist to the body's coding to turn

blood into super blood," the young doctor had told Bennett as he sat on an exam table in a pair of scrubs. "No more disease. Drunkenness? Off the table. Heart attacks? Clotting? Stroke? Things of the past! Your blood will fight off any foreign invader, break down any internal problems, and self-regulate to maintain optimal levels of oxygen and nutrients throughout your body!"

It had been three months since Bennett's dishonorable discharge and, desperate for money, he'd responded to the ad seeking a medical test subject. Sitting in the exam room, he raised an eyebrow. "It sounds too good to be true."

"We thought so too," the Doctor said. "But we've completed our animal testing and are ready to move on to human testing. You fit all the criteria, and if you're willing, the job is yours."

"Are there risks," Bennett had asked.

"Immortality?"

~ * ~

Monthly injections followed, with large cash payments each time.

"Any side effects?" the doctor asked when Bennett returned for his fifth visit.

Bennett shook his head. "Nothing. I feel great."

"You should," the man smiled. "We've very excited about your progress. This will be your last injection, but we'll still need you to come in for monthly monitoring. In a few months, we'll be able to expand our testing to other live subjects."

"Good," Bennett said, a knot growing in his stomach.

The doctor laughed. "Don't worry, we'll still need you. As we make progress, being able to compare our progress to the original subject will be helpful. The money won't stop coming."

Bennett smiled. "The money has helped. It's been more than generous."

"It's nothing less than you deserve. You're helping with a scientific advancement that will change the world!" He patted Bennett on the shoulder. "Let me get the injection."

"Okay." As the doctor left the room, Bennett noticed a folder on the corner of the desk labeled PROJECT: NOAH. That was unusual. Usually the desk was clear, no folders or other materials left in case he got the urge to snoop. He knew he shouldn't look, but he was curious. It usually took the Doctor fifteen minutes or so to get everything together. Reaching for the folder, he opened it and began to read.

The first page had a single line of type: *Genesis 6:5-8*.

Flipping through the pages, he found what he was looking for.

ABSTRACT

NOAH is an effort to restore the earth to its purest state by purging the wicked elements of humanity. This will be done by protecting those who have found favor with a broad-spectrum antidote (EUCHARIST) while unleashing biological and chemical warfare (BRIMSTONE) upon the rest of the world, resulting in chaos which the favored will rise above to create a pure earth (BABEL) under the leadership of YAHWEH.

Bennett sat the folder down and exhaled. "This will make Hitler look like Mother Teresa," he whispered to the empty room.

Billions dead, ugly deaths, pain and suffering sweeping the world as society broke down and anarchy took over.

That's what the injections were. They weren't testing something positive, an advancement. The antidote flowing through his veins would change the world, but not for the better. It would wipe out most of the population, the "unfavored" from the planet, leaving only a few chosen elites.

Toward the back of the file he found a list of project members. Law enforcement, congressmen, government officials. Enough power to stop him if he tried to tell anyone what he'd learned. And he had no doubt he was meant to know it. The folder had been left there to recruit him.

What to do? What to do? He put the folder back on the desk and waited for the scientist to return.

~ * ~

The body lay on the floor in front of the desk, the head twisted to an impossible position. An empty needle rolled away from his hand, the last of the injections needed for John's immortality.

Now it was time to deal the man's research a crippling blow.

Taking the dead man's pass, Bennett moved through the building until he found the laboratory. Plenty of flammable things to work with.

He spread them through the building, giving special care to the Doctor's office and body. Computers were doused, doors propped open, vials smashed, everything he could do to ensure complete destruction of the project.

It was dark when he stepped into the lobby and set a match to the trail of alcohol he'd set as a fuse. The flame rose, moving quickly into the rest of the building as he got in his car and drove away.

~ * ~

"There's a mountain of evidence against you," the Public Defender had told him. "Three different security cameras saw you leaving the scene, your bank records showed massive transfers into your bank account, and your appointment was in the Doctor's online calendar. The District Attorney isn't even offering a plea deal, he's going to send you to the gurney and ride the notoriety to a Congressional seat."

"Good," Bennett had said, the fluorescent lights bouncing off the ugly concrete walls of the jail's visitation room.

"Good?" the defender had asked. "Good? You're a dishonorably discharged soldier facing murder charges with no possible defense, yet you expect to plead not guilty? How is any of that good?"

"It just is," Bennett said, drumming his fingers on the table as he looked out the window.

~ * ~

The Warden put down the phone, then knocked on the door to the executioner's room again. Opening it, he stuck his head in. "The Governor has granted a thirty day stay of execution. Don't touch anything. A team is going to come in and go over everything with a fine-toothed comb."

Standing, the executioner shrugged. "I'm not sure what they think they'll find. I've done everything I know to kill his ass."

~ * ~

Two years later, Bennett sat with his attorney in a courtroom. The first month after his failed execution had been spent being poked and prodded by medical professionals, trying to determine why the lethal chemicals hadn't worked. After that came two years of legal battles, the State and Bennett's lawyers each laying out a case for killing or releasing him.

Now, the honorable Judge Wyatt M. Kershaw had a decision to

make. Could the state attempt to execute Bennett using a different method, or did the failed first attempt mean his sentence had been carried out, and he should be a free man.

"All rise!" the Bailiff called, and the rest of the courtroom stood. The gray-haired woman was there, standing with the priest behind the defense table, while the victim's family gathered behind the prosecutor. A bald man in a suit sat with them, sunglasses covering his eyes even though he was indoors. In the back of the courtroom, the reporter hovered. This case had made her career, gotten her into the running for a Pulitzer and earned her several job offers from newspapers in bigger cities.

Judge Cutshaw didn't betray his thoughts as he entered the room and walked to his chair. "Be seated," he ordered. Opening a folder, he looked up.

"The heart of this issue is simple. The state contends that because Mr. Bennett's execution was not completed, they have the duty to continue trying to kill him until they succeed. Mr. Bennett argues that since the sentence was carried out, in some cases exceeding the state protocols, the sentence has been fulfilled, even if the desired result was not achieved. To continue to allow the state to try to kill him, indeed, to hold him in prison at all, is double jeopardy and false imprisonment." The judge paused to look at both tables, the two grim attorneys at the prosecutor's table, surrounded by those hoping Bennett would finally get the same sentence he had given their loved ones, the well-dressed, pro-bono defense attorney who had taken the case for the sheer variety of it, and finally, Bennett himself, sitting tall in his chair, looking straight ahead, trying not to get his hopes up. Behind him, the priest reached out and placed a hand on his shoulder. Bennett jumped, but regained his composure.

"It is the opinion of this court," the judge continued, "that the sentence of execution by lethal injection has been carried out under state law."

Behind the prosecutors table, a woman screamed as those around her burst into tears. A man tried to embrace her, but she stood, pointing a finger at the judge. "You call this justice?"

The judge banged his gavel as the prosecutors and other family members worked to calm her. "Order! I understand the emotion inherent in this case, but I will have order!" Waiting, he watched as two others led the woman from the courtroom before continuing.

"As the sentence has been carried out, even if the desired result was not achieved, the state has no right to continue to hold Mr. Bennett. He is to be freed."

John threw his head back as the gavel came down again, closing the case. "Thank you!" He mouthed to the ceiling as his attorney lifted him from the chair in a hug. Across the aisle, the prosecutors shook their heads.

"My full decision will be filed by the end of the day," the judge told them, standing. He shook his head as the bailiff began to announce his departure. not wanting to disturb the celebration at the defense table or the grief of the victim's family as he left the courtroom.

~ * ~

"It's so nice to have you home," Frieda Bennett said the morning after his release, reaching across the table to take his hands. A tear came to her eye, and she smiled. "You've been given a new life! What are you going to do with it?"

John looked down at his bowl of oatmeal, then shook his head. "I don't know. It's been years since I was imprisoned, and it feels like the whole world has changed. It'll take some getting used to."

"Oh, John, you'll be okay. You've always been so smart, so adaptable."

A smile crept across his face. "Yes, mother, I'm adaptable."

"What's so funny?"

"Nothing, nothing," he said, leaning back in the chair. "You just reminded me of someone I knew before I went to prison."

"Oh. Well, maybe you can find them now that you're out." She looked hopeful, like she wanted him to resume a normal life.

He sighed and shook his head, as a knock on the door interrupted their conversation. Walking through the house, he pulled it open to find a man in a suit standing there. He was bald, with dark sunglasses and an even darker car parked on the street behind him.

"Can I help you?" Bennett asked.

The man smiled. "Mr. Bennett, my name is Yahweh, and we have some unfinished business."

~ * ~ * ~

Joe Stout is an east Tennessee based emerging writer who focuses on short stories and flash fiction. He dabbles in many different genres, but his favorites are historical fiction and horror. Although he used to be a mortician, he now works the night shift in a plastics factory, a career he thoroughly enjoys. His short story "Breaking Souls" was published in the Non-Binary Review and his story "Trick or Treat" was published in the Wicked Shadows Press Anthology "Halloweenthology: Trick or Treat."

When he's not writing, he enjoys exploring the Appalachian Mountains, visiting museums, geocaching, and spending time with his children (Atlas and Wednesday).

You can follow him on Facebook at Joe Stout Writing or at Instagram @joestoutwriting.

The Price

Dana Bell

Heart pounding, gasping for breath, Keira lifted her shaking hand, wondering why she hesitated before knocking three times. She paused, before rapping three more times, glancing nervously behind her.

For several terrified metras, she feared no one would answer. Maybe she'd used the incorrect code.

The door creaked open revealing a girl with long dark hair, eyes the color of the sea Keira had only heard stories about. "You seek safety?" Her green dress shimmered in the breeze.

"Yes," she managed, unsure if the girl would allow her inside.

The other motioned Keira to enter. "Come." Turning to go down a narrow hallway she ordered, "Follow me."

"Thank you." Her eyes darted to an opening revealing cushioned seats, with several potential customers waiting. The second floor provided the living for the entire house.

Another opening gave Keira a look at the busy kitchen, bustling with cooks and servers. Pots boiled and enticing smells reached her nose. Her stomach rumbled reminding her she hadn't eaten all day.

"Wait here." The girl pulled aside a gauzy curtain.

Alone, she examined the small room. A desk with barely room for one person perched on the stone floor and another chair sat before it.

Trembling, Keira eased into the other chair, trying to still her hands on her coarse skirt. What if no help was given? Many had told her to come here. The owner helped anyone who came. What if, because of whom her pursuers were, she got turned over to them? What if she had to continue hiding on the dangerous streets, easy prey for those who would betray her for the reward offered?

"You seek help."

Keira started. She hadn't heard the Charon enter. A furred head of white with black stripes, tucked into a flowing gown of glittering gold, with the dark eyes of a predator. Unwillingly she gazed at the sharp claws, knowing they'd been made to kill. The tail tip peeking from under the fabric seemed out of place and she barely controlled her laugh.

"Yes," she squeaked.

"All who come here are offered aid," the large feline reassured Keira.

She swallowed. "You may not want to help me once I tell you who's after me."

A slow blink. "Tell me."

"I'm in so much trouble," she blurted out. Nervously she pushed back her dirty black hair.

A paw she knew she should be afraid of lightly touched her shoulder. "You are in no danger here."

Not wanting to tell her whole story, Keira took a deep breath. "The Arkon's hunters and—" She had to force the words out. "The vampires."

A snarl filled the small space. "The reason?"

Focusing her gaze on her folded hands she replied, "I have something they both want."

"Per the Arkon's decree vampires are not allowed anywhere in the Five Systems or Borders. Only their own world." A claw tapped the desk. "What do you have child they would risk certain death to retrieve?"

How could Keira explain? Even she wasn't certain how it had happened. An accident of birth? Genetic manipulation? Although she doubted the latter. Simians only designed animals. Nothing intelligent.

"I don't know how to explain."

"Vampires hunt." She heard the clicking of claws. "Never under my roof."

Knowing she'd placed everyone in the brothel in danger, Keira rose. "I should leave."

"You stay," the owner firmly told her. "Keya!"

The girl reappeared.

"Make certain our guest is served a meal and given a place by the fire for the night."

"At once." Keya gave the Charon a half bow.

The feline's eyes again rested on Keira. "When you have eaten and rested, we will talk again."

"What about the hunters and vampires?" She couldn't see how they could be kept out.

"They never come for what is offered here."

~ * ~

After a meal of hearty vegetable soup and fresh bread, Keira settled on the mat she'd been given and pulled a heavy blanket over her body. Warmth from the kitchen crept into the sleeping alcove, along with the scent of fresh baking and spicy dishes served to their guests.

The brothel, owned by Tamzin, had the reputation of being the best in Arkona. Her guests varied from the nobles to the Rovers and many others. On the streets, it was known to be the place for a free meal and a warm place to sleep when needed.

The Charon seemed quite certain Keira's pursuers would not come there. While Tamzin hadn't exactly said so, for some reason none of those after her would dare enter. She wondered why.

The hunters, an honor passed down from one generation to the next, had been among the Arkon's guard for centuries. They had the training to deal with the vampires, if they dared to leave their home world and come to Aris. Their violation would cost them their head.

How could she possibly be worth the risk?

~ * ~

Cannon shifted trying to ease the pain in his side. Blood trickled from the wound and he could smell the life-giving fluid escaping. No matter how much he fed, it never healed. What he needed hid below, if the report made to him had been accurate.

"You're bleeding again." Duncan moved to inspect the tightly bound bandages. His travel companion and bodyguard frowned. "They need to be changed."

"There isn't much to be done." His eyes watched another patron knock on the door below. A brief light flared in the darkness as they entered and he blinked at the brightness. "You're certain this is where the trail ends?"

Duncan chuckled. "I'm your best tracker."

Cannon nodded. A fact he well knew.

Pointing his chin Duncan continued, "I know the scent." With a growl he pulled Cannon away from the roof ledge. "Hunters," he warned.

One of the hunters boldly knocked on the brothel door. "Open up," he ordered. "We demand entrance."

The door partly opened and a girl replied, "You are not welcome here and entrance is refused." She began to close it.

"Don't you dare close that door!" the hunter bellowed.

"Per our charter, approved by the Arkon himself, we have the right to refuse or welcome all who knock."

"We have the right to search!"

A snarl answered their demand and a feline shape replaced the girl. "Unless you wish to explain to your master why you have new scars—"

He heard the hunters gasp.

Long claws extended from huge paws. "I suggest you leave as you are not welcome."

The pair back off. "We'll be back."

"I doubt it." The door slammed shut, the echo twirling down the alley.

Grumbling, the hunters left. He doubted they'd go far.

"Interesting twist," Duncan observed,

"We wouldn't fare any better," Cannon reminded his companion. He groaned as pain lanced through his side and more blood escaped.

"We don't have much longer."

"I know." Cannon slumped against the brick ledge. "I need to feed."

"I'll find you easy prey." Duncan rose. "Stay here until I return. While I'm gone, change your bandage." His bodyguard vanished into the night.

Cannon closed his eyes, changing out the blood-soaked bandages. His action wouldn't make any difference. His time was running short.

~ * ~

Morning dawned gray with drizzling rain. Keira watched it through a back window overlooking a lavish garden. Flowers opened guzzling the liquid, while branches bowed to the onslaught.

"My private place," Tamzin commented behind her.

Keira turned, holding a hot cup of tea. "It's lovely."

"Reminds me of home." The Charon's eyes met hers. "We must talk."

She followed the feline back to the tiny office and took the chair. The cup she held steadied her hands.

"Hunters tried to gain entrance last night," Tamzin told her. "Those who watch for me reported two vampires on the roof top across the alley."

Keira wanted to slink away. "I've brought you trouble. I'm sorry."

"Trouble I can handle." Tamzin rested both paws on the desk. No claws extended. "What I wish to know, is why both seek you."

How could Keira explain? She didn't really understand it herself. "I don't know how to…"

"Several Rovers owe me favors and it would be simple to smuggle you off world. However, I will not collect unless I am made to understand why they should take the risk."

Keira hadn't expected a way to be offered for escape. She finished her tea and set the cup on the desk. "My blood."

"We all have blood."

"Not like mine."

The Charon waited, looking regal in a simple long black tunic.

"I don't know how they found out," she began since she couldn't think of a good place to start.

Leaning forward, Tamzin's eyes held interest.

"You know the hunters developed a poison to kill vampires?" She waited for the Charon's response.

"I've heard rumors."

"Seems my blood counteracts the poison."

"So that is the reason the hunters seek you." Tamzin tapped a claw on her desk. "The vampires as well."

Keira nodded.

"My observers found blood on the roof. One of the vampires is injured."

She felt faint knowing why they hunted her.

"You will not be easy prey." Tamzin rose. "You will stay with me until I speak with our local healer."

"You have a wise woman here?" With their limited numbers the presence of one on Aris surprised Keira.

"I have many secrets." Tamzin seemed amused. "Keya needs

help with a few tasks today."

"You want me to help her." No doubt the price for keeping her safe until she could be smuggled off world.

"If you do not mind."

She didn't mind at all.

~ * ~

Duncan found them lodging when the rain started with a couple who owned a small inn. They only housed maybe a half dozen lodgers at any one time. For a price they provided clean water, rags and bandages. Most important they asked no questions.

Cannon had fed on a man who lived in the alley, only taking enough to take the edge off his hunger. Leaving bodies would bring the hunters straight to them. In his weakened state, he'd quickly lose his head.

"You should rest," Duncan reminded him again.

He glanced at his companion. "I'm fine."

"You're lying." He pointed at the bed. "This place is free of vermin."

"They don't like us."

"True."

Knowing he wouldn't win an argument with Duncan, Cannon removed his cloak and crawled under the heavy furred blanket. He didn't need the warmth. Still, there were times when remembering what it had been like when he'd been human, appealed to him.

How many orbits ago had it been? He couldn't remember.

~ * ~

Keira wiped her sweaty brow as she washed dishes. There weren't as many as she feared. Eating wasn't the most popular activity. Everyone who currently resided as staff or those in need of help, washed their own.

The heat of the kitchen, pleasant while she slept, seemed unbearable despite the chilly day. A couple of women and a small child mixed ingredients for bread and chopped vegetables dropped into a kettle of hot broth.

"When you finish there," Keya instructed her, "you may take a rest." She held an armful of linens.

"Thank you."

The girl disappeared in the direction of the back stairs. No doubt to change the much-used beds. She dried the last pan, hung it on the hook overhead and returned to the alcove. Tamzin treated her help well. Most of the nobles only gave their servants mats and nothing else. She'd never understood why.

Not that her life had been one of comfort. Her mother had turned her out during her sixteenth orbit. "You're old enough to make your own way." her mother had said as the door slammed behind her. She heard the cries of her siblings and hoped they would not be sold to the mines. The work given to children caused early death or so she'd heard.

She'd taken work where she could find it. Slept on the streets when she had to. It had taken a long while to work her way to Arkona and she'd hoped to fare better. Then came the night she did not remember. The painful bite and then nothing. When morning came she'd lived. An injured creature, or so she'd assumed by the red stains on its clothes, stared at her with wonder. He'd reached for her and she'd run.

How long ago had that happened? She had no idea. All she did was run and, still, they pursued her.

Keya stuck her head in. "Tamzin wants to see you in her office."

"I'll be right there." She took a deep breath, wishing she had a change of clothes or even the chance to bathe. Too afraid to ask, she went to talk to the Charon.

~ * ~

"I have spoken to the healer," Tamzin told her as Keira entered the small office. "You are of interest to her."

Not in a good way Keira surmised. She tensed, preparing for the worst.

"She will be here momentarily."

"The healer is coming here?" Such a visit surprised her.

"Those who serve me have found the vampires," the Charon continued.

"I don't understand."

"The healer will explain."

A woman entered the office wearing a hood over her head and draped in common robes. Keira heard the curtain drawn closed, wondering at the other's importance.

Tamzin bowed. "Your Grace."

Eyes of green looked at Keira. From inside the robe a satchel appeared. The healer drew out several instruments and motioned for her to sit. "I will make this quick."

Securing a tight band over her upper arm, the lower part was cleaned and something pierced her skin. She gasped at the unexpected pain. "What are you doing?"

"Taking samples of your blood." Several small vials were filled and a larger one. "The vampire will be given what he needs and be escorted off world."

"Why?"

"He is of importance." She didn't explain further. Her blood samples disappeared into the bag. "The captain of the *Aralon* would be best," she told the Charon.

"He is currently a guest." She called, "Keya!"

The girl poked her head in careful not to look at the healer.

"Find Captain Talu and tell him I have a favor to ask."

"At once."

"Good choice," the healer agreed. Her gaze turned to Keira. "Be safe on your journey. May the Great Mother watch over you." She slipped away.

"Who was that?" Keira asked.

"One it is best you forget you ever saw."

~ * ~

Cannon woke famished and knew it would only be a day, maybe, before the poison killed him. Blood soaked his bandage and the bed. He groaned.

Duncan moved to his side. "You're worse."

A light knock on the door startled them both. His bodyguard rested his hand on his dagger.

"I don't have to hunt." He opened the door and gasped.

"Who is it?" Cannon managed as pain radiated when he tried to sit.

"My lady sends her regards." The woman stepped inside. From her garments he knew she worked in the Arkon's palace. "She has sent a gift."

"Why would she help me?" Cannon demanded, puzzled by the unexpected assistance.

"There will come a time when she will ask for your assistance. You will answer." In her hand she held a large vial of blood. "You are not to pursue the person from whom this blood came."

"But—"

"You would argue?" The woman calmly looked at him. "Drink this. Heal. Leave undetected."

"The hunters?" Duncan asked.

"Diverted." She smiled slightly. "You were reported to have left the city for the mines."

"Inventive." Cannon accepted the vial, his hand unsteady.

"My lady knows a day will come and she will call on you. You will come to her aid."

The woman left.

"Unusual price," Duncan commented, a frown creasing his face.

"One I might regret answering." Cannon removed the cork and drank the blood. Fire flashed through his veins and he cried out. He felt Duncan's hands on his arms forcing him to be still.

He tumbled into burning darkness.

~ * ~

Days later, Keira relaxed as the Rover captain opened the hatch. "Welcome to Marllon."

She peered out nervously. "You're sure they're expecting me?"

The Rover chuckled. "Here they come."

Two bright colored dragons landed, folding their wings against their backs. One had purple scales accented with gold tips and the other black with silver.

"They're a mated pair."

"Oh." She swallowed. "They won't eat me, right?"

The Rover chuckled. "We don't taste good."

She stared at him.

He shrugged. "They have an odd sense of humor."

"You're sure I'll be safe here?"

"Safer than you would be anywhere else."

The purple dragon moved closer eyeing her.

"That's Zathena. Her mate's name is Zohl."

"Are those cats?"

"Mated pair of Felcats."

She'd heard about the intelligent cats, but never thought she'd see any.

"They'll keep you safe."

Straightening her back, she walked down the ramp, hoping she didn't regret her new life.

~ * ~

Home again, Cannon stared out into the darkness. Somehow the Charon had managed to smuggle the woman off world, and no one knew where she'd been taken. Their one chance at a cure for the hunters' poison gone forever.

"You look better." Duncan entered his room.

He turned away from the window, the night breeze filled with the scents of flowers, which bloomed only at night. Cannon kept a simple room, with a bed, a place to store his clothing, and a door leading to a room for bathing.

"I'm still surprised I lived." He didn't remember much after he'd drunk the blood. When he'd awoke, Duncan sat next to his bed. The bodyguard had never explained how they'd gotten back to their planet.

"I don't think you would have been asked to come when called if killing you had been the goal."

"Agreed." Dressed in robes, as was his right, he glanced outside again. "I dread the deal I made."

"I wonder what we are committed to." Duncan came to stand beside him, dressed in traditional armor.

"When the time comes, I suppose we'll know." He sighed. "No sign of the woman?" He'd hoped they'd find her, but suspected she'd been well hidden.

"None."

He closed his eyes and shook his head. "We dare not leave our home world again. The risk is too great."

"Perhaps when the Arkon—" Duncan began.

"Don't say it. I do not wish to give the ruler any excuse to destroy us as a race."

"Of course."

Silence fell as Cannon searched his thoughts. He'd survived being poisoned. For that he gave thanks. The woman who held their salvation—gone. He knew he had little choice but to accept events as they had happened.

Their planet was their prison.

They would never be allowed to escape.

~ * ~

The Princess Royal examined the blood and smiled at the findings. She knew why the woman's blood destroyed the poison the vampire had absorbed. A rare protein and a mutated genetic sequence. The woman had been born with the change.

Tucking her findings into a secret vault and sealing it, so no other would find what she'd discovered, she left her lab. She had duties to attend to, a blurry future she needed to see and had not yet had a clear vision to prepare for.

As she stepped into her audience chamber, she stared up into the sky. One day, she would need the help of the one she'd chosen to save. He would answer the call. Willingly or not. Her price had been clear.

The lives of many would depend on him.

She'd burn their world if he failed.

~ * ~ * ~

Dana Bell is a Colorado author who has two cat overlords, who want her full attention anytime they're not napping or eating. Many of her stories feature or star feline characters who take the reader on a delightful adventure in the wilds of space, a celebration of the holidays or anywhere else they please. Her books *Winter Awakening* and *God's Gift* plus a short story collection *Bast's Chosen Ones and other Cat Adventures* are great examples.

She has edited numerous anthologies, too many to list, and launched the careers of many up-and-coming authors.

Her own stories have appeared in more anthologies than she can remember and she's an award-winning poet.

Writing paranormal romance as Belle Blukat, her first novel, *Blood Bride*, yes, there are cats in it, is available along with short reads on KU.

Hobbies include doll houses, arranging flowers, and collections that got started due to roaming the aisles in thrift stores. Also enjoys traveling and then adding them to her tales.

Up and coming releases include *Winter Emergence* and *Homefall Search.*

Virgins R Us

A.P. Sessler

Russell Hadley felt like a canned sardine in the office he had previously considered spacious. If not for his commitment to fashion, he would have removed his dark purple vest and long sleeve shirt to cool off. The number of film crew and burning hot lights crowded around him made the air so thick it justified cranking the central air to MAX, but nothing could ease the discomfort of the dozen eyes glued to him. He began to wonder why he even agreed to the interview. *Exposure. Free advertising. Oh yeah, that.*

He looked into the calming eyes of his son in the framed photograph atop his desk and tugged at his silver necklace. He took a deep breath and glanced down at the lav mic on his lapel. It was tempting to adjust it, but he'd already been scolded once for doing so.

Directly across from him sat Allison Carter, journalist for the live televised news show *Off the Press.*

Jerry's handheld camera panned the office to give viewers at home a look Allison had taken at least three times herself: plants, tribal masks, and the larger-than-life company logo behind Russ. But what her gaze fell to was the large arcane symbol on the floor encircling the desk.

"I'm curious about the circle beneath us. What does it represent?" she asked, and the camera took a look, too.

Camera 2 was trained on him with Diego behind the lens.

"Protection," Russ said in a matter of fact tone. "Though salt works, too."

"What does any of that protect you from?" Allison asked.

Mickey stood behind Camera 1, capturing her likeness in three-quarter view.

Russ smiled. "Customer complaints."

"Which would appear at a minimum considering your sales figures," she noted.

Russ shrugged. "Business is good, and we'd like to keep it that way."

"Who would you consider your demographic?"

"Religious cults."

Somebody snorted, but Allison didn't miss a beat. "Seriously?"

Russ nodded. "You also have your smaller, unaffiliated covens or individuals interested in summoning the Dark Lords."

She gestured toward the company logo behind him. "So, why the name?"

He did a quarter counterclockwise turn in his chair and looked over his shoulder at the VIRGINS R US logo, as if he hadn't ever seen the thing. "Well, I'd think that was obvious," he said and swiveled clockwise back toward her. "We are the leading exporter of virgin blood in the continental United States, and I'm Russ. It's a play on words."

"Some have suggested you are, in fact, involved in the sex slave trade."

"I'm sure you've followed the money. We don't exactly do business under the table."

She fought to hide her contemptuous sneer. He did not hide his.

"As I'm sure you've discovered, all our suppliers are both of legal age and consent," he added.

"At least that's what the paperwork says," she tried to trump him.

"And their social security numbers and birth certificates, if you care to dig that far."

She tried another angle of attack. "Do you feel your company exploits women?"

"We're an equal opportunity employer, whether male, female or fluid—all our welcome."

"Would you say the demand for CIS male and trans-female blood is equally that of CIS female?"

"The only real demand is that it be virgin blood."

"Why is it so important the blood be from a virgin?"

His expression twisted into one of surprise. Wasn't the answer obvious? "You can't go summoning a demon from the Fourth Order using spoiled product. It's just plain stupid and downright dangerous."

Her head tilted slightly, as if she were about to shake it in disbelief. "How do *you* define 'virgin?'?"

Elbows on the table, he twirled a finger in the air. "Well, a few demonic entities are real sticklers over broken hymens, but the rest are only concerned with penile-vaginal penetration, which is great for our gay and lesbian suppliers as they can enjoy a satisfying sex life and still earn a living."

Arms folded across her chest. "So demons are part of the patriarchy?"

"Are you kidding?" He laughed. "They *created* the patriarchy."

Legs crossed to match her arms. "Isn't that then a form of discrimination against women?"

"If anything, demons discriminate against heterosexuals, which is why we experience a high turnover in that regard. So again, our gay and lesbian suppliers really have the greatest chance at having a successful career."

"How exactly do you guarantee the 'purity' of your product?"

"We don't. We provide a disclaimer on every package as well as point of purchase. Customers waive their right to pursue any and all legal action against Virgins R Us LLC, its founders or suppliers resulting from improper use of our product. Product is sold *as is* and no warranty is given that blood is in fact virgin blood."

"But your company's called Virgins R Us."

"LLC."

"Yet you assume no responsibility to verify your suppliers are in fact virgins?"

"We make every reasonable attempt to do so. You can't force someone to tell the truth."

"What do you consider 'reasonable attempt'?"

"Our application asks, 'Are you a virgin?'"

The sneer she had withheld thus far finally made a cameo appearance. "Yes, we actually have an application, printed from your website," she said and produced a manila folder, and from that, a form. The handheld got a closeup over her shoulder. She pointed at the line of text. "Right here."

He gave an affirmative "Mmm hmm" and "Yep."

"That's it?"

He ran a finger over several lines. "It also asks for Name, Address, Social Security, Phone—"

"Yes, I see. And here, at the end it warns prospective suppliers of the 'potential consequence' for committing fraud or perjury. The consequence being 'death'?"

"Yes ma'am."

"And that seems reasonable?"

"It's implicitly implied they will come to a horrible and violent end should they lie about their sexual status."

"When you say 'implicitly' what do you mean?"

"We say 'If you lie about your sexual status you will come to a horrible and violent end.'"

"That's not implied. That's forthcoming."

"Eh, *to-may-toes, to-mah-toes.*"

"While your product may be sold *as is* how can buyers be sure you aren't off having sexual relations with your suppliers in some back room?"

"Are you kidding? Only a fool would throw away that kind of money."

"You claim you've never had sexual relations with your suppliers?"

"None whatsoever."

"Then why did your wife, now ex, file for divorce and full custodial rights of your son?"

His smile had all but melted, perhaps from the heat generated by the sudden and rapid grinding of his teeth. "We had as they say, irreconcilable differences."

"Court papers mention a gag order."

He nodded, too angry to speak.

"So in your own words what would you say took place between the two of you that would cost you your house in Beverly Hills and full custody of your only child?"

He squirmed in his seat. "I'm not at liberty to discuss that."

"Through the Freedom of Information Act we were able to procure this," she said, sliding a document out of the folder and across the desk, "from the Los Angeles County Superior Court that records a charge of child abuse—"

His eyes bounced across the text. Fingers tightened around the document. Paper crinkled. Dave winced at the unpleasant sound piping through his headphones.

"How did you get this?" Russ asked, his face red. "That's supposed to be sealed—"

"So you admit to abusing your child?"

"This interview is over."

"Why don't you just answer the question."

"That's the last answer you're getting. You can see yourselves out."

"I only have one more question for you."

"Not interested."

"I was hoping to ask about a specific supplier."

"That would violate our confidentiality clause. Now leave before I call security."

She placed the folder on his desk and pulled a paper-clipped stack of papers out, a black and white photograph of a woman on top. "What do you know about *this* supplier?" she asked and slid the papers before him.

The lens of Camera 2 extended to get a closeup of the sweat beading on his brow. It was like blood to a shark for Allison, who had to purse her lips to conceal her gloating smile.

Russ' gaze settled on the picture. Its subject seemed familiar, though he wasn't exactly good with faces. "Where did you get this?"

"Do you recognize her?" she asked, her chin resting on her hand like a yearbook photograph.

An unblinking gaze met hers. "Can't say I do," Russ said.

She reached for the photo to take it back, but his hand rested heavy upon it. His tight-lipped smile stated he wasn't about to release it.

She quickly folded her back-length hair into a ponytail and slid on a pair of glasses. "What about now?"

His smile shrank into a worrisome pucker. The woman in the photograph was clearly the same as the reporter. "This concerns me," he said, the utmost sobriety in his voice.

"Are you afraid customers will find out you're selling unverified product?"

"I'm concerned because you don't look like the virgin type."

Her brow leaped. "You were convinced three months ago."

He tapped the photo. "I mean the *real* you," he said and pointed at her. "You look like the type who landed this role on a producer's couch. Am I right?"

"Your sexist comment and how I arrived at this point in my career aside, I am qualified enough to report the truth and expose fraud."

"We're done here," he said and pressed the intercom button. "Security."

Mickey gestured for her to keep going, his gaze fixed on the camera's viewfinder.

"I have another surprise. Right this minute my *spoiled product* as you so eloquently describe it, is being used in a ceremony to summon one of your alleged 'demons'."

His face went bloodless white, fittingly so. He mashed the intercom button again. "Security! Get your ass in here now!"

From the opposite end of the building Mike pressed the walkie button. "On our way. Over," he said and faced his partner. "Jeez, what's his problem?"

"Suppose we better double-time and find out," Terry said, picking up his pace.

They turned a corner to enter the long hallway. At its end lay a brood of snaking cables that spread from electrical outlets into the office.

Russ sat on the edge of his seat, eyes glued to the ritual unfolding at some undisclosed location upon the monitor, specifically facing him for the reaction shot. Blue flame shot up from the floor in a circle and in its center stood a hideous thing of odd-numbered limbs and numerous eyes.

It looked around the room long enough to locate the summoners.

Russ pushed his chair away from the desk.

"Do you have a problem being confronted with your own fraud on national TV?" Allison asked.

Russ spun the monitor toward her. "That's the problem, missy."

"Don't call me—"

The screams from the monitor silenced her. She faced the screen to see the demon make mincemeat of her coven-for-hire.

"Holy shit!" Mickey said.

Dave swung the boom mic counterclockwise a second too late to avoid picking up the expletive.

Allison faced Russ.

He stood. "You need to get out," he said and held the intercom button down. "Secur—"

His voice was tripled from the walkies as the doors opened.

"What's the problem?" Mike asked, hand on his pistol.

Russ pointed to her. "I want her out, now!"

The guards stepped toward her but were confronted by the film crew.

"Nuh uh," Mickey said. "You touch her and I'm filing a lawsuit, she's filing a lawsuit, not to mention the network."

The guards eyed one another to assess the current threat level, and setting their sights on Mickey they wrestled him into handcuffs. Jerry and Diego captured the action as it unfolded.

The building shook, the mere movement enough to freeze every soul in place. A shower of motes fell from the ceiling like an ominous, portent rain. When the dust settled the melee commenced.

"Fine. I'll take you out myself," Russ said.

He circled the desk and grabbed her by the wrist.

Toya picked up a reflector and pounded him with it. "Let her go!" she shouted.

He swatted the contraption, sending Toya off balance and stumbling back into the back light which toppled over with a loud pop and the room darkened by a third. Russ took a slap from Allison, but refused to release her.

Jerry laid down the handheld to aid in the ladies' defense, Diego still filming on Camera 2. Russ wasn't prepared for Jerry's cracking punch to the nose, which immediately drew blood. Allison pulled free, now ignored as Russ went for Jerry right over the protective circle's line when a large, unwelcome guest burst into the room, tearing the doors off their hinges.

All eyes turned toward the demon, including Diego from behind Camera 2, who was the first to experience the monster's wrath. A limb shot forth like a frog's tongue, right through the viewfinder, into Diego's eye then whipped back with a profusion of blood and brain matter.

Diego dropped to the floor.

Toya made it to her feet and threw the harmless reflector, then raised the felled light pole as a lance to jab at the demon. A single of its limbs wrapped around the pole and shoved it straight through the girl, pinning her to a wall.

"Forget the cameraman! Shoot the demon!" Russ yelled.

Mike swiveled on a knee to engage from a kneeling position. His first shot unfortunately caught the escaping Jerry in the neck. Terry rolled onto his back. The two guards fired off a few shots collectively before being sliced into halves—one lateral, the other medial—in a blurring radial saw-like motion of limbs that sent their steaming innards spilling, shooting in every direction.

Not paying attention to Toya's grave mistake, Dave shoved the boom at the thing, getting himself pinned to the ceiling but he immediately slid off the metal pole face-first onto the floor. He managed to crawl two feet toward the doorway before getting his head squashed to pulp by the demon's enormous cloven hoof.

Allison screamed at the sight of her slaughtered crew.

Another whip-like motion and Russ found his arm gripped by a spidery hand.

"I got something for you!" he shouted and went for something beneath his vest, but he would never reach it.

The demon lashed at him with all its hooks, slicing him to ribbons like paper through a shredder.

Mickey, whose attempt to play dead throughout the attack had thus far been successful, was all the more convincing when a well-placed hoof found his spine.

Allison screamed again, not intending to draw the demon's attention. It found her between the standing key and fill lights, perfectly illuminated in all her vulnerable, paralyzed fear.

A tongue flicked. The scent was hers, alright: the blasphemer who dared summon it with her foul, unconsecrated oblation. It stepped toward her, sending her back first into Russ' desk and tipping the father-son photo over. It raised a leg to step over the circle but a blue flame shot up and sent it retreating, step by snarling, growling step, cursing in its infernal tongue, backwards till it passed through the doorway and out of sight.

She would be safe…for now.

~ * ~

Blood. Everywhere. Not the premium kind sold for top dollar. Not the kind desired for rituals nor the kind that could save life, not when sprayed on ceilings and splattered on walls, dripping from desks and chairs and plants and fixtures, coating the floors in a wet sheet of red.

She hyperventilated, trying her hardest to catch breath that eluded her grasp like a greased pig. Fingers fumbled as if searching through darkness in search of the chair Russ had sat in only moments before. She collapsed into the seat, not at all comforted by its deep cushion or reclining springs.

The doorway stood before her like a portal to Hell itself, a Hell she now knew was every bit as real as Russ' outlandish supply and a demon's demand.

"What are you doing?" she asked herself, barely aloud. "Don't just sit here, dummy! Get out!"

She stood and made her way toward the exit, first stepping from the confines of the protective circle, then over an arm, a leg, a torso, each movement a nightmarish labor that took the breath right back out of her.

"Close your eyes. Keep moving," she whispered and took another step, her foot snagging on some corpse. A cry escaped her lips and she opened her eyes to see what had hindered her movement: the mangled face of her longtime friend and lighting grip Toya.

Allison doubled over in grief-stricken pain. She raised a trembling foot and planted it on the opposite side of the body. Her other leg was following suit when a paralyzing-deep growl came from somewhere in the building.

It's still here? Of course. Why wouldn't it be? Go back! The thoughts raced through her mind, but the reflex, the instinct to retreat malfunctioned. *Move! Hurry!*

Another growl. This one closer.

"Move, damn it!" she scolded herself, though she knew precisely what kept her stuck to the floor.

It was during her expose on illegal tiger poaching in India. A village fed up with suffering casualties to man and beast due to tiger overpopulation took matters into their own hands despite the threat of fine and imprisonment from authorities.

Conditioned by her Western mindset, she took the government's side to spin man as the true aggressor, condemning villagers as brutal and inhumane for taking the initiative to protect themselves from future attacks. While researching the subject of human-tiger encounters, she was informed of the tiger's supposed ability to paralyze prey with its infrasonic roar.

While she found it hard to swallow, she witnessed the effect firsthand when escorting a band of poachers. The gory image which had so haunted her since that day now seemed, by comparison, as tame as a common house cat.

It came back to her in vivid, violent detail: Ahead of her lie the animal rights activist who acted as guide and translator, still alive though pinned to the earth beneath an enormous tigress. Allison made a futile effort to shoo the beast away when it released the fabled roar. She was frozen in her tracks. The only bodily function that seemed to operate was her bladder, which promptly emptied its contents down her leg.

Knowing she was no longer a threat, the tigress took the guide's head between its jaws and with an effortless bite, cracked his skull, killing him instantly.

Allison watched helpless as the mother dragged the man's body to a dead tree her young waited beneath to dine on the fresh kill. The journalist would have stayed in that very spot till the tiger came back for her had the poachers not picked her off her feet and hurried her to safety.

The experience changed not only her but her story. She had determined from then on to always get to the truth of the matter, vowing to expose swindlers, scammers, government corruption and overreach. Yet here she was, so sure she was doing just that with Virgins R Us, and now she knew, much like Hell was real, she was wrong. Again.

Something else occurred to her: if she was wrong about Hell, maybe she was wrong about God. The invisible Man in the Sky. The Flying Spaghetti Monster. The crutch of the intellectually vacuous and tool of the power-mad, the Grand Pusher of Divine Opiate.

"Please, God. Please, Jesus. Just let me—"

Her nerves awoke. She let out a gasp and retreated to the safety of the circle double-time and took back the breath she had lost in deep lungfuls.

"Thank you, thank you, thank you," she said with eyes raised.

"Now, find something useful! There has to be something in here," she told herself and began sifting through the drawers of Russ' desk.

Her face twisted with disgust when she opened the long top drawer to find a half-eaten sandwich and packets of ketchup, mustard, and mayonnaise. A ringed coffee cup and a small, open jar some crystalline substance that obscured other contents, so she removed them and placed it on the desk. In the back of the drawer sat a streaked butter knife alongside a pickle spear atop a paper towel.

"Who lives like this?" she asked aloud, quickly reminded it was the type of guy who sells blood and gets himself killed by a bloodthirsty demon because of her. She faced the mutilated corpse just long enough to make eye contact. "I'm so sorry."

She pushed the drawer shut and tried another. Scissors, sewing thread and needles. A wax doll with a lock of human hair stuck to its crown. An assortment of candles lying flat: red, black, white. A pack of matches. A piece of chalk.

Another drawer contained two leather-bound books: a King James Bible and a much thicker, larger book bearing the strange symbol on its cover like the one drawn on the floor beneath the desk.

That symbol! The circle itself seemed to provide protection, but Russ hadn't reached for either of the books. Would either have saved him?

She pushed the drawer shut and leaned back in the chair, closed her eyes, and prayed for the second time since she was a child for a way out of the mess she had so foolishly made.

~ * ~

"The road to Hell is paved with good intentions," the voice said.

"Huh?" She opened her eyes.

It was a dream, but whose voice was that? Fuzzy vision gave way to the cruel reality she had nearly forgotten. She shut her eyes again, hoping it was a nightmare though she knew better. Had she truly been able to sleep amid such devastation?

Reluctantly she opened her eyes, careful not to look at the floor even though the reflective, red surface skirted the bottom of her vision like rising floodwaters. She focused instead on the entrance. She knew the demon had left through it, and she was certain it would return, though she wondered why it couldn't just materialize where it wanted.

She looked to Russ' corpse wishing she could get an answer—he was in no mood to talk.

Her gaze returned to the doorway. She stared so long it appeared to grow larger and larger until it filled her vision. She became aware of her breathing, her inhalation a short rise and exhalation a steep drop.

Something dropped from the ceiling in the hall, making her start. When her breath and heartbeat resumed, she saw it was the hinged cover of the fluorescent lighting. The lights flickered out and she found herself retreating to the far end of the circle, still careful not to step over it should she expose herself to harm. With the desk between her and the door she felt only slightly safer, though in truth the circle was the only thing that provided any protection. She opened drawer after drawer in search of some weapon.

A silhouetted figure stepped into view from the hall. She found the pair of scissors and clutched it to her breast as if in pledge to a flag.

The figure ducked to avoid the swinging cover then paused to look at the massacre left in the demon's wake. "What a mess," he said.

He stepped over a mangled body and stood beneath the track lights which illuminated his form in full.

"Larry?" she asked and placed the scissors on the desk.

When he faced her his back went straight. The sandy-haired and over-tanned producer wore an immaculate three-piece suit that was far too clean and crisp to occupy what amounted to a supernatural crime scene. "Allison. You don't look so good yourself."

She couldn't believe it. "What are you doing here?"

"Well, you put out the highest-watched episode of nightly news in television history and don't show up for work the next day, one can't help but wonder if another network gave you a better offer."

"What? Highest watched?"

He smiled. His perfectly straight, white teeth made many wonder if they were real. "The Nielsens love you. We love you. All of America loves you. They're talking Emmy. You even have the Amazing Randi ready to give you his million-dollar reward."

"The who?"

"Never mind. Just know you turned the whole world upside down last night."

"How?"

"You just gave them proof of the supernatural. There's no such thing as an atheist now because of you. Now come on. Let's get you out of here."

"But what about Toya and Mickey and Dave? Jerry? Diego?" She saw each one in her mind as she mentioned their names.

Larry looked at the pile of meat on the floor. "That who that is?"

She whimpered.

"Forget 'em, babe. You're going to the big leagues."

"Shouldn't we wait for the police or something?"

"They're right outside, waiting to come in. They just need you to get out of here so they can go to work. Now come on."

"But—"

"Come on. I'll take you to Spago's. You have to be starving."

The sight of viscera, not to mention the odor, made her stomach turn. "I can't even think of food."

"Fine. We'll have drinks. That'll calm your nerves. Now hurry!" he said, his open hand waiting for hers.

She looked around the room at the carnage one last time, then closed her eyes to shut it all out. She placed her hand in Larry's.

"That a girl. Let's get out of here," he said and took a step toward the door, pulling her one foot out of the circle.

She remembered the folder on the desk, filled with a month's research. "Wait! I forgot something," she said and stepped back, pulling Larry's arm, sleeve and cufflink across the circle, revealing it to be one of the demon's spidery hands.

She gasped. "Larry?"

He looked at his black hairy arm and glared at her, lips peeled back to bear gritted teeth. "Come, Allison. Join your friends, so you can all rip in pieces," he laughed.

"No!" she yelled and reached for the scissors. She plunged them into Larry's neck which only seemed to make him angrier.

"Did you really think that could protect you?"

Of course not. Why should it? If only there was some real protection beside the circle. Russ' words replayed in her mind: "Protection. Though salt works, too."

Salt? Was that what the jar on the desk was filled with? She thought it was merely a condiment. She leaned back with all her weight, stretching to reach the jar on Russ' desk, hoping to God it wasn't sugar or coffee creamer.

The Larry-demon gave a tug and pulled her back upright, one foot outside the circle.

She did what she had always wanted to: stood her ground and kicked Larry—or his doppelganger anyhow—square in the family jewels. "How's that feel, you slimy son-of-a-bitch?"

He smiled. "Good. Do it again, Mommy."

She extended two fingers. "Sure thing, Daddy," she said and

poked him in the eyes.

A demon hand shot up to nurse the injury. She used the opening to lean back, this time reaching the jar, which she emptied onto the demon's arm from his wrist up to his shoulder and neck.

Tendrils of acrid smoke rose from bubbling flesh, as if it had been doused with hydrochloric acid. The hand released hers and for the second time the demon exited the room.

She turned and swept the coffee cup and folder off the desk, then lay on her back.

"I won't fall for that one again," she said and closed her eyes to rest.

~ * ~

A noise disturbed her half-nap. She raised her head to view the entrance. All clear. But she knew better. She stood and circled the desk to rifle through the drawers a second time.

"Has to be something I'm missing. He wouldn't have left himself so vulnerable. Not if he believed this stuff."

Half-eaten sandwich. *Check.* Empty mayo packs. *Gross.* Sewing kit. *Crafty.* Voodoo doll. *Freak.* Books. *Okay.* Two more drawers. Battlelites action figures. *Nerd.* Divorce papers. *Divorce papers?*

She knew his ex had filed for divorce and won full custody of their child. She took the framed photo of he and his son off the desk to examine it closer. It looked unnatural: a weird, soft look. It clicked.

The photo had been enlarged—shot at a lower-resolution, its pixels interpolated during resizing and blurred to minimize the obvious effect. Russ must have cropped out his ex. What was the kid's name anyhow?

She went back to the divorce papers and skimmed through the text.

"Forfeits full custodial rights…Child…Son…Age 7…Russell Faustus Hadley."

Faustus? Damn. What kind of father…Never mind. Exactly the kind of father Russell Hadley would be. What a jerk. With his neck beard and his pompous, pretentious, purple vest and gaudy jewelry.

She glanced over to the mutilated corpse, her eyes settling on said gaudy jewelry around his neck. The cameo brooch looked familiar, or at least similar to the company logo. She looked over her shoulder at the giant silver emblem on the back wall. There was one striking difference: the illustrated jewel on the wall was black, while the jewel on Russ' mangled neck was red. Onyx black to ruby? That made no sense. Onyx. Blood-red ruby. Blood. Red. Could it be?

She leaned just far enough out of the circle to take Russ by the feet. She pulled and immediately the right leg came off in her hand and sent her falling on her butt. She went to scream but vomit bubbled out. She wiped her mouth with the back of her hand and tossed the leg outside the circle.

Taking hold of the left leg in both hands she pulled again, hoping it wouldn't separate from the shredded corpse as its partner had. When his hips came over the circle she spun his body counterclockwise and dragged him in so she faced his upside down head.

She raised his head to take the necklace when it snagged on the thick piece of torn skin just above his severed carotid. Her stomach heaved and she almost vomited again. She chose instead to undo the necklace latch and put it on her own neck. She looked at the jewel and rotated the brooch 45 degrees clockwise and center. Was that a tiny bubble of air moving inside? It wasn't a jewel. It was blood!

And considering Russ Hadley's business it could only be one kind.

His words echoed in her mind. "I got something for you," he had said when the demon attacked. The scene rewound to time-sync with the voice. *Roll sound. Roll camera. Speed. And action!*

She screamed at the sight of her slaughtered crew.

The spidery hand wrapped around Russ' arm.

"I got something for you!"

Russ reached inside his vest…

Wait. Did he?

She raised the bloody vest expecting to find a harnessed gun. Nothing. If he had one he wouldn't have been shouting for security. He wasn't reaching inside his vest. He was reaching for the necklace, more precisely the blood-filled brooch.

Was it an offering? Could it have appeased the disgruntled demon offended it had been duped by defiled blood? Was this blood so special it could guarantee peace? She turned the brooch over.

Her eyes went wide. *The monster!* Engraved in silver was the name: R. Faustus Hadley. His son. His seven-year-old son. No wonder he tried to offer it—and no wonder his wife divorced him!

The blood of a child could only be virgin, and only the purest of.

The timing could not be more perfect.

The demon ducked to enter the office. Drool oozed from its jaws and hung in long, viscous strands. It stepped toward her.

"It is time, my dear. Either you step from that circle and die like a saint, or remain inside and burn like a sinner," it said, and if she should doubt the veracity of its offer, it turned a spider palm upright, where a blue fire appeared and extended into a three-foot flame.

Her eyes rose to the ceiling where several fire sprinklers were mounted. Its gaze followed.

"Don't bet water against the fires of Hell, girl. You'll lose every time."

She cleared her throat. "I have a proposition as well."

The monstrous mouth would have appeared to smile. "Do tell."

She held the brooch forward. "The blood of a child. A true *virgin* child."

It gasped in orgasmic awe and reached for the brooch, only to have it pulled out of reach. "Give it to me!" Its smile most certainly became a scowl.

"I get to walk out of here unscathed. Forever."

It was about to speak when she added "And I want my own show. Bigger than Oprah, Barbara Walters, and The View."

The drool increased ten-fold, pooling at its feet in a half-inch deep puddle that sizzled into green steam upon touching the circle. It nodded. "Done. Now give me!"

The brooch exchanged hands.

~ * ~

Faustus sat with his mother on the plush, microfiber sofa. He pulled down the collar of his Fortnite tee-shirt and pushed his brooch aside to scratch the two-inch scar over his heart.

"Stop," Becca said.

"But it itches," he whined.

"I know. Just try to ignore it," she said and unconsciously stroked the matching, red-jeweled brooch between her breasts.

A great blue flash of light came from behind, drawing their attention to the large bay window.

"What was that?" he asked, leaning over the sofa.

Blue smoke rose from gaping cracks around the disturbed grave of Russ' beloved and quite virile cat Crowley.

"Nothing. Finish your cereal," she said and approached the bay window.

Becca remembered when Russ came to her with a silver bowl filled with their child's blood. The bastard had the nerve to suggest they each wear a brooch filled with it as a means of protection—an insurance policy against the Dark Lords. She silently consented and had a jeweler craft three matching brooches with fillable glass chambers, only she made certain Russell Hadley would never be near or possess any part of her son ever again after what he had done.

She stroked the brooch. "That's what you get for cutting my son," she grumbled. "Now burn in Hell."

~ * ~ * ~

A resident of North Carolina's Outer Banks, **A.P.** frequents an alternate universe not too different from your own, searching for that unique element that twists the everyday commonplace into the weird. When not writing fiction, he composes music, makes art, and strives to connect with his inner genius. He lives with his dog Kahlua and a nameless cat of unknown origins.

Praxis Tattoos

Jamie Zaccaria

The bell over the shop door dinged, and Erin groaned inwardly. All she wanted to do was close up early so she could go home and make dinner with her girlfriend, have some lazy wine-induced sex, and sleep for a solid eight hours. Depending on what this customer was about to ask her, those plans could be out the window.

Erin walked out from behind the violet curtain to see who dared be her late-night walk-in. Her scowl immediately softened when she spotted a petite young woman, wet from the rain, standing awkwardly in front of the counter. Her dirty blonde hair was tangled around her face, and black makeup smudged around her eyes.

Shit, Erin thought, *she can't be any older than 18, maybe 19.*

"Welcome to Praxis Tattoos. How can I help you?" Erin asked smoothly, knowing this woman didn't have an appointment as no more were scheduled for that night.

"I, um, heard you could…" the pale girl stammered, looking down. Erin waited patiently. She had a feeling she knew what was coming next. The girl looked around as if checking that no one else was in the store. Then she looked right into Erin's eyes,

"I need a Fury Special," she said, then followed it up after a slight pause, "Please."

Erin sighed deeply and then moved to the front of the store, where she promptly switched the Open sign off and locked the door. She turned towards the young woman and motioned for her to follow as she walked back behind the curtain.

"Have a seat," she said, pointing to the large black pleather chair. The short woman scooted up, her wet clothes making eerie noises against the material.

"Are you sure you want this? You understand what you're asking for?" Erin asked, looking straight into the woman's hazel eyes.

"Yes. I'm absolutely sure," she responded, with no trace of fear left on her face.

Erin nodded, biting back the urge to say sorry. She learned a while ago it wasn't her place to apologize to these women or to pity them. It was her job to provide justice.

"How much?" the woman asked.

"Don't worry about it," Erin replied, her back already turned as she gathered supplies.

"Are you sure? I…" Erin interrupted her by gently grabbing her arm and laying it on the table.

"You're good," she said firmly but not without compassion.

The girl watched Erin set up her tools, her eyes tracing the serpent tattoos that snaked around the older woman's arms. They were intricate images of black mambas, chosen because they were some of the world's most dangerous snakes. Black mambas were surprisingly quick in size and possessed venom known to kill humans. Erin also loved how the inside of their mouths were black, as if they themselves were poisoned.

Erin grabbed the small scalpel that sat in a jar of antiseptic. She dried it off before turning on a burner and holding the tiny blade over the fire. After a few seconds, she removed it and extinguished the flame. After waiting twenty seconds for the blade to cool, Erin turned again towards the blonde.

"This will be quick, I promise," she said, making a small slice in the girl's forearm, watching the blood quickly seep out of the cut. She placed what looked like a matte black test tube under the wound, collecting the few drops of the red liquid.

Then, swift and efficient, Erin cleaned the cut and secured it with a bandage. And with that, it was over.

Erin carefully carried the vial to the counter, where a bowl of ink awaited. She tipped it slightly, whispering under her breath in a language the other woman could not make out. Erin swirled the scarlet droplets into the black ink with a small blade, breathing her magic into the potion.

Watching the emulsion, she wondered if it was different for her mother when she mixed women's blood into her pen ink years ago. Did pen ink mix differently with blood than tattoo ink? Did they swirl in the same direction, meld into one dark color in the same way? Did her mother feel the same harsh emotions as herself when she pulled the dark liquid across the paper, creating poetry out of pain?

Erin turned towards the young woman, handing her a yellow

legal pad and a pen. The blonde looked back at her quizzically, prompting an explanation,

"Write down the name and address." The woman took the supplies and complied, handing the pad back once the man's information stained the paper.

"Okay," Erin said, bringing finality to their transaction. The girl got down off the chair but stood a moment longer.

"That's it?" she asked.

"That's it." A beat.

"Thank you."

Erin gave the girl a tired smile. "Get home safe." The other woman headed to the front of the shop, while Erin packed the blood and ink mixture with her portable tattoo gun, gloves, and other supplies into a well-worn backpack.

Moving to the front of the shop, Erin unlocked the front door so the young woman could exit the store. She took a few breaths, then threw on a black raincoat, covering the scarlet mini-dress she wore over patterned tights. She closed the door to her shop and locked it, pulling her hood over her half-shaved head as she started walking to her car.

Plugging the address into her GPS, Erin wondered why she even bothered. She already knew who she was going to see and exactly where he was. It was part of her gift. But still, she wanted to get in and out as quickly as possible and just maybe salvage some of her night.

Driving through the dark, Erin listened to the wipers on the windshield and half-stared at the drops coming down the glass. Her thoughts turned once again to her mother and hers before.

Her grandmother had been a painter but not a professional one. Her works were too dark, too damaged to interest anyone in the art world. When women came to her in the dark of the night, she took their blood the same way Erin did, mixing it into her paints and creating portraits on canvas. She freed women from their pain through brush strokes the way her daughter did through her pen.

Erin pulled up to a townhouse that sat back from the street. She did not worry about being seen; her gift would provide cover. Her black combat boots splashed through puddles, spilling the dark water across the pavement as she approached the door.

Knocking twice loudly, Erin waited for a beat before kicking the door in and entering. A shirtless man on the couch jumped up, spilling his beer and cursing in surprise at seeing the pink-haired woman in his living room.

"Hello, asshole," Erin greeted the man, walking inside and shutting the door behind her.

"What the hell do you…"

"Sit down." Erin interrupted him, and he did as she said, his muscles under her command. His mouth opened in surprise, but she ignored him and his questions. Erin pushed the man down on the couch.

Erin unpacked her tattoo kit methodically, knowing he was still struggling to regain control of his muscles to fight her off. She swallowed down nausea as the man's vile aura spilled out. This was a particularly rotten one.

Turning on the tattoo gun, Erin moved toward the man's bare chest. She whispered in the same mysterious language as before as her tattoo gun moved across the man's skin. She was not being careful or precise, and despite his paralysis, he cried out in pain.

As she pulled the vibrating needle across his skin, chest hair singed, the smell adding a sense of urgency to the air. She carved the words into his chest using the blood ink, focusing on transfusing the pain and the shame that was mixed inside.

Erin willed the man to feel everything the young woman was feeling. She willed this monster to inflict himself with the young woman's pain, sucking back in all the hurt he had caused. This was her retribution, and the woman's, and womankind's.

Every time she completes the ritual, her fingers tingle with feminine power. She worked to contain her wrath and focus it on her task. So long as women come to her with their pain, she will continue her work doling out vengeance as her mother had done before her and her grandmother before that.

Erin turned off the gun and sat back on her heels, admiring her work. This design was especially large and painful. She flicked her eyes upwards to look into the man's (the criminal's). Tears were welling, and she saw the torment written across his face as the woman's experience was transferred into his consciousness.

Erin exited the couch, packed her kit, and headed for the door. She turned back once more to the man,

"Night night," she said before walking outside and back into her car. Erin checked her phone and saw it wasn't quite bedtime yet. She was only 20 minutes from home and might have time to enjoy a nice meal with her girlfriend after all. Splendid.

~ * ~ * ~

Jamie Zaccaria is a wildlife biologist by trade and writer by pleasure. She currently works for an ocean exploration organization, serves as the Wildlife and Endangered Species Committee Chair for the New Jersey Sierra Club, and writes fiction in her spare time. She has been published in over a dozen anthologies, online magazines, and her debut short story collection Lavender Speculation was released October 17, 2023 by Wildling Press.

She lives in NJ with her furbabies and wife.

Mortal Karlat

James Tallett

Blood sprayed into the crowd, blessing those rich enough or lucky enough to force their way to the front. As it pumped, the executioner lifted the decapitated corpse high, pouring the cruor upon the ecstatic crowd. The head, unneeded now, rolled gently away, the dire imprecations it had spouted in its last moments frozen upon its face.

A frisson of energy shot through the executioner, jolting his thoughts, and Karlat, for that was his name, glanced to where his hands held the corpse and saw a drop of blood, sliding down his fingers. *The touch of the gods.* That burst of energy, that moment, was why people fought and clawed and paid their way to the front of the crowds. It was a gift, the divine touch, wrung forth only with proper ceremony and holy sacrifice, and it meant everything to the people of Ashrai.

And to him, it was same old, same old.

He did not receive the blessing of the gods every day, but as a primarch executioner, it was his frequently, more frequently than many of the exalted priests who sat above him in the temple hierarchy. They received allotments, a crimson gift held back from the sacrifice, but the potency was diminished, never as strong as when the hot gift of life was still within it.

Because of the way society about him scratched and scrabbled to feel one more drop, he felt like little more than a seller of narcotic leaves, always peddling the next high. It wasn't that he didn't believe—he believed firmly in the gods, having felt their presence throughout his life. And it wasn't that he thought society was failing—the Ashrai could honestly claim the title of "empire", should their ruler be so inclined. More it was an exhaustion in himself, a feeling he was no longer truly alive.

The gods had poured their will into and through Karlat for so long and so often that without it, he didn't feel he had a purpose. They had gifted him a body strapping and tall, easily able to wield the ceremonial akrafena for the executions and carry the corpses that resulted. They had given him a mind more than suited for the role which he had undertaken. But now…

Now he wasn't sure of himself.

So, he raised the corpse high one last time, the symbolic raising to hell, that barren place beyond the sky and cloud, and let it thump down, discarded. It would be taken away and butchered, the meat served to the needy, those who could afford no better than corpse flesh.

That was not for him. And so Karlat turned, his doubts circling him about, and disappeared into the sanctuary.

~ * ~

The next day was a day of rest for Karlat. It left the priest with the opportunity to head into the city, explore the markets, find a brothel. But none of those things truly appealed to him, not in the way he felt a passion for philosophy or art. And so he disappeared into the catacombs beneath the temple, home of once-holy statues now all but forgotten.

The icons and relics housed there had formerly possessed meaning to the people of Ashrai, each stained or painted a deep crimson, emblematic of the blood that had flowed over their surface. But for one reason or another, be it age, damage, a changing of imagery, they had been put away, left to decay in silence and darkness.

It was with a soul lantern held high Karlat was forced to visit them, for only it provided enough light to truly see the details worked into their forms. A torch would have been easier and less exhausting, but the flickering reddish hues it cast were poor illumination for what he wished. So, he had bound himself to the lantern, its glow the slow seepage of his spirit into the material world, and now found himself before a particularly grotesque effigy from which limbs sprang hither and thither, ending in claws, suckers, mouths, any form of rasping protrusion that could drink blood.

Once, it had supposedly done so, animated by the will of the gods to provide a channel for souls to be given into their divine grace. But now it was little more than an ugly, stained, relic from the past. And yet for all that, Karlat found it uniquely appealing. He had sat and stared at this piece before, sometimes for hours, because it stirred within him questions about the nature of his religion…who he was.

Was the deity who created and inhabited this statue the same as the one to whom he sacrificed men? Was the little frisson of excitement that passed through him from a creature like this? Or was it from the much more humanoid forms which adorned the temple walls aboveground, their marble conspicuously newer than that of the surrounding structure? In the hearing of other priests, these would be dangerous questions to ask—there was only so much one could challenge the hierarchy, and changes accrued slowly, over time. An overt belief the priesthood might have broken with the past, throwing the history of Ashrai into doubt, would be swiftly squashed.

Yet…

Karlat filled the chamber with a nasal chant, building in words and intensity until his voice reverberated off the overhanging stone and echoed back, a chorus of one. Until he stopped, and only the dying imitations sounded. They, too, then ceased.

Replaced by the sound of a blade slicing flesh. Karlat's dagger cutting deep into his palm, blood welling thick and fast as he placed his hand atop a stone mouth.

The only thing I'm going to get out of this is a sore palm and questions I'll have to lie about.

His blood dripping into the mouth, he waited.

With each passing moment his hopes faded. Perhaps this statue was awoken by other means, other rituals. Perhaps it had been fed the soul of an unbeliever, not a believer. Whatever the case, the inhabiting god did not answer his call.

He turned to go, suddenly disgusted with the strange carvings and himself. Why did he seek solace in the past and not the future?

There was the faintest rasp, stone upon flesh, and then his hand was bound about with limbs, cold, firm, forceful, strong, *hungry*. They pulled at him, a tongue lapping from the depths of the statue, forcing itself into the wound, satiating itself with blood.

I've done it! But…what have I awoken? Can it speak? Is it sane? Will it interrogate me for being unfaithful?

As those thoughts and more roamed through the priest's mind, the statue rippled, the flesh less polished rock, more…leather.

And wholly alive.

Where once there had been a statue now stood a writhing twisting mass of limbs, a god given form and flesh. Lacking such niceties as a proper face, the creature still managed to encompass Karlat with a leer, more than one mouth watching him with predatory desire.

And yet, for all that it tried to intimidate him, Karlat felt nothing. Perhaps he was too world-weary, or perhaps he had spent too long in his contemplation of these gods, locked away in their stone vaults. But now that he had one alive and in the flesh, he merely circled it, eyes fixed upon a form not seen in many ages.

"What are you?"

A GOD, MORTAL CREATURE. YOUR GOD.

"No, I think not. I think you are something we once worshipped as a god, you and your kind. And one day, we threw off your yoke, finding our new gods in the blood."

AND YET YOU WORSHIPPED US WITH BLOOD. BLOOD GIVEN FREELY FOR THAT MOMENT OF POWER, THAT QUIVERING OF THE HEART.

"What do you know of such things, trapped down here in your forgotten hollow?" As he continued to pace and stare at this creature, Karlat cursed himself. Why had he not foreseen the icons down here might have been little more than vultures preying on the Ashrai?

A head, or indeed many heads, tilted, and a fist of invisible force lifted Karlat, slamming him high into the wall of the chamber and pinning him there. And with it came the same surge of energy that flushed through him when his akrafena slashed through the neck of a sacrifice.

A GREAT DEAL MORE THAN YOU BELIEVE, KARLET. ME AND MINE ARE BEYOND YOU.

Given he was currently being ground into the wall by a mystical force from a creature barely resurrected, the priest was forced to acknowledge he had misjudged the situation. Badly.

Although…

Struggling against the wall, he dragged himself down it until he stood on his own two feet, scraped and battered from the energy constantly shoving him into the unyielding architecture. *It would appear my doubts were somewhat unfounded. But now that I've woken this being, what happens next?*

With an abrupt halt, the pressure on him stopped.

"Why did you let us lock you away in graven images, forgotten? It seems a strange thing for a god."

***YOU* DID NOT. *WE* DID. WE HAD FED, LONG AND LUSTILY. GORGED ON POWER, WE RETREATED FROM THIS BURDENSOME PLANE AND LET OUR THOUGHTS WANDER EXISTENCE UNDISCOVERED.**

A roiling, hacking noise echoed off the walls, born of too many throats slightly out of time with one another. Before that horrible noise even Karlat's iron will quivered, and he doubted himself.

Until he realized the deity he had awoken was *laughing*. Laughing at him, at the world, at its own existence, at the joke of being dragged from contemplating the cosmos by the uncertainty and curiosity of a single mortal Ashrai.

"Why return at all? Surely you could have ignored my call, the touch of a soul's blood upon your lips?"

CURIOSITY.

"You are not immune to that desire?"

NO, MORTAL KARLAT. WE ARE NOT. WHY SHOULD WE BE? SHOULD WE ROAM THE WORLDS UNCOUNTED, YET TAKE NOTHING AWAY, EXPLORE NOTHING? OR SHOULD WE REVEL IN VARIETY, IN DISCOVERY, IN THOUGHTS NEWBORN?

Questions abounded in the primarch executioner's mind, ones that had entangled him during those long ceremonies in which he stood stern faced and bored. But to voice them…would the divinity smite him down for his impudence?

"You have learned then. Learned and become more. Can I learn and become greater, too? Discover a purpose lost in a sea of blood and repetition, politics and dreariness?"

GODS DO NOT GIVE PURPOSE, MORTAL KARLAT. THAT IS THE CURSE OF THE LIVING, TO THINK LIFE HAS A PURPOSE.

"We exist for no reason? What kind of creation have you and yours engendered!"

ONE THAT IS INTERESTING FOR US.

"You tell me the purpose of my life is to be nothing more than a source of entertainment for you? That is all that creation is?"

BUT OF COURSE. FOR WHAT OTHER REASON WOULD WE CREATE A THING THAN THAT IT BE OF USE TO US?

"Because of the beauty of the creation, and to see what creatures do when given a goal? You created the flower to breed and spread beauty, the wolf and the coyote to hunt, the bird to soar through the air as it travels from place to place. Each of these has a reason for their existence, inherent in the very thing they are. And yet, for those of us who are of a higher order, who are not constrained by our very nature into one task, you have given us only what we can create for ourselves. Why is that?"

WE GAVE YOU RELIGION.

Karlat stopped and stared at the writhing statue of flesh. *Religion? They gave that to us…in order that we might feed them. We're* cattle. *We're their food source.* The priest then tilted his head to the side, a revelation coming upon him. *And yet they have not needed to feed upon us in a long time, and we have replaced them with other gods.*

"You did. But why? You do not need to feed upon us, at least not much. You have explored the worlds uncounted, as you so name them, without ever returning to this one to sup upon the power of the blood."

YOU ASK SO MANY QUESTIONS, MORTAL. THAT IS A TIRESOME THING. BUT YOU ALSO AMUSE US, WITH YOUR SEARCH FOR UNDERSTANDING OF THAT WHICH IS BEYOND YOU. WE ARE GODS, LITTLE MAN, AND OUR ACTIONS ARE OF SUCH DISTANCE FROM YOUR OWN THAT TO EXPLAIN THEM WOULD BE TO RENDER THE EXPLANATION MEANINGLESS.

Karlat looked upon the figure of this creature, this former god of the Ashrai, and pondered. Clearly, the creature was capable of power far greater than a mortal, and had transformed itself from stone to flesh with but the merest taste of blood, far less than that of even the single corpse he had bled upon the crowd. And despite its earlier demonstration of strength, it had shown no real desire to harm the priest, more the mannerisms of a cat toying with its prey, with something so far beneath it, it was without meaning. What this meant…he would have to think upon it greatly.

Bowing, Karlat performed the obeisance proper from one of his station towards the gods. "If you permit, I shall return when I have clear thoughts upon what to ask."

That awful sound, that cacophonous symphony of bitter amusement, spilled down on Karlat, bathing him in dissonance and pandemonium.

YOU MAY GO, MORTAL. BUT DO NOT THINK TO SUMMON US AGAIN. YOU WILL KNOW WHEN YOU ARE SUMMONED.

With that, the writhing of the statue ceased instantaneously, the leathery tendrils and maws of ravenous teeth freezing into stone once more, but this time caught in that moment between spotting prey and devouring it, poised to leap upon whatever came to it next. The posture was a threat, Karlat knew, a reminder of what would happen should he fail to heed the warning he had been given.

Struggling to comprehend all that he had been told, but perhaps most of all that the gods in the temple above might be no more than ingenious fakes to replace these darker, older, gods who clearly existed, Karlat grasped the soul lantern, feeling once more the pull of the mystical object on his spirit, and went forth to resume his duties.

~ * ~

Karlat gave himself over to the study of philosophy and the collection of power, both blood and otherwise, and throughout the years he rose from his position of primarch executioner to the very pinnacle of the priesthood, the leader of all the faithful, the sanguinary. He had won his role through debate, and through means less honest than that, sometimes employing the gift of the gods as a weapon against his rivals. He had felt unclean in those times, and had assuaged his feelings with devout fasting, hermitage, and flagellation. Each of these bouts had rendered him more holy in the eyes of the general clergy, and when it came time for the last appointment, he was carried forward by a swell of approval.

In all that time, however, he had had no contact with the gods, heard not a thing from them. There had been days where that frustrated him, unable to commune with the deity who had led him to his purpose, but he consoled himself with the knowledge there was to be a reckoning one day, a debate between mortal and immortal that would answer the questions he had to ask.

Many times had he gone to the depths of the catacombs, soul lantern in hand, to sit and stare at the graven image of omnipotence, knife at the ready. But never had he broken the commandment to wait, and while many arguments had spun back and forth between imaginary debaters in his head, those words had not been spoken aloud.

Even as the rippling body of youth passed into the strength and knowledge of middle age and thence to the wisdom of seniority, Karlat did not falter in his behaviour. He did, however, start writing down his thoughts, his beliefs, what he had once experienced and now understood to be true. These words he kept secret, hidden from those around him, for he was uncertain how the priesthood would react to the knowledge the gods of the public spaces appeared to be little more than a cleansing of things hidden much deeper in the archives.

Even so, he laid the groundwork, assigning those he trusted to compile grand historical epics and other treatises, works that, of necessity, required delving into forgotten sections of the temple and seeing what lay below. Some priests who had read the old tomes less carefully than others were horrified at what they found in those depths, and counselled the artefacts be destroyed, lest they have a corrupting influence. Others, and it was amongst this number Karlat carefully placed himself, decried the thought of despoiling holy objects, for did they not still have the touch of the gods upon them?

With careful and reasoned arguments, he overcame their objections and slowly and subtly returned the old gods to the knowledge of the priesthood, although not that of the general public. To change out the benevolent beings with whom they were familiar for the awful and powerful creators who appeared to be true deities would likely have been a step too far. Even so, by the time the decrepitude of old age had crept over Karlat's body, knowledge of the true gods of the Ashrai had become commonplace and accepted, and belief in the new beings had all but disappeared.

While perhaps the changes and the drive that had pushed Karlat to such ascension were unnecessary or fated to happen with or without his intervention, when at last the images of the graven gods began to creep out of the catacombs and into the public spaces, he knew he had achieved his life's work.

~ * ~

I shall never hear from the gods again, shall I? Karlat lay abed, extreme old age having stolen his health, his sight, and now the last remnants of his breath. *But I shall go to my passing knowing that for all the questions raised, I found answers within me. And accomplished much.* He smiled, inwardly only, for his face lay frozen in the rictus of a grimace left by a stroke.

He lay alone, within the chamber of the sanguinary, having been left in that post throughout the passing of the years, a mark of respect from the clergy who had replaced him in all but name. And while many had clamoured to be about the bed, seeking to capture the last words of a great man, he had banned them all many years ago. He would find no peace in the chattering of men, but only within the contemplations of wisdom.

As his heart counted down its final beats, Karlat let his mind wander over problems of philosophy and religion that had confounded his mind, but most of all, that one, sole, solitary conversation with the divine. Had those been the words of a god? A demon? A creation of the Ashrai using talents long forgotten?

To this day, despite all Karlat had done in their name, he was unsure. He had accepted those as the words and promises of a divine being, as knowledge from a realm beyond their own, had taken it all on faith. A faith that never answered the question of whether it was true.

Karlat's last thought, as breath rattled in his lungs and his heart slowed to a final pulse, was *At least I'll know the answer soon enough.*

~ * ~

WE DID NOT FORGET, IMMORTAL KARLAT.

~ * ~ * ~

James Tallett is a dedicated lover of fantasy and science fiction, both in book and computer form, and a person who has memorized entirely too many song lyrics for his own good. When he's not found at his computer for work, he's found at his computer for fun. Or outside on the mountains near his home, hiking, skiing, and being harassed by his collection of terriers. Who keep demanding he write a book about them (he never has).

The Iron Née of Life

The short, bloody story

Anka B. Troitsky

"To tell a good fairy tale, you must study science a little..."
From the homework of the 13-year-old schoolgirl.
Essex 2008

It has been almost fifty years since we took over the Earth. Now we are your rulers, masters, top of the food chain. We used to be fictional characters for you. We did not exist. You thought you imagined us, put us into horror stories and fairy tales. You called us creatures of the night and other stupid names. You had a very wrong idea about what we look like. Pale skin, red eyes, long fangs and bat wings? Ha! Now you know...and you don't laugh any more.

You learned we do not lurk in the mist or fly across the night sky. Garlic doesn't repel us, and fire is a convenient escape method. We neither fear sunlight nor wear Halloween costumes. We are perfect in our disguise. We adapt our anatomy to look exactly like humans, and the only giveaway would be that we don't age, don't sleep, or eat your food. Since we prevailed, we don't have to pretend any longer. Well... We love castles and palaces, though.

The collaborators among you are always useful. We would not succeed without them, but lucky for us, those believers would do anything for the hope to be turned and become immoral too...I mean, immortal, of course. Fools. They still wouldn't accept that they couldn't become immortal, precisely because they were already immoral. After a bite, a fanatic and faithful servant sometimes goes on for a few years, happily convinced he or she is one of us. But then, we must terminate such insignificant fools to stop the truth from coming out. After that, no one would even remember they existed. So much for immortality!

It is true we drink your blood, but only as a starter. The rest of you is used for tissue renewal. When we are done with you, not only is every cell of your body integrated to support ours, but also every atom of a particular element is decayed inside our digestive system. The process is similar to natural decomposition and radioactive decay but more rapid and directed inwards. The real secret of our immortality is the energy from turning iron into cobalt inside our core. It does not work with just any iron bar or ore. It has to be part of haemoglobin.

Don't make that face at me! I never thought you would understand, but this should answer other questions you might have. Why don't we reproduce? We don't need to replace ourselves. We don't die; the same few who arrived with me four centuries back are still here. Some have been dormant since nineteen forty-five. Good for them, since something started to happen that we did not plan for.

~ * ~

The man in front of me is not very appetising. He is old and dry and chewy, and the salty perch on his plate probably looks the same to him. Seafood and fish were our first food on this planet. The blood of other animals used to work, but now their flesh gives us the most painful cramps. Some humans taste terrible now, too, but we must rely on them as a last resort. That is, if we don't find the solution to our problem.

"Why are you talking to me?" The man asks.

I know he is hungry. Fish is a privileged food in his position, but tonight, we are dining together. The thinnest tube of the blood transfusion device stretches from his broad collar to my long, intricate bracelet, covered with controller buttons. Drop by drop, his blood becomes mine. We don't have to make a mess by biting into their necks anymore. No need to waste precious liquid. I have no intention of draining him. I just need my share of supper.

"How old were you during the *Global Referen-doom*?"

"Thirty-one".

"How did you manage to live to over eighty? You are the oldest man I have seen in our livestock."

He doesn't answer, but I am not that interested anyway. I am trying to figure out how to get his agreement to help us. He doesn't believe in turning and has no reason to sympathise.

We are studying each other across a table. I wonder what he is thinking. His face does not express anything but hate and weariness.

Finally, he coughs and asks, "What do you want?"

"Your knowledge and expertise. Do you know where we came from?"

"From hell."

"Others might believe that, but not you."

"Do I need to care?"

"It might help you to understand."

The man's face changes for the first time. A minor change. His brows relax a little. I wonder what question forms in his mind, but he does not ask. Instead, he nods, "Go on then."

I look at him again. He is old and will die soon. It is safe to tell, especially since the last time I did it was in that interview some time ago. The man wrote things on the paper I burned, and he was young and delicious.

"We are from a faraway world that does not exist any longer. Four ships went in different directions, searching for a planet with promising characteristics. I don't know what happened to the other three, but our ship was pulled in and swallowed by that gas giant you call Jupiter. I was a crew leader and managed to reach the Earth with a handful of my servants in the escape pod."

Man sniffs. "A captain who was the first to leave his sinking ship. What happened to the pod?"

"Probably, it is still where we left it, in the ice near Antarctica. Our ship was not made of metal. To you, it would look like a unique and fossilised coral. Our bodies were completely different, too, back then. We looked like your slugs, only larger. Our long and narrow core had a very thin casing. We could not move on the Earth's firmament. We barely crawled to the water and swam along an underwater mountain range. We consumed the animals we came across along the way. With each new species, we adapted more and more to the flesh of the inhabitants of your planet. By the time we reached the tip of the mainland in what was later called Patagonia, the flesh we covered ourselves with was completely terrestrial.

We thought, in error, the rest of the planet was also inhabited by savages, but the bipeds in those parts made us feel at home for the first time. We already had four limbs, but that's where we found our feet. This is how we discovered the Americas and reached its equatorial regions almost simultaneously with its European discoverers."

"So not all the eaten sailors were eaten by the aborigines?"

"You better ask where the aborigines got the tradition to eat the meat of their own kind. And where did they get the idea eating an enemy would grant them that enemy's strength? But I don't want to talk about them. They believed we were divine animals which took human form to rule them. They were not completely wrong but were very unpleasant to deal with. The Europeans were different. Their blood and flesh turned out to be a real reward for the long journey. When our skin turned a different colour and our speech became more coherent, we ended up in Europe with them. That was our evolution, if you like."

"I'm beginning to think you are also behind not only cannibalism but all racism, fascism and chauvinism," the man says, frowning.

"Maybe. But getting what you want is hard if you hide in the crowd or move with stealth. Some of us had to take leadership."

"When did you have any problem just killing people? Seems much easier in the darkness of the night. Why take charge?"

"At some point, we suspected the physical properties weren't the only thing we adopted. Especially since some of us decided to become females. They get obsessions first, mainly with appearance. Then, the rest of us realised we had developed a different type of thirst. A thirst for power…"

"Now you have it… You took what you wanted. You turn us into your cattle. What's the problem now?"

"If I knew, I would not ask for your help. Taking the random traveller or lost child is not satisfying any more. Selecting the right person became harder and harder. We had to become counts, kings, führers and presidents to access the unlimited and necessary resource with impunity."

The man before me looks me in the eye. I do not sense any surprise in him. More of triumph and contempt. I am starting to feel the desire to kill him right there, but this time, I must be patient. He is the last scholar I have.

He shakes his head. "I won't help you find those hiding. They are rebels who are way out of your reach. I was in your captivity and know nothing about them. Even if I knew, I would not betray humankind's last hope to repopulate this planet."

"No, that is not why you are here. I want your skills. You are a scientist of…whatever kind knows about biochemistry. If you work it out, I promise you will not regret it, and the rest of your days will be very comfortable."

"I was a scientist, yes." The man looked at his disfigured and broken hands then sighed. "My scientific curiosity is still pushing me towards knowledge, especially of such an important domain."

"And before you get too clever, you must know you will stay here, in this fortress, and never get out to tell your comrades."

"I know, but doing something gives me purpose." He thinks for a whole minute then asks, "If I do what you want, will you give me what I need?"

"Anything. Better food, better conditions, you can even wear clothing again. I cannot promise you a female, as we have not seen one for years… And I will stop this transfusion…" I lifted my hand to my bracelet to switch off the pump.

"No…no, carry on. I want you to take more. I need data. You said you are having problems finding satisfying blood. I guess you want me to figure out why you get less and less from humans you kill. Am I right?"

"Yes. What do you need? What sort of data?"

"I have questions for you and for your clan… Can you describe their symptoms and patterns?"

"I might be able to answer for all of us."

"Okay. First, your reaction to your…food. You already told me some people you consumed made you feel unwell. Can you tell me more? You started by eating animals and never had this problem before."

"That's right. In the fifteenth century, we looked a lot like humans; we became a part of society and had almost unlimited access to food. Most specimens could disappear without anyone noticing; some were believed to be killed by wild animals or maniacs. Soon, we noticed that not all prey is good for us and started sampling their blood before consuming the whole body."

"And people noticed those bites left by you and started telling stories."

"Yes, we contributed to the legends and various folklore. One thing was clear: some humans were better to eat than others. We decided to split, and each went to different regions to find the perfect supply. One of us wasn't careful enough and became known by you in Romania."

"He wasn't a myth, then?"

"No, but you're killing him—was. He discovered blood types before you did, although there are no scientists among us. But, it wasn't a blood group that was the problem."

"What is your theory?"

"I don't have one."

"Don't you think the desire to get to the top in every way is related to the inability to digest just anything?"

"How?" I rise and stand over the table in my sudden anxiety, "Our instincts always lead us to the best course of action! Why, this time, do our choices bring us to all this? It must be you! Your fault!"

The man does not move. "Physically, we did not change. Our blood did not change. We have the same iron in the same haemoglobin."

"Then tell me! What do you think?"

He sits back, picks a piece of dry fish with effort and chews it slowly, talking with his mouth full. "You used our structural proteins to construct your bodies, and you consume us to support them, but still don't belong here. Before you came, this world lived by its rules and still does. You don't. No matter how much you follow your instincts, you can't become part of this ecosystem. Your instincts don't belong here either."

"So, what happened? Is something wrong with the iron? Different isotopes?"

The man shrugs, "You do terrible things to us to obtain what you need. You take, kill, and don't care about anything but your precious iron and your thirst."

I return to my chair. "You have predators on this planet. The secondary consumers do the same."

The man spits a fish bone on the floor. "They exist in the balance. They coexist. They have a role in their habitat, and they are not useless. You, on the other hand, are not just a predator; you are a poacher. You do not care about your new home's future, causing the extinction of the species, including your own."

"You are mistaken. There is still plenty of food for us to eat. You don't explain why we can't."

The man finishes eating and takes a few greedy gulps of water from the cup. "That is my next point. You said it yourself: You are what you eat. Your problem started when you consumed creatures capable of thinking, feeling and wanting. We also have instincts; they are genetically pre-programmed into every cell you swallow. The instinct of self-preservation is a powerful thing. What if this is the way we fight you? Mm? What if this is how the whole planet rebels against your parasitic invasion. It was tolerating you when you were grabbing an unfortunate victim from the shadows, but now you cross the line. Mother Nature is trying to regain her children, freedom, and her maiden name."

He talks calmly and slowly, like a teacher explaining a biology lesson to a child. I want to rip the skin off his face, so I grab the tabletop with both hands to contain myself.

He continues. "If you can use logic, try and see for yourself. There are plenty of good and bad people on Earth. By absorbing their drives and desires, you also absorb their conscience and ethics. You lived long enough to notice the dark ages were over, the wars stopped being everyday things and killing become, let's say... frowned upon. More and more people don't find killing as easy as they did in past centuries. They are more peaceful and civilised. Eating them gives you indigestion because adopting their good nature will prevent you from killing more. For you to exist and to be immortal, you must be immoral. As soon as you become capable of seeing the difference between good and bad, you are aware that what you are doing is wrong. We now have more good than bad people in this world. You want murderers, tyrants, and corrupt scams. Eating them grants you abilities to get what you want without feeling guilty. Guilt feels like a sickness to you, doesn't it?"

He smiles a little for the first time. Does he want me to kill him on the spot?

"Are you saying that eating weak and gutless people turns us into them?"

"Not weak, but good people. You cannot be good. You are evil and can only survive as evil. Let see... Women are easy targets, but most have mother instincts and are usually less aggressive than men. They can be very strong and protective. I don't count in some power-thirsty bitches. I am talking about our worthy and best half. Noble men and women whose power in their skills, abilities and creativity will not improve your evil nature but..."

"Corrupt it!" I exclaim with sudden understanding, "So it is your fault! And now you have concurred all that is left are victims and resistance? No one collaborates with us these days!"

"You got it. Everyone is fighting the common enemy; you are the only evil left. Iron allotropy has nothing to do with it. Our philanthropy is your poison. Without it, we would perish like extinct animals."

"What will happen to us?"

"I don't know. You have no other ship. Mankind did not have time to build a good enough spacecraft for you to search for another planet to devour it. It is your own doing; there was no need to start wars, lead mafia structures and provoke religious confrontations. You don't think you can die because you have never been in this situation. What will happen to your sluggish core if you don't get suitable iron isotopes because the nature of the host is incompatible?"

"I…I don't know." I am feeling strange. This feeling is not normal for me; I must have absorbed it from humans, too. Is it… fear? It could not be from him. He looks fearless.

"I see only one way for you to exist without dying out with this planet."

"What? What is it?"

"You want energy to live and power to kill people. You can't have both powers. You should give up the latter. You adapted once, you can do it again. Convert to the simple creatures, save your core, and return to slug form. You will not survive in this world any other way."

"What? No! How dare you? We want to be above men."

The old man lifts his head slowly, and the morning sun from the window lights up his face. The candles are gone for a long time now. Only now can I see his every wrinkle, his grey and very thin hair. He is in pain. I realise he allowed me to pump his blood out all night. I can tell his strength has expired, and he will lose consciousness any second now. Not only that, but I realise with absolute horror I can't attack him. I am feeling another human emotion. Compassion! That's impossible! I don't want it. I would rather be a slug than feel pity and other sickening things. He did it deliberately. He knew!

The man speaks again, and these words are his last. "To be truly above men, you must first become a real human. It is not natural for rational beings to kill each other. Only the lowest of the lowest did that in our history. You simply have to absorb enough of us to feel the effect. This last straw… Humanity is in our blood."

~ * ~ * ~

Anka B Troitsky was born in the USSR in 1968, grew up in Kazakhstan and left for the UK in 1993. She is a Philosopher, Artist, Science Teacher, and Translator of books, police cases, court hearings, and National Health care. She reads tons of books yearly, always takes courses to learn new skills, and has no sense of humour. Being an independent author, Anka shares things she realised and discovered in her hard science fiction novels and short stories in various genres, including LGBTQ+. Her 3-part Novel, *Who is Vist*, is a futuristic series.

The content of her most recent work is greatly influenced by the current war and political crime against the Ukrainian people. In her stories, Anka studies the nature of the people responsible for the worst and the best things happening in the world. To deliver her message she doesn't mind breaking rules of writing, playing with languages and even frustrating her editors a little.

More Great Anthologies from WolfSinger Publications

Space Brides – edited by Dana Bell

Tired of those lonely dark nights? No one in your settlement suitable? We are here to help! We will help you find the bride or husband to keep you company, raise your children, and be your partner building a dream together. Contact us directly and give us your specifications. Success guaranteed.

In this collection of 15 testimonials read about the challenges and triumphs of some of our clients as they found love on the frontier of space.

From aliens to vampires, we brought these couples together and together they found acceptance and love—each in their own way.

A man with three kids finds an unexpected match in the brother of the woman he had contracted to marry when she runs away.

A woman running away from an abusive marriage finds acceptance and respect with a colony group that marries everyone to everyone in order to ensure they know they belong to a family.

A woman constantly rejected because of her skin color and origins finds acceptance and love with a wounded soldier.

Even though we encourage absolute honesty in your profile and correspondence with your potential spouse—many people don't. However, like some of the testimonials you'll read here; they still manage to expand their horizons—together.

Contact or walk into any of our offices 24/7. We are here to help you find that special someone and start a new future!

Other conditions apply.
Please ask for more information before contract is drawn up and signed.

The Dragon's Hoard – edited by Carol Hightshoe

Dragons are well known for their hoards—but not all hoards are created equal.

A young dragon starts his hoard with some very precious gifts.

One dragon shares her complaints about taxes with a friend as they wait for a lunch delivery.

Another dragon defends her most precious treasures against a group of greedy goblins.

And yet another may hold the solution to saving the Earth after a devastating apocalypse in his collection of bottled treasures.

In addition to the normal gold, silver and jewels here you will find dragons who collect many different treasures. 25 storytellers invite you to enter The Dragon's Hoard and share the treasures within.

Tails From the Front Lines 2 – edited by Carol Hightshoe

Come meet some of the four-legged members of Law Enforcement who also serve and protect.

Here our authors will introduce you to the brave K9 officers who serve alongside their human partners. They are their eyes, ears, noses and sometimes when necessary they are their shield, protecting others.

Proceeds from this anthology will be donated to the El Paso County (Colorado) Sheriff's Office K9 program in memory of K9 Jinx who was killed in the line of duty on April 11, 2022.

Ring of Fire – edited by Dana Bell

Enter the Ring of Fire, as unpredictable as the land masses shaking a city and volcanoes erupting covering the landscape. Could there be other reasons for these events? Or could these rings be more than a geological location.

They may be dragons playing tricks
or magic portals opened to mysterious realms
or sacrificing the best work of a lifetime.
Perhaps a rescue during a forest fire
or an attempt to raise the dead
or even while attending a high school reunion.

Journeys are taken to far off lands, another world, and through caves, each with their own unique twist.

Each tale presents a new idea on what the Ring of Fire could be. It is more than what many have been led to believe. Pull up a chair and warm yourself by our fires—just don't let yourself get burned.

Out of the Darkness – edited by Carol Hightshoe

Mental Health issues have long been stigmatized, with those facing them pushed into the shadows, often unable to deal with the darkness they find themselves trapped in.

In this collection, stories explore many types of darkness—Suicidal Ideation, Death from Suicide, Survivor's Guilt, PTSD, Chronic Pain, Chronic Illness, Depression, Death of a Loved One, Secrets, Bullying, and other forms of darkness are explored. Some related to mental health issues and some not, but all of them offer very human perspectives. As in real life, some stories have happy endings and sadly others don't.

We offer these stories of darkness without judgement, but with hope and compassion. Some roads should never have to be traveled —but we understand that for many they are being traveled alone.

Proceeds from sales of Out of the Darkness will be donated to the American Foundation for Suicide Prevention—for more information on AFSP please visit their website at: afsp.org.

For those who may be in crisis—PLEASE call or text 988 to connect directly to the 988 Suicide and Crisis Lifeline. For those outside the US please connect with your local lifeline

Never Cheat a Witch – edited by Carol Hightshoe

Magical curses. Arcane revenge. Being transformed into a frog. Things evil witches do to mere mortals who cross their path. But, what if there is more to the story…

Deals made with a witch are magically binding and can bring dire consequences to those who even think about breaking them.

Whether they are seeking revenge for wrongs done to them, helping others or simply trying to live their lives—it is NEVER wise to try and cheat a witch.

Open your spell book and join our authors as they relate tales of witches and mortals. From classic fantasy witches to modern day witches and even the legendary Baba Yaga. Good and Evil as well as every shade of gray in between. And, yes—there is a prince who is turned into a frog.

Time Capsules – edited by Carol Hightshoe

Time Capsules–history and mystery–a gift or a message from the past to the future. Messages that can easily be misunderstood.

What were the reasons for passing along a pair of pink, fuzzy handcuffs?

A glass vial containing a perfect dandelion puff?

A Japanese Katana?

A red and blue scarf?

A wooden spoon?

What magic do these items contain? What stories do they tell?

From the past to the future. Mysteries and meanings abound within these pages, as well as reminders of the things people find precious. What will you find?

US/THEM – edited by Carol Hightshoe

Fear of the *Other* breeds hatred of the *Other*

They aren't like us—so they must be bad…inferior… dangerous…

Humans are by nature social animals, but we tend to bond with other humans with whom we have something in common: beliefs, experiences, likes and dislikes, etc.

With the expansion of humans across the planet, it seems that, even as our numbers grow, we find ways to whittle our groups into ever narrower, specialized, and exclusive blocks. We target the *Other* for the most minor differences and interpret everything from *THEM* as an insult or an attack.

Within these pages you will witness hatred, intolerance and fanaticism as well as love, understanding and acceptance. Most of all, I, and the authors, hope you discover stories that will cause you to pause and think before condemning someone as being *THEM* and not *US*.

Crunchy with Ketchup – edited by Carol Hightshoe

It has been said that one should never meddle in the affairs of dragons—for you are crunchy and taste good with ketchup.

Come enter the dragon's lair.

Take your chances with other would-be heroes and heroines who decide to face off against one of the biggest, baddest predators ever.

Witness a dragon civil war.

Hear the true story of the Battle of New Orleans.

Find out what it's like in the belly of a dragon.

Discover why cats can spell disaster when stealing a dragon's egg.

Meet a group of dragon riders who protect us from nuclear devastation.

Follow legends of modern dragons, only to find something very unexpected.

And more…

Crunchy with Chocolate – edited by Carol Hightshoe

It has been said that one should never meddle in the affairs of dragons—for you are crunchy and taste good with chocolate.

Come enter the dragon's lair and roll the dice. Within these pages you will still meet some of the biggest, baddest predators ever—but if you are lucky, you will also discover some that have a sweeter side.

Meet a dragon with a soft spot for hard luck cases and another who is a hopeless romantic.

Enjoy a musical battle between a dragon and the specter of one of the greatest guitarists to ever play.

Meet a dragon in trouble with other magical creatures because he enjoys hanging out with human children.

Join a mother and daughter and their teams of dragons on a dangerous cross-country race.

Reconnect with an imaginary friend—who is not so imaginary and escape the isolation of the pandemic.

And more…

So enter in BUT tread carefully—remember you are crunchy and taste good with chocolate.

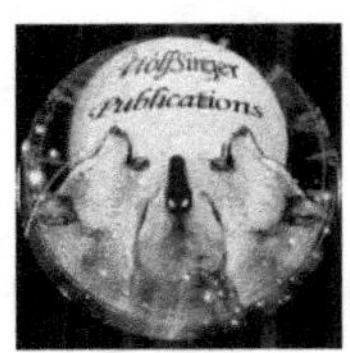

www.ingramcontent.com/pod-product-compliance
Lightning Source LLC
Chambersburg PA
CBHW051508260626
47162CB00008B/2876
* 9 7 8 1 9 4 4 6 3 7 4 9 1 *